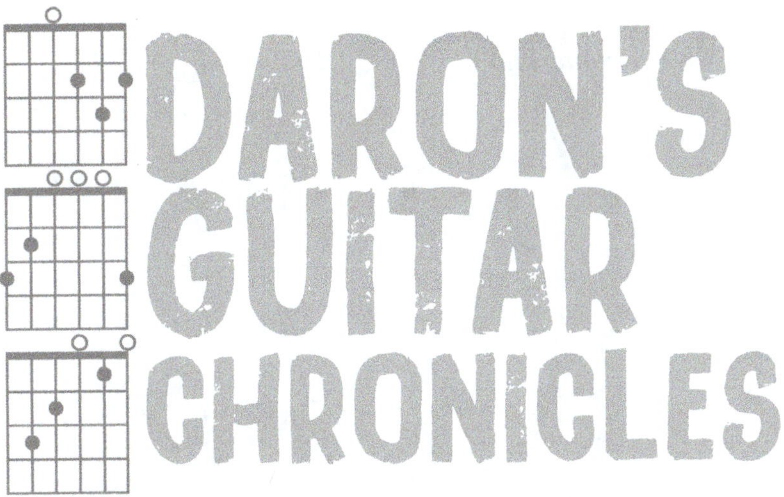

DARON'S
GUITAR
CHRONICLES

for everyone who has made DGC online such fun

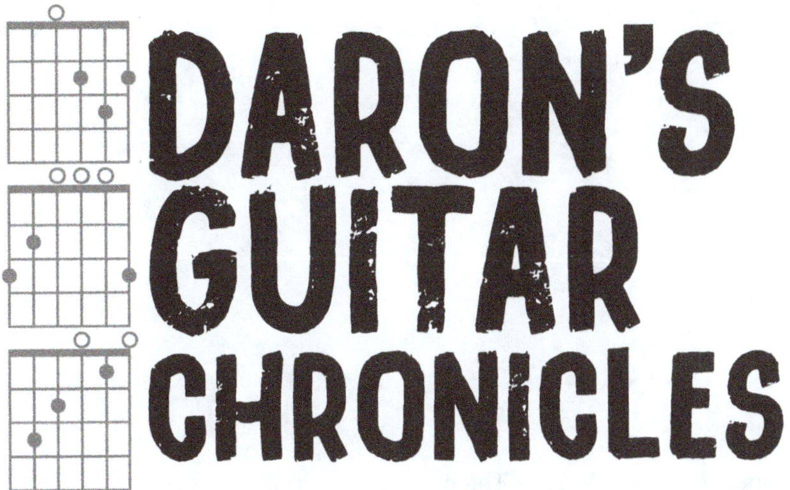

DARON'S GUITAR CHRONICLES

VOLUME 3

CECILIA TAN

CONTENTS

151. You're All I've Got Tonight
152. The Low Spark of High-Heeled Boys
153. Electric Avenue
154. White Room
155. Breakfast in America
156. Burning Down the House
157. Hey Hey, What Can I Do
158. So Far Away
159. One of These Nights
160. Games People Play
161. Take Me to the River
162. Don't Fear the Reaper
163. Instant Karma
164. Walk Away
165. I Still Haven't Found What I'm Looking For
166. We Will Rock You
167. Same Old Song and Dance
168. Another One Bites the Dust
169. Pretzel Logic
170. You May Be Right
171. No More Words
172. Blister in the Sun
173. Long Distance Runaround
174. Go West
175. Rocky Mountain Way
176. Break On Through
177. Get Off My Cloud
178. Over The Hills and Far Away
179. Won't Get Fooled Again
180. Going to California
181. Centerfold
182. Loves Me Like a Rock
183. The Wild Night Is Calling

Part Six

Spring 1989

Mirror In The Bathroom

So what do you do after you have a literal panic attack after getting off? If you're me... a lot of rehearsing. Ziggy and I didn't try again. I felt fine the next day as long as I didn't think about what had happened. He did not bring it up and I was not seized with the urge to scream again. I kept my distance and he kept his.

Essentially, we went back to play acting that the only thing we cared about was the band, the songs, rehearsal — the things we'd actually argue about.

On March 1st the producer Mills wanted — a pretty hip, late-twenties guy named Jordan Travers — arrived in Boston. He'd produced a slew of other acts for BNC, some rock, some pop, even one or two R&B albums, which I thought was both cool and strange at the same time.

By then we had fourteen songs to choose from, some better than others. He came to the studio straight from the airport with his bags. We were taking a break when he arrived so we heard him coming up the stairs. He had the same leather BNC jacket as me, skinny wrap-around shades, and more hair in his goatee than he had on the rest of his almost-shaved head. He waved from the doorway like he was waiting to be invited in. We invited him in, gave him the quick tour of the fridge, video games, sound console, and then ran down names.

"You sure about these names?" he asked, as he jotted them into a day planner. "Some bands all have different nicknames they insist on in person," he explained. "I'm happy to call you whatever you want."

"These are already our nicknames," Chris explained back, and we got down to work.

I had to struggle to forget Jordan was there. If I thought I was too self-conscious before, the feeling was ten times worse knowing he was standing there listening. At least Jordan seemed like a relaxed kind of guy, more like us than like Mills. He strolled back and forth and sat in the window looking out at the traffic while we ran through a bunch of tunes. He said nothing for hours. I spent all of Wonderland and Intensive Care sitting on a crate with my head bent and my eyes shut. He didn't say anything until we took a break for dinner.

He was a rice noodle man, meaning we took him to Chau Chow, the el cheapo Chinese place around the corner—I mean, every place in Chinatown is pretty cheap, but some are cheaper than others. This place had more the atmosphere of a diner than an ethnic restaurant, which is to say none. Red vinyl banquettes, green formica tables, and a bevy of white-shirted waiters who sat at a round table in the back and waved you to a booth or table when you walked in instead of standing up. They were always the same waiters, no matter what time of day we went in.

We knew from eating there often that if you wanted a glass of water, it was better to ask the younger guy with the glasses. With the older guy who always looked unhappy about something, each person at the table would have to ask individually for water and then he always brought the glasses sort of suspiciously three-quarter full. Some nights it didn't matter who you asked, you could get twenty pots of tea and still never get a glass of water. But the food was awesome. Somehow, sometime, someone had gotten me to try the chow fun noodles with beef brisket and I'd gotten sort of attached to the huge white rice noodles covered in blobs of beef fat and soft meat. Every time I ordered it the waiter, no matter which one it was, would double check that was what I really wanted. Jordan Travers dittoed me on the order and after the waiter was gone Chris shook his head.

"I don't know how you guys can eat that stuff." He'd ordered chicken and vegetables on rice and a Diet Coke. Christian was not what I'd call overweight. But he was not only the tallest of us four, he was also the only one with any bulk. He was always complaining about how I seemed to be able to pack away as much food as I could without ever getting paunchy. The typical exchange went something like this:

> Chris: Jeezus, how can you eat all that? You must have a hollow leg/tapeworm/bucket in the back...
> Me: Can't talk, eating.
> Chris: I mean, jeezus, where does it all go? If I ate like that I'd look like Chaka Khan/Jabba the Hut.
> Bart: He's making up for not eating yesterday.
> Me: Forgot to.

Chris: Here, take mine. Maybe I can transfer some of this beer
    gut to you.
Me: Give me your beer instead.

Et cetera.

Tonight's exchange though, being performed for Jordan Travers's benefit went sort of like this. After the opening comment, Jordan, who was downright skinny, said, "I really need a lot of calories or I get burned out. I eat instead of sleeping."

Chris came back with, "Is that like smoking instead of eating?"

Jordan shrugged. "Mills tells me you're all non-smokers."

Chris held up his hand boy-scout-pledge-wise. "I quit. Can't say about these three babes in the woods."

"Just never started," Bart and I said in unison. Ziggy didn't say anything, but put a hand to his delicate throat and cleared it with a high pitched "ahem."

"But seriously," Chris said, bringing the subject back to food. "You'll be amazed at what these little twerps can pack away. I mean, use McDonalds as a baseline measure, okay? Your average adult is supposed to eat, what, a Big Mac, large fries, and a large soft drink, right? Now, you figure that includes men and women, young and old. So factor in that Daron here's twenty..."

"Twenty one!" Bart said emphatically and grinning like a fool. I don't know who I was more embarrassed for, him or me.

"...one," Chris corrected and went on. "And possibly still growing, and so say you make that two Big Macs."

"Quarter pounders with cheese," Ziggy said. "You're the only one who likes the Big Mac."

"Whatever. So this little guy orders three Quarter Pounders, a large fry, an apple pie, and a large drink."

"But he never finishes the drink, you know," Bart put in.

I began to feel downright silly with everyone talking a mile a minute about my eating habits.

"I always get to finish his Coke," Bart explained to Jordan, "so I only order a medium."

"ANYWAY," Chris said with a smoothing motion of his hand like he was planing off wood, "The point is, he takes in like twice what a normal-sized person does, and he's not even the size of a normal person, and yet, look at him, he's a stick. What do you weigh, now, ninety eight pounds or something?"

"That's because he burns off all his calories worrying," Ziggy said.

I stood up. "Taking a leak," I announced, so my sudden departure wouldn't seem weird, though I knew it did.

"Probably *purging*," Chris called after me as I rounded the table of waiters to the little back hallway that housed the restrooms.

Chau Chow's restrooms are phone-booth-sized and cleaner than anything you'll find in Manhattan, which isn't saying much, I know. I didn't really have to piss, but I did anyway now that I'd bothered to go back there. And then there wasn't much to do while waiting what I hoped was a long enough time that the subject of conversation would have switched to someone else.

I looked at myself in the mirror. If I took my hair out of the pony tail it hung to the middle of my shoulder blades in the back but there were still parts of the front that didn't stay in the bunch, and I was constantly sticking them behind my ears. I wondered how Digger had looked at my age. Other than the bits of my chin that I shaved every other day I felt like I looked essentially the same as I had when I was fifteen or sixteen. I cracked my knuckles. It wasn't like being in here alone was any better really than being out there with them. I didn't like the scrutiny either way.

The other thing we like about Chau Chow is how fucking fast it is. You don't really have a relaxing meal the food comes so fast. The other four were already digging in to hot plates of food when I sat back down.

For the record, I weigh one hundred and twenty pounds.

Pop Will Eat Itself

"Everything come out alright?" Chris said.

"Yeah, fine." No one said anything for a few minutes while we ate, mouths full. And then Jordan started the talking the next time.

"So how many tunes do we have to work with?" He was picking pieces of fatty beef out of his noodles with chopsticks and eating them one at a time.

"Twelve, fourteen, maybe more if we want to work on anything half finished," I said.

"I heard what, ten already today?"

"About that." I made a show of eating, forking up noodles and looking at my tea cup. But my heart had started to beat fast.

Jordan wasn't looking at me, either. He would chew a bit and look around the restaurant while he talked. "We are in fine shape, then, I think. The real danger with the second album is a kind of backsliding. The second one has to be a leap forward. If it's too similar to the first album, it seems like backsliding, dated."

"Backsliding," I repeated, more to keep the conversational ball rolling than anything else. The others, so talky before, were now silent, and watching me and Jordan not look at each other.

"Speaking in the most purely commercial sense, you guys have the potential to be blockbusters. I mean like R.E.M. who have not only broken out, they continue to sell well every album. Or U2, talk about a band that sells records. Their last one was considered a flop by their record company only because they had hoped for something even huger than what they got. Naw, they did fine." He waved his hand as if to dispel a bad smell. "Do you know you're the first new rock act that Mills has put onto the Billboard Top 40?"

"No."

"You are. He's done it with older AOR rock acts with new albums, some established acts switching labels, but Mills is essentially a pop man. An Olivia Newton John, George Michael, what's the word... Laura *Branigan* kind of guy. So from his perspective, anything you do musically, new, innovative, whatever, he's listening for its Top 40 potential. He was right when he said Candlelight could become a hit if given the right push. It wasn't AOR that put that record into the countdown, it was pop stations. You know I heard it on a soft rock station the other day?"

Ziggy made a hiccuping noise. "Don't tell me that."

"Oh yeah, the adult contemporary stations are very big on 'alternative' acts. These are the only stations who are still playing Culture Club, The Thompson Twins, Howard Jones. The thirty and forty-somethings who listen to it don't know you're a bunch of scruffy, weird-hair, postpunks. What do they care? It's a ballad, it sounds nice. You have to be able to take the song out of its context, and see where it can go, like hey, what about a dance remix of this? Do you get what I mean?" His hands fluttered like he was trying to figure out what to do with them.

"You mean," I said slowly, "we should keep our minds open to different interpretations."

"Kind of." He laughed to himself a little. "What I'm really trying to say is that it's my job to think about all that other stuff, hear the songs out of context, and make my suggestions for how they can have the widest appeal without seeming like they're..."

"Compromised?" I suggested.

"Yeah." Now he looked at me. "So in a way I want you not to worry about it so much, don't try to aim at these commercial targets. Don't want you to end up like, I don't know, any of ten million other bands who went major label and ended up boring, bland, bad."

Okay, if everyone knows I'm a worry wart, why hide it. "If you're telling us this to make me feel less anxious about working with you, Jordan, I hate to tell you it isn't working."

He waved his hand again and I wondered if he was wishing he had a cigarette between his fingers. "I'll make you a deal, Daron. I won't ever tell you anything 'just' to make you feel better."

"And what do I do in exchange?"

"You tell me how you feel."

"It's a deal." And you know, I did feel better. There wasn't a word he'd said that I didn't agree with, either. In all the ways I could analyze it, I felt like I (and we as a band) should get along with Jordan swimmingly. What I couldn't explain was why I felt so tense. But, well, that was getting to be a normal state of being; I was almost used to it.

Blues from a Gun

Spring in Boston comes a lot later than it does to New York. When New Jersey is yellow with forsythias and daffodils and stuff, up here we're still looking at gray skies and piles of dirty snowplow snow. We're talking way into March, sometimes April. People still have ski racks on their cars and snow shovels in their trunks at Easter.

The nice days we do get are like Mother Nature saying "sike!" (or is that "psych-"?) and just make people like me even more pissed when we get up the next morning and its shitty out again. Oh yeah what do I care, I spend all my time indoors, right? If only. Even Jordan remarked how crappy the weather was when we were getting ready to wrap. He'd been with us two and a half weeks and was Fedexing tapes to Mills every other day. We'd done nothing but work during the day, eat in restaurants, and then go back to work—except for a few times when we'd gone to see a show, some band we knew or that Jordan wanted to check out. That's how I got to meet Tom Petty, and David Knopfler (Mark's brother). But I spent most of these shows backstage, half-there, my mind still in the studio trying to get some kind of perspective on the whole thing. (Though I admit, meeting Petty was cool.)

The more Jordan told me not to worry about perspective, the more I worried. The more he told me Mills liked what he was hearing the more worried I got that maybe *I* didn't have any idea whether *I* liked what I heard. I just couldn't tell.

What bothered me the most, maybe, was that Ziggy and I didn't exactly put aside our conflict in order to work together. We dug in and cooperated less. There were some songs that were "my" songs, some that were "his." I felt like we'd been more collaborative before, when I was writing almost everything and he was adding lyrics and putting his own spin on stuff, which meant we could be more collaborative as a band. Now, it was competitive, even if we never said that aloud.

"Okay Jordan," I said one night when he and I sat in the stairwell and shared some grass while the other three went off to pick up some take out. I didn't fake toking; I figured I needed to be as calm and quiet as I could get for this. "If you're Mr. Perspective, can you tell me something?"

He passed the pipe back to me—a weird carved job made of some kind of stone he said he'd picked up in New Orleans—and held his smoke for a bit before answering. "Sure, what."

"Can you tell the difference between the songs Ziggy wrote and the ones I wrote?"

He thought about it a moment while I fired up the bowl. Then he said "Do you mean, can I tell the difference, or is it you want to know what the difference is?"

I shrugged—whichever.

"Okay. I'm hearing a more, I don't know, *exotic* sound from the stuff he writes. But sometimes it sounds like he's reaching. He pulls it off because he can really perform it, and because he comes up with hooks. With you, you give yourself more room to write a complete texture, it's not just the lyrics, it's the total surface of the music with lyrics and lead. But hey, what else would you expect from a singer-songwriter and a guitarist-songwriter?"

"Yeah," I said. "But does this make some kind of difference in the grand scheme of things?" Grand Scheme of Things was a Bart phrase he'd been using for years but for some reason all of us had started to use it with frightening regularity.

Jordan played with his goatee. "I shouldn't be telling you this."

"Telling me what."

"That I think Ziggy's got the pop pulse right now. He's just weird enough to bring it above bubble gum. I think it's his songs mostly right now that will be singles, if that's what you're asking. The stuff I'm hearing from you right now is, what, the stuff that gives the overall album its ballast." He held up his fingers like he was counting. "Of say ten songs we end up with on this record, three have Ziggy written all over them. And I'd bet money those three will be the singles. Provided the thing does well enough to spawn three singles of course."

"Granted."

"Yeah, so..." He gestured for me to give the pipe back, which I did. I think it was carved in the shape of a snake's head, or something like that. I didn't look too closely. "Yeah, anyway. But the other seven songs I see as you."

"Please tell me it doesn't sound like we wrote a couple of hit-ready songs just for Top-40 and they are totally obviously like, not part of the rest of it."

"I promised I wouldn't tell you anything just to make you feel better."

"Yeah so, and what's the answer?"

"What was the question?"

In that marijuana kind of logic I had to wait until he packed the bowl again and we each took another hit before I could retrace where we'd gone astray. "The question is, does it sound like we wrote a couple of hit ready, yadda yadda?"

"Ah." He looked like a man chewing a cud. "No, it doesn't. For what it's worth, if you'd just sent me the tape and I'd never seen you play, I wouldn't have known some of the songs were yours and some were his. Your average Joe Listener isn't going to have any clue. Do you know what percentage of people actually read the liner notes of albums, and look at stuff like songwriting credit?"

"No, what percent?"

"I don't know man, I thought you would know." We both laughed even though I think we were both a little depressed by the fact that probably not a heck of a lot of people gave a damn. But cheer up, I told myself, that was the point. You wanted to know no one would be able to tell the difference.

A few days later we had all major tracks in the can, and Jordan went back to New York and suddenly I had a tour to think about.

Long Distance Dedication

I'm glad that Jordan turned out to be an incredibly cool dude, and that he didn't turn the album into Top-40 crap, and that he and I spent a lot of late nights talking about music and history and stuff. That wasn't the only eventful thing in the spring besides my birthday of course. We also got flown to Arizona to film the Why the Sky video and got good and sunburned in the process. And all that time, Carynne was working on putting us on a warmup tour on a shoestring budget. Digger had negotiated a nice deal with BNC, but we'd agreed to handle a lot of the financial responsibility ourselves. BNC and WTA were working on an extensive tour for later in the year, but I just couldn't wait that long.

Oh yeah, and Christian and I bought the Allston house with some of the advance BNC'd paid us.

And Ziggy and I ignored each other.

I could not wait to get back on the road.

Carynne had pulled in a bunch of promoter-to-promoter favors, using Mike Fink's name, and had raided Waldo's Rolodex, and the result was what looked to be an intense four weeks: Cleveland, Chicago, Detroit, Ann Arbor, Pittsburgh, Philadelphia, DC, Chapel Hill, Athens, New Orleans, Austin, San Antonio, Boulder, San Francisco, Portland, Seattle. Getting a decent date in LA or New York was impossible, apparently, without bigger favors or longer lead time. I put a map of the USA on my wall and traced our route in red. Man but the West is fucking big. That thought would occur to me again while we were trying to drive across it. But I'm getting ahead of myself.

Carynne built our entourage this way: Herself as road manager. A friend of hers and Colin's, Kevin Altman, as stage and equipment manager—essentially an uber-roadie. And we hired Colin as roadie because what the fuck, he needed the money and I'd rather have someone we knew than not. Digger would be along for the first few dates, then get off at Philly to go back to his office, and then join back up with us in San Francisco. And of course there would be the four of us.

We rented an equipment truck and a big van, the kind with three benches of seats. BNC released Why the Sky as a single and the video was thrust into heavy rotation on MTV, which we hoped would help fill seats. Remo said he'd try to fly up to San Fran to see us when he got back from London. And on April 2nd (Carynne insisted we could not leave on April Fool's Day) we were rolling in a two-vehicle convoy westward on the Mass Pike.

The first leg, I rode in the truck with Kevin because we didn't know each other well and for some reason right then I felt like it might be good to get away from the other guys for a few hours. Kevin worked sometimes for the same temp agency Colin did, so had respectably short hair, which I didn't hold against him.

He drove first, which suited me fine, having never actually driven a truck yet, even a smallish one like the rental. We were just pulling through the toll booth onto the Mass Pike when he said, "Dig out a tape, will you?"

He pointed to what looked to me like a black zippered shaving kit. I opened it to find it packed with cassettes. "I brought some too," I mentioned.

"You can pick when it's your turn to drive," he said. "We should make it a rule. That way everyone will want a turn behind the wheel."

"Okay so, driver picks the music. Makes sense."

"Exactly. And no backseat drivers, either. Okay, now remind me what the hell I put in there."

I read off the handwritten labels. "Fleetwood Mac, the Eagles, the Beatles, Supertramp, Joan Jett…"

He decided to start with "I Love Rock and Roll" and I decided I liked Kevin a lot.

A while later we swapped places. I'd brought all kinds of stuff myself, mixed tapes, Steely Dan, Frank Zappa, U2, Violent Femmes, Tones on Tail, Warren Zevon, and Jackson Brown. I got to feeling superstitious about *Running on Empty* though, something too weird about an on-the-road theme album as road music, and in the end I decided not to play it for the entire trip.

By now I had some idea of what to expect out of touring, though this low budget excursion meant some changes, like, we always stayed in a motel instead of driving all night. Carynne had done me a cost analysis on getting sleeping buses and trying to skip hotels some nights but it just wasn't worth it, especially when we couldn't always schedule shows that close together anyway. I was very glad I'd never tried to set something like this up myself. Just a glance at Carynne's day book was enough for me, as I thought in my head, for every detail she had ironed out in there, that was what, six phone calls? ten phone calls? I couldn't imagine myself now making hundreds of phone calls to total strangers. Booking a band in town is not like putting a band on the road.

Carynne and I had pre-planned the rooming arrangements, pretty much. I didn't think about that because I thought I might blush, like I had when she and I were going over the details, on the floor of my room:

"With an entourage of seven, we're four rooms with me the only female being alone, if you guys double up."

"Naturally."

"And with Digger along, we can either go to five rooms, he and I each alone, or I can bunk with Kevin, and one of you guys can bunk with Digger."

"Five rooms is fine."

"You're sure."

"I'm sure."

"You and Ziggy together, or apart?"

"I don't know." That's when I blushed.

"Are you guys getting along okay?"

"That's what I don't know."

She had pursed her lips. "I'll put you together. If it doesn't work out, we can switch you around."

I wanted to forget that there was something to remember. Why couldn't everything simply... work out? I knew guys, musicians, who never seemed to be too concerned about anything, like they were oblivious to the fact that there were things to do or be taken care of. They floated through life while other people scrambled around them, girlfriends, roommates, bandmates, etc. such that, from the guys' perspective, everything did seem to work out. But I also thought of these guys as lazy-ass space cases, and none of them were particularly head of the class when it came to musical success either. I didn't believe in blind luck enough to think that I could let it all go and I'd get what I wanted delivered on a silver platter shaped like a Stratocaster. But, somehow, I thought about the way things had... come together on the last road trip, and I am sure now that that's what I was hoping again.

The drive from Boston to Cleveland was motherfucking long. Somewhere in upstate New York we rotated and I took a spot in the van and then fell asleep to the sweet discord of King Crimson, "Discipline." Don't ask me why, I've always fallen asleep easily to loud music.

Late In The Evening

Close to midnight we pulled in to the motel in Cleveland, and Digger and Carynne did this little vaudeville act at the side door of the van. ("After you." "No, after you." "Ms. Manager, I insist." "Oh no, you first Mr. Manager." and so on until they both moved at the same time and bumped heads.) And then we were all in the lobby, with essential gear and bags of clean T-shirts and jeans, and the ritual key distribution took place.

And thinking about the lazy-ass space case that I did not want to be, but also thinking about the churning stomach and gnashing teeth worry wart I also didn't want to be, I basically just stood there paralyzed and let it take place around me.

I was half sure I didn't want to be with Ziggy all night and half hoping that maybe if we spent some time alone we'd figure things out. But there was Carynne, keys in hand, chomping a piece of chewing gum in an authoritative fashion. She handed one to Digger, handed one to me, tossed one to Bart who caught it by trapping it between his hands with a clap, and gave one to Kevin. She said nothing about who should go with whom. As it turned out, Colin and Chris has gotten into some kind of cribbage grudge match and wanted to keep playing, and Kevin gave his key to them and asked Bart if he could move in with him, which left Ziggy and me to ourselves.

We went on down the row to our rooms—it was one of those single floor places where each room's door opens onto one long exterior sidewalk—and while Colin and Chris played, we hung out in their room and Bart got out the Miller and played (yes, Bart can play the guitar, too) and me and Ziggy generally hung around and we shot the shit and told jokes we all knew we were going to be tired of by the end of the month, but hey, there was a kind of slumber party mood, I guess, and no one wanted to go right to sleep even though the drive had been long. Well, I don't know what Carynne or Digger or Kevin did, but the five of us, four bandmates and three housemates—yeah, you'd think we saw enough of each other back in town, right?—stayed up until Colin declared he was saving the rest of his weed for the drier states and things kind of broke up.

I washed my face. And looked through my clothes for what I was going to wear tomorrow. And puttered around with other such bullshit while Ziggy lay there in all his clothes on top of the bedspread, channel flipping. I was just sitting down to get undressed when he clicked the TV off and looked at me.

"You okay?"

I was stuck for a beat and then I said, "I was, until you asked me."

"I mean, are you happy? Does everything seem to be going the way you want?" He used his business-y kind of voice, earnest and a little quick.

I shrugged. "Seems okay thus far."

"But time will tell. So tell me about the place we're going to play." Entirely too business-like.

"I don't know a lot about it. It's about the size of the Orpheum I think. Show's almost sold out, or it was last we checked. It might be by now."

"Cool." He hugged himself a little, the clicker still in his hand. "You think we're going to do alright?"

You're thinking about Christmas aren't you. "That was over four months ago, Zig."

"Yeah, but do you think...?"

"I don't know." Hey, Mister Guitar, didn't you make a promise not to say those words anymore? I put on a false smile and felt weirdly cheered up by it. "No use worrying and making it worse."

"Hey, that's true." He put the clicker down. "So did you see that desk clerk? She just about wet her pants when she saw us."

"I didn't notice." I was too busy thinking about how the fake plants in the lobby looked suspiciously familiar.

"I think she's like eighteen at most, working the night shift at a motel, reading a paperback book, and in we come. And it's like, *holy shit!* I saw her mouth move, she said 'holy shit.'"

"It's nice to know we bring some joy to the world."

"Do we have any tickets to the show or what have you? I bet we could rock her world."

"If she's really a fan she probably has tickets already," I pointed out.

He shrugged. "I'm going to go out and see if she's still there."

I said nothing.

"You want to come? I mean, jeez, it's got to be a pretty boring job."

"Always the philanthropist, you?" I already had my sneakers off. "No, you go ahead. It's going to be you she's into, anyway, Mister Singer. I'm not the one who gets recognized on the street."

He didn't stay around to argue.

I lay down in the dark and the only thought I had was *here we go again*.

Cold As Ice

There's not much to tell about the next day. We had some tech glitches with the live rig, but between Kevin and Colin and me and Christian and the guys from the venue they were eventually worked out. Soundcheck was a non-event, as if we were all working so hard not to be nervous about our opening night that we ended up less enthusiastic than usual. Deadpan, even.

Deadpan, in fact, is a good word to describe pretty much everything from our waitress at Denny's to my performance itself. The more stiff I was, the more frenzied Ziggy got, fretting and strutting and screaming to the audience like he could make up for it. And the more wild he got, the colder I felt, the more rooted to the floor.

The audience cheered anyway. I played the right notes. They didn't know to complain, I guess. How were they supposed to know that I felt like I was doing some kind of rehearsal, a live-audience rehearsal, going through the moves with a singer who tried too hard to please them and a rhythm section whose eyes I wouldn't meet during the show?

When we came off the stage Colin said "good show" in an obligatory sort of way, and Carynne chewed the end of her pen and hugged her day book to her stomach. Everyone kind of made small talk about this or that, shook hands with the local crew who didn't seem to notice anything amiss, and the first person to say anything about it at all was Digger, when he and I were sitting in the bar (Rogan's Rodeo Room, which had a couple of horseshoes on the wall but otherwise was as generic a dark wood and dart board and neon Bud sign kind of bar as you could get) next to the motel. They didn't card me. I was drinking something that was a step above Jack Daniels, I forget which whiskey, and Digger was having the same, and bar peanuts, salty skinless peanuts that he'd crack into two halves between his fingers and then eat each half one at a time, making the bowl last longer, I guess.

"Kind of a rough night?" is what he said.

And I'm thinking, this is my father asking, here. This is my manager, too. Maybe he'll actually have some advice or something. "Yeah."

"Heh!" He cracked a peanut and joked, "Better shape up or we'll have to fire ya."

Okay so maybe one of the reasons I didn't talk to him before, and one of the reasons why after Remo left I stopped spending much time with the old man, was because he never did give any good advice. Right then he wasn't even giving the impression that he cared, particularly. The booze was hot in my throat. I was thinking c'mon, even with the best of intentions, what's he going to tell you? What kind of advice does a former shoe salesman turned media exec have for a professional musician with some kind of performance block going on? I mean, what the fuck did I expect? At least he noticed. At least he asked.

All this went through my well-lubricated mind in a flash, leaving me feeling not angry or sad, but empty. When I didn't laugh or smile at his joke, Digger's eyes drifted to the baseball game on the TV screen overhead and he popped another half-peanut into his mouth.

We were going to lapse into an uncomfortable silence, I thought, but suddenly he looked at me. "This isn't about your mother, is it?"

I was too startled to do anything but blurt, "What?"

"This thing," he said, meaning whatever my problem was, "you're not feeling guilty about her now are you?"

"Why would I—?"

"Because you got to wonder, if I saw you in a magazine, Claire might've. I see those teeny boppers in the audience and I think, sheez, Courtney could be one of 'em."

I half-wondered if he hoped to find them by tagging along with me. But, no, that'd be stupid, he's the one who ran off without them.

He swigged his bourbon and stared at the game while he talked. "Don't you worry yourself about them. They ain't starving. I left them well-taken care of. It wasn't like some spur of the moment thing, my taking off like that. I planned it pretty good."

"Then why the fuck didn't you tell me?" My hand was tight around my glass and a funny pain burned like booze in my chest. "I had to hear it from Remo, forgodsake, six months after the fact—!" My mouth stayed open as I trailed off realizing that, although I'd waited years to tell him off about it, I didn't really have anything else to say.

Digger didn't really look at me, he looked down at my feet wound in the rungs of the barstool, at my shoulder or just over it, his eyebrows knit and protruding like a small, folded up awning on his face.

Finally he muttered, "Pot calling the kettle black, hey Mister Moondog?" The name had never sounded more stupid before that moment. "You're pissed at me, because I took off, cut you off, and your reaction to that is, what, take out a personal ad? Give me some credit, Daron, I ain't dumb."

I wanted to know how he kept from blushing, when my face felt molten hot.

"I had some good reasons doing it like I did. 'ats not what matters now anyway."

"Don't..." I started to say *don't give me some cockamamie tough guy story because I ain't buying it*. But a couple of things were hitting me at once. One, he was kind of right about me doing exactly what I was pissed at him for doing, and once again I was struck with the fact that my image of myself as nothing like him was false. Ouch. And two, whenever we drank and/or argued, we both said 'ain't' instead of 'isn't' and other shit like that. "Just don't."

"Don't what? Kiddo, you don't know what you're talking about."

"The fuck I don't," I said, though it sounded childish even to me. I stood up—or got down, as the case may be with tall bar stools—and decided to leave him with the tab. "Getting up early," I said as a surly goodbye and walked out.

Well, that was one sure way to get my mind off Ziggy for a while. Oh I was just making friends all over the place, wasn't I?

Yours Is No Disgrace

I wasn't lying about getting up early. We had to be at the Chicago venue by like four o'clock, which meant a six hour drive, leaving at ten a.m., and actually we had to leave earlier than that so we could have time to stop and eat. The wake up call would come when it would come.

In the room, Ziggy was in bed in the dark with the TV on. The whites of his eyes looked like two little blue TVs in the darkness. I sat down on the other bed and got undressed and then sat there like I was too tired to lie down.

"Do you want to talk about it?" he said, his finger on the MUTE button.

It. I could think of so many things that "it" could be. The show, my mood, the elusive "it" of our relationship or lack of one, the fight I'd just had, yadda yadda. "I'd just as soon sleep on 'it,'" I replied. "What's to say?"

"I'll tell you tomorrow," he said, and clicked off the TV and rolled over, cocooning himself in the sheet and bedspread. I mirrored him on the other side, then of course lay there wondering what he was going to tell me, trying to guess, but too proud or too stubborn or too *something* to roll back over and ask him to tell me now.

Before we left in the morning, we had to sign two black and white glossies, one for the night clerk who I never did meet, and one for the manager to frame and hang in her office. Digger had brought plenty of them, he assured me. The weather was hazy but cool and self-consciousness was at an all time high as I chewed my calluses and watched the road going by and fretted about my fucking *signature* of all things—was it too mundane? Did it make me look like I was still a five-year-old putting his name on art projects? I hadn't really had to sign all that many things in my life. I did not get out a piece of paper and practice it because I knew damn well the ridicule that would ensue. No thanks.

I spent all of Indiana in a foul mood but I don't think I missed all that much.

Sentimental Hygiene

Ninety percent of the time spent on any tour is preparations. One moment you're on stage, the next moment you're off and already preparing for the next one, whether preparing to travel there or thinking about laundry or making sure to buy more strings.

The good thing about it is one can fall into a rhythm. We hit Chicago on schedule and went through the motions: Out of the van, load in, check out the dressing rooms (nice, the kind with lighted mirrors), meet the local band opening for us, soundcheck. We were standing there on the stage while lights went on and off and light techs did their thing when Bart and Chris broke into some Def Leppard riff. Much as I wanted to jump in, I waited for them to die down and then hit the opening of "Windfall" and we played half of that.

We heard Why the Sky on the radio while we were eating dinner and I tried to remember what recording the song had been like, but my memories got all tangled up. I pictured the Chinatown loft even though we'd recorded it before that. In the show, I was playing it semi-acoustic, with the Ovation, but I'd recorded it with the Fender. I think. I felt a little pit of unease in my stomach, wondering if I'd maybe smoked too much pot that day and addled my brains.

And then there was the getting dressed. For this tour Ziggy had settled into a costume of these black army surplus pants with extra pockets and such all over them, a mesh tank top, and either a leather jacket or a billowy white shirt, either of which he would shed by the third song. The pants were a little big in the waist and hung low on his hips, making his stomach look very long and flat. He had this little move he'd do sometimes while singing, pressing his palm to his chest and then sort of skiing it down his front and off into space—sounds stupid to describe but it was sexy to watch.

Bart played every show in one of two ratty-looking vintage tuxedo jackets, sometimes with a bow tie, when he was in the mood. And Chris, Chris could have been dressed up like Bozo the Clown and still nobody'd really see him behind the kit.

As for me, Ziggy'd convinced me to give up wearing sneakers on stage and wear combat boots instead, and I alternated between a pair of black jeans and a pair of artfully ripped blue ones, and a collection of cool-slogan/graphic/local band T-shirts I'd accumulated over the years.

He also cornered me before the Chicago show with a bottle of liquid eyeliner. I resisted at first, but the look he gave me said essentially, look, things can't get worse. Just try it.

So I sat in a chair and tried to look at the ceiling while his hands held my face and lined me. "Watch the *Kilroy Was Here* video again," he was saying, as if I needed reassurance. "Even Tommy Shaw's wearing eyeliner."

"Tommy Shaw's blond," I said, for argument's sake.

"So he's not wearing black liner, jeez. And boy they really caked it on to Dennis De-Old."

"Hey, if you can still sing like that at his age, you won't quit either."

"True."

It was kind of nice to have Ziggy touch me like that.

Never Stop

The opening band was called the Rebellious Doodads or something and I was reminded of a lot of the Providence bands we used to see, sloppy in a fun sort of way, earnestly jokey. We gave them high fives and that kind of thing and then took our turn.

I've talked about video filming before, the repetition, the weird double-vision thing that happens when you have to imitate yourself doing something you already once did, pretending you're doing the same thing, feeling the same thing, etc. Well, playing the same song again and again isn't really supposed to be like that, at least, it never had been before. But by the time we came around to the encore, Candlelight, I was feeling a little too much deja vu for my taste. I couldn't wait for the solo to be over and was the first one to leave the stage after the last cymbal crash died away.

Once again, nobody told me how much the show sucked. Because it was obvious and no one could do anything about it. An awkward situation like, I don't know, having a relative in a wheelchair and everyone studiously ignoring the fact that grandma can't actually get over the door jamb from the living room into the dining room.

We bugged straight out from the show back onto the road so we could get to a place in the Detroit/Ann Arbor area and, luxury of luxuries, actually sleep there three nights in a row. The ride was four hours from where we were to where we were going and three in the morning seemed like an imminently reasonable hour to arrive. Kevin and Colin were all set to drive the whole way but I drove the first hour in the van. Nobody said much except Carynne, who merely noted aloud that she was going to try to get us shower facilities at future gigs if she was going to be getting into a van with us post-show. It was too chilly to open the windows.

Carynne dispensed keys as if we were all permanently partnered, no one argued, and to our rooms we went. This was a nicer place, more on the business-y side than the tourist-y side. A place with room service that stopped at midnight and its own restaurant that also closed at midnight. (Not that I was in any mood to eat or that this did us any good at three a.m.)

I stood in the shower for a long time, making the water hotter and hotter, until when I got out my skin was lobster red.

When I came out Ziggy was sitting cross-legged on the bed, toweling his hair dry.

"Sorry," I said, for taking so long and making him borrow someone else's shower.

"Huh?" He squinted at me through damp black strands of hair, then flipped them back. "What for?"

"Everything," I said, loath to explain suddenly. "Just everything."

"Well, quit it," he said, coming over to me but leaving the towels behind. "Because we both know it's all my fault, right? It's all because of me. So quit worrying."

"I can't."

"You can. Will you forget all the bullshit for a while?"

"Just exactly which bullshit are you referring to?"

He let out an exasperated noise, his lips tight. "Didn't you say you wished things could be the way they used to be?"

"When did I say that?"

"During that anxiety attack on your birthday."

I'd forgotten about that. He'd tried to make up with me then and I'd had a panic attack. It was only the once so I hadn't thought about it since.

"Well, I'm trying, I'm really trying—"

I felt a chill.

"—but other things are not as they used to be, Daron. We may as well have you on tape up there, you know. You used to run around, you used to tell these little musical jokes with Bart in the middle of songs—"

I'd never thought of riffs that way but I guess that's what they were.

"—and now we get you a wireless rig finally and you're like glued to the spot, won't look at anybody. People notice this shit."

"I know."

"So, what's it going to take for you to lighten up?"

"I wish I knew." I was standing there, my fingers tingling with the realization that his skin was soft from the shower and that if I wanted to I could probably reach out and touch him.

He seemed to realize this, too. He almost whispered. "Do you remember how it was—"

I heard the sound of someone at the door before the actual knock. I turned away from Ziggy and looked through the peep hole. There was Digger, still in his suit, an unlit cigarette in his mouth. I put a hand on my towel and opened the door a crack.

"Hey, kiddo, just wondered if you were up for Denny's."

"No. Just going to get some sleep."

"How 'bout you Zig?" he said louder. I don't think he could see him through the crack.

"Nah, tomorrow though."

"Me and Kev are going to take the van."

"Yeah, okay." Whatever. I closed the door and leaned my head against it. I was so numb I didn't even feel worried or guilty or scared or anxious that Digger might have seen the two of us simultaneously damp and in towels. My heart was not pounding, my hands were not sweating, and incredibly I did not feel nauseous.

What I felt was cold.

I could almost see how things would have been if it had been the "old" us, me shaking like the proverbial leaf, Ziggy coming up behind me and doing me, and making me forget.

When I turned around he had on a pair of faded jeans and was digging a shirt out of a drawer. "Changed my mind," he said, pulling his boots on and then hurrying out the door to catch them.

I looked at the Miller's case on the floor, shook my head, and got into bed. I started thinking of a song, with a lyric: tomorrow—is just another day, then decided that was so clichéd I shouldn't even write it down.

I realized I'd lied to Ziggy when I'd told him I wanted things to be the way they used to be. Now just exactly what I *did* want, that was another story, one I didn't know how to tell.

Under Pressure

Detroit struck me as kind of an ugly town, at least the parts of it I noticed, haphazardly burned out and deserted right in the midst of otherwise normal-looking cityscape. I suppose New York is similar, only New York is so crammed it makes for a different effect.

The inside of the music hall was about the same as anywhere else, though. After soundcheck we met a reporter from a local magazine or newspaper who didn't have very many questions and looked to be more interested in the band who were opening for us, a local act that BNC was courting much the way they had courted us. Soundcheck was uneventful except for the way Bart flubbed the ending of Why the Sky and took off his bass and left the stage. I can't describe it as storming off because he seemed neither angry nor in a hurry. Chris and Zig shrugged at each other and then Zig looked at me and said, "Must have been something he ate."

I didn't go running after him—why?—Bart would tell me what he thought when he was ready to.

I was walking down the hall toward the men's room when I ran into Digger, literally; our shoulders bounced off one another and we both said "ow" in the same voice. And then we were looking into each other's eyes.

"Sorry," I said.

"Hey, kiddo, that's okay. Are you doing alright?" This time I heard what I would have to call fatherly concern in his voice.

"Yeah. Yeah, just a little tense."

He looked over one shoulder, then the other, and then he crooked me a smile. "Ah, I seen it all before. At your age especially, kiddo. Let me tell you something. I know you're trying hard to be real professional here, and do this right."

"Uh huh." I could not guess what he was driving at with this, so I tried to hang in with encouraging nods.

"Sure thing, I see it. She's sweet, and I know she's Remo's friend's daughter, but come on, boy, she's been going to bed alone every night, by herself, you know? That girl has a huge sweet spot for you. I know I'm supposed to be speaking as a manager here, but just man to man, I really think you'd feel better if you'd quit being a pansy about this and give her what she wants." His voice dropped low on those last three words as if they were too obscene to say aloud, even without polite company.

"What she wants," I repeated, a bit dumbfounded by the whole exchange.

"You'll feel better. This kind of tension isn't healthy. And I tell you what else, if you don't, one of these other studs is going to get on her. That's why they're all so antsy; it's an unresolved thing, like a pack of dogs and only one piece of meat, you know? Just do her, set the rules, you know, you'll make her happy that way. It's you she wants. She talks about you all the effin' time. I think it'll help you relax, too."

I'm sure my face was red, not with embarrassment, but outrage. He'd just likened Carynne to a piece of meat, and my friends to a pack of dogs. I wanted to tell myself: he doesn't mean it that way. But that's just the thing, he *did* mean it that way. And then I had another icky thought—he probably thought of himself as one of those dogs, too, like he was eligible to have a crack at her if I didn't do my duty. Ick. My pulse picked up and I stammered out "Yeah, I'll think about that," and took an obvious step toward the men's room door.

"You do that," he said, sounding jovial, to my back. "I guarantee! You'll feel better!"

Tears for Fears

In the men's room I splashed my face and stood with my hands leaning on the sink, watching the water go down the drain. The numbness had changed to a tingling, and some of my old nausea came back, my mouth and eyes watering a little. *I can't believe he said that* were the words in my mind, but I believed it just fine; this was the kind of behavior I'd expected from Digger all along. The water sounded like the roll of a faraway drum as the stream fell into the uncovered drain of the metal sink. When I straightened up my hands shook and I pressed them together like prayer hands.

I'd been so hot to get back on the road. Ziggy had said it himself, I had wanted things to be the way they were, onstage and off, before things got weird between us. But just being on tour wasn't enough to push us back in time. And I didn't know how to go forward.

Ziggy came in then and gave me a head-cocked look before he went into a stall.

I thought of a good word for the way I was beginning to feel, now that I felt something rather than nothing. Unglued. The word was unglued.

I decided that right before a show was a sucky time to come unglued and I marched to the dressing room, sat down at a mirror with Ziggy's makeup kit and decided to glue myself back together. It took several tries, but I eventually got a reasonable amount of pencil under my eyes. I picked up his tube of hair gel, the words *Alcohol Free!* in neon orange letters on the side. I couldn't imagine why there would be alcohol in hair gel in the first place and had a vague memory of the Michael Jackson/Pepsi conflagration. My own hair was too long to gel now, but I decided maybe it could do with a little taming anyway. I ran gel through the sides with my fingers and combed it smooth before tying it up in an elastic. My eyes looked huge now, with no loose strands to cover them and rimmed in black.

I sat with the Miller in my lap for the next hour while I waited for show time, running my hands over the rosewood fretboard and the silky finish, but there wasn't anything I felt like playing. I felt better, more together, with the guitar in front of me though, like some big fucking wooden teddy bear.

We lined up at the top of the little half-flight of stairs that led out of the wings, Chris in front, then Bart, then me, and Ziggy last. "Break a leg" Chris said, because he always did, as the lights went down, and then he started moving.

We took our places. On the first chord, the lights would hit, and everything would be fine, I told myself. The waiting's over, and now you can just *be*. But I didn't convince myself, apparently, because as the lights came up and we started to play, I found myself doing the same thing I had the past few nights, staring out into the crowd where individual faces wouldn't resolve, as if my eyes and my hands were from two different people. We opened with Welcome, a song which has a kind of upbeat chorus on the title, which makes it seem natural to open a concert with, but the verses are a lot of references to spiders and flies, and other sneaking suspicions.

And here came Ziggy, crawling toward me like said spider, on three limbs while one hand held the mic, the white shirt rippling as he bobbed his head and weaved snake-like, all the time toward me. I knew how stupid it would look if I ignored him, so I faced him, playing and watching his eyes, waiting for him to break off and go skipping back to the other side. But he didn't, he held my gaze and kept coming, until he was climbing up my front, first a hand on my knee, then his shoulder rising up to the level of my waist and two fingers walking up my torso as he straightened up to full height. His voice dripped innuendo as he leaned in as if to kiss me and then, then, he slid back, a cat move, as the chorus hit again.

I felt like I was short of air even though my breaths were long and deep. Worse, I felt myself rushing the riff, and could feel Christian pumping the kick drum more emphatically, as if sending me the message, *here! the beat is here!* Get with the program *ass*hole! I closed my eyes and concentrated on playing, on getting it right, which felt wrong, all wrong, to do with music I had written, like the song was some arduous thing I'd had to learn and practice and now could maybe give a recital of if I tried my best. This made me angry, that playing should be such a fucking chore, that songs that had come pouring out of me once should now be some kind of torture to get right.

I got so angry I broke a string and had to change guitars between songs.

Colin was there with the replacement guitar at the edge of the stage and he handed it to me and gave me a little pat on the arm like "buck up" or something. Bart was laddering notes nervously in the empty space, like sending me a message to hurry up. I hooked the strap and was ready for business and had to cross back to my side of the stage. Ziggy, his back to the audience, watched me with moon-round eyes and a puckered mouth dark with lipstick.

The next few songs were not as eventful, shall we say, as he kept to his area and I kept to mine. I saw Bart playing facing Chris a few times but I was not tempted to join them. The feeling of arduousness lessened a little on the older songs but crept back up on some of the newer ones. It's not that I didn't write them, I told myself, since the worst one of all had been Welcome, something I'd written without any input from Ziggy at all.

In Way of Life I could almost have been said to have begun to hit my stride, finally, and during the solo I even dropped to one knee, my worry-center short circuited for a short time by a great riff and a momentary feeling that the notes would come out right without my even trying. But then I thought about that, and I slipped up a little, sat back on my foot and pointed the neck toward the ceiling as I played. I was just shifting my weight to stand up again when I felt a hand on my shoulder from behind—Ziggy, suddenly there since I had no way to hear him approach, his hand sliding down my chest and cupping under my chin. He turned my face upwards so I had to look at him sing while I kept playing. "I won't live your way of life," he sang down to me, as he pressed my head back into his pelvis, and ground his hips. People screamed. I tried to butt my head backwards a little but we were pressed together too tight, and Ziggy gave a little animalistic howl into the mic as he arched his back like he was fucking a hole in the back of my head. Finally I jerked away and he skipped backward, the follow spot staying with him and leaving me in relative dimness to get back to my feet.

We were supposed to segue directly from Way of Life into Rain but I stood there panting, my back to the audience, pretending to cough while my mind whirled around trying to latch onto something. Chris was giving me a concerned look over the top of a ride cymbal. Colin and Digger stood side by side in the wings, Digger's dark suit making only the V of his white dress shirt visible in the purplish lights.

I took a step toward the crowd and heard Christian count off. Now I stood facing the band, the crowd on my right, as if I could somehow keep an eye on how they were doing, as if that might distract me from my own playing, as if that might keep Ziggy away from me but put me back in synch with Bart & Chris. Ziggy stayed out at the edge of the stage, pacing it like a zoo animal, while I stayed back out of the spot. Bart's eyebrows threw me a question: what are you doing back here?

We closed the set with Why The Sky, the crowd giving a proverbial roar of recognition and approval as we hit the opening notes. And here came Ziggy, sliding across the stage on his knees when I stepped forward for the solo, lying at my feet with his legs under him, undulating like a harem dancer. I had flashes of other shows, of how I used to straddle over him, him clutching at his heart as if every chord sank deep into him, or get down there with him, his arm over my shoulder as he sang in my ear. And here I was now, standing up like a soldier, stoic, looking down on him like he was some kind of street beggar I wished would go away. I could not let myself go. His eyes begged me to, Chris's bass drum nudged me again and again—if I looked up I might even see Bart give me a thumbs up or something. But I stood there and the moment passed and Ziggy stood up to take his bow.

The applause for the encore was respectable but not raucous and we went back out after the allotted pause, Chris with sticks held high. Ziggy told the crowd we would play a new one, from our forthcoming record, (Intensive Care, which I felt like I needed) and then came good old Candlelight.

By then, I just wanted it to be over. I felt like my nerves were frayed or like I was bleeding somewhere and if I didn't sit down soon I was going to bleed to death. The feeling of urgency grew as the solo approached and, my head down, I started to play note for note what I played the night before, what was on the record, a careful mimicking of what was once a piece of good playing. And Ziggy was coming toward me again, now that I was in his space, in the spotlight. He had left the microphone behind in a stand or somewhere, leaving his hands free, one reaching toward me, one sliding down to the loose waistband of his army pants...

He rubbed his crotch through the fabric and mouthed things at me, and I took a step back, and he kept on coming, and I took another step back until I bumped against something, PA, amp, something, and then he was getting ready to press me in close.

I don't even remember putting the guitar down, or taking it off, but I must have, because I didn't have it with me when I ran down the half-flight of stairs and down the dark hallway to the dressing room and stopped halfway across the room. I turned back to close the door behind me—too late, Bart was there slamming the door behind him.

He pushed a chair against the door and sat down in it. He folded his arms over his chest while I stood there panting, wondering what I was going to say, wondering what there was to say.

Disintegration

Bart's face was stony calm but his voice wavered as he said, "Do you mind telling me what the fuck is going on with you?"

Fuck hit me like a mic pop and I flinched. My hair hung in sweaty strings down my face and I slid to the floor, my legs crossed under me. I couldn't catch my breath and I couldn't figure out where to put my hands. My heart was pounding and I stuffed my hands under my arms and rocked back and forth. "Bart..."

"Is it your father? Is that what it is? We never should have—"

"It's not my father." That sounded so weird: *my father.* I put my hands on my knees and repeated it, still rocking, words coming out of my mouth too too fast. "It's not my father. Maybe, maybe it was at first. I mean, maybe I got a little nervous with him around—"

"A little nervous!" Bart started to get up and then crossed his legs as he planted himself in the chair again. "You... okay, if it's not him, what is it."

I kept looking at the spot on the floor in front of me. I couldn't catch my breath and my heart felt like a fist was squeezing it. Panic attack. "It's everything."

"Daron, give me something I can work with here. What can I do?"

"Nothing, there's nothing you can do." I wanted to lie down where I was and wait for everything to pass over me, wait for the feeling of the storm and churning to subside. "I've just lost it, that's all. It's just gone."

"What's gone?"

"The..." I didn't have words for it. Even trying to put words on it felt like a jinx to me, as if by describing it I'd make it stop working. But it had already stopped working. "You know how when you're a little kid, you go do something incredibly exciting, I don't know, you go to a movie or your parents take you to an amusement park or something. And there's this thing that happens, where you forget yourself?" Talking felt like vomiting does when you're sick— awful but a painful kind of relief at the same time. "It's like you're so happy that it's almost like a dream and you don't even realize it until you wake up." I dared to meet his eyes through the weeds of my hair and he was chewing his lip while he looked at me. "It's like you go away, you're in the magic place, until something brings you back."

"Yeah, I guess," he said.

"Don't be saying that just to get me to go on." I pulled my knees up, stage sweat chilling my neck and shoulders and making me shiver. "Do you know what I mean?"

"Like when you spent the day with your crazy uncle doing all kinds of cool stuff, but later when your mother asks you what you did, it's like you can't even remember."

"Yes." I'd never had a crazy uncle, but I suppose Bart did. "Yes, that's it. It's like you forget yourself, you're there doing it, but you're free somehow..."

"Like onstage," he said then, suddenly dropping both feet to the ground and leaning toward me. "I can never really remember that later, either."

My hands were shaking and I pressed them together. "Stay with me on this one, Bart." Now that I had started, I felt like if I didn't tell someone I was going to fly apart into a million pieces. Unglued.

"Okay."

"So, picture me, growing up, and every time I had that feeling, someone or something, usually my mother, or my sisters, or my father making trouble, would yank me back in. And then I discovered a way that I could get away, that I could make it happen." I held up my hands and looked at them. "Maybe, once in a while, I could get it just from listening... but I could always, always, do it by playing." My hands clutched at the air and I buried them under my arms again. "So picture me, miserable kid, spending every waking hour I could playing. Yeah, okay, it wasn't all bliss. I studied and I practiced and I learned new things. Because the better I got, the easier it got. The easier it got to let go."

The door thumped behind Bart, who shouted "Not now! We're busy!"

The muffled sound of Digger's voice came through, but not the words he was saying.

"In a minute!" Bart hollered then turned back to me. "I'm with you, man. Keep going."

The floor was cold, and I was cold, and I wasn't sure what I was going to say next. "Well, you get it."

"This magic thing, this forgetting, letting go, that's what you need."

"I can't play anymore, Bart. It doesn't work anymore."

"So what happened?"

"Ziggy happened."

"I was afraid that's what you were going to say." Another thud shook the door. I hid my face in my hands while he opened it, saying to whoever was out there, "Jeezus, what is your problem?"

Digger was there, I could hear the click of his expensive shoes as he shuffled into the room with someone else. I looked up to see him holding Ziggy by the arm. My father pushed him onto the couch and stared down at the two of us like he'd caught us joyriding in my mother's car or something. Family lecture time, I guess. Carynne tiptoed in behind him and closed the door.

"I...." Digger began, then threw up his hands. "I don't know what to say." (As I recall he had sucked at family lectures, and gave them up around the time we started sneaking out together.) "We've got a problem here, boys, and it ain't something I can fix. I can only do so much. I need to know from you where this is going. I need to know if we're going to cancel dates, or if this is a passing thing, you know?"

"Where's Christian?" I said.

Carynne spoke from behind Digger. "He's on the phone."

I guess it wouldn't have mattered what she said. My nerves weren't going any farther that night, my energy wasn't carrying me along one more second. I laid my arms across my knees and buried my face in them. I was always a crybaby as a kid. Realizing that right now tears were pouring out of my eyes and that I wasn't going to be able to hide it for long only made me cry harder. I wasn't sobbing, I wasn't hiccuping. It was not a hysterical kind of cry, it was just that I've-sprung-a-fucking-leak kind of cry that I had no power to stop.

I was still crying when I put my head up and said, too loud, "I'm tired." At least the panic was starting to subside. I no longer felt like my heart and lungs were going to pop.

Everyone did look at me, of course. I remembered for a moment that I could be in charge if I wanted to. I was amazed I could talk and cry at the same time. "We're going back to the hotel. We'll... we'll have a meeting in the morning."

Digger shot a glare at Ziggy but did not argue. No one said anything. I closed my eyes and sat there feeling the hot tears run down my neck and into my cold, damp shirt. The sounds of people packing around me came as if from far away. After a while I was alone in the room, and I stood up, and went out to the van.

Desperate But Not Serious

Of course they were all sitting there in the van, waiting for me.

Colin and Kevin stayed to supervise the load out with the truck but the rest of us could go back to the hotel. Everyone stared at me as I climbed, still in my damp stage clothes, into the seat closest to the sliding door and shut the door wearily. If Ziggy and I had ignored each other all those months, now everyone was ignoring me, studiously playacting that nothing was wrong.

Carynne drove, and kept looking in the rear view mirror at me, but said nothing. I felt defeated. I'd gone out there to do battle with my demon and barely survived. The drive to the office park area outside the city where our hotel blazed brightly was a silent one. As Carynne pulled the van into a space she said, as if it had been her idea, "Meeting at eleven, okay guys?"

In the lobby bar Digger started bantering with the cocktail waitress. Bart and Chris got into the elevator. I hung back and they waved to me as the doors closed.

Carynne closed her hand over my arm. "Do you want to go upstairs?"

"I..."

She pushed the up button and leaned her head on my shoulder, which was kind of tough because in her heels she was so much taller than me, and said in a soft, mellifluous voice, "Don't give me any shit, Daron, just say *yes*."

"Yes."

"Okay then."

The doors opened, and we stepped in, and as we turned around to choose our floor, I saw Digger give a little wave from the overstuffed chair he had parked himself in with a bowl of nuts. Ick.

The elevator was permeated by the sounds of genuine elevator music, an orchestral arrangement, with saxophone solo, of a Neil Diamond song. No, Barry Manilow, "I Write The Songs." As if I wasn't nauseated enough.

"Can you believe him?" I said when the doors had closed, relieved somehow to be able to talk about someone other than myself. "Earlier today he said all my problems would be solved if I would just sleep with you."

She shook her head and rolled her eyes. "Your father is a character."

"A sexist pig, you mean."

"I was trying to be polite."

"Well, I'm sure he thinks we're going off to do that thing right now." I sighed.

"Let him think what he wants. I thought he already thought we were?"

"Apparently not. Or, I don't know. He thinks maybe I gave it up for the tour, for professionalism, maybe?"

"It would have been sweet of you if you had." She kissed me on the cheek and the doors opened.

In her room she produced a bottle of rum and a two liter bottle of Coke, sat me down with them, went to get ice from the machine, and then came back and sat herself at the little desk table across from me and began pouring like a chemist, one glass for each of us. She sipped hers with a smile that spread like a warm glow and I almost smiled myself. She sipped and sipped until the glass was empty and poured herself a glass of unadulterated Coke.

"So, you mind telling me what is going on with you and Ziggy?"

"Nothing, nothing's going on."

She hiccupped slightly and I noticed how red her cheeks were under her pale skin. "Oh, don't tell me that. After all the arranging I did to get the two of you together so no one would notice? Oh Daron, don't tell me you're squandering this golden opportunity for decadence."

"I am."

"Ziggy must be heartbroken."

"Maybe he is. Car, I don't know what the fuck to do." The Coke was sweet and the rum was sweet and I felt like my stomach was on fire. "Jeezus, do you really want to hear this?"

"Daron, sweetie, do we have to go through this again? Hello? This is *me* you're talking to." She waved to me, the fourth person in a row to do so tonight, as if I were at a distance.

"Yeah, yeah, okay." I proceeded to finish the rum and Coke and tell her the basic gist of how, at this point, Ziggy seemed basically to want to get back together or to start sleeping together again or whatever way of saying that you want, but that when we'd tried, I'd had a panic attack. More or less just like I had tonight. I summed up the whole bit about how I used to lose myself when we had sex, and now I couldn't—not only that but I couldn't lose myself in performance, either. "Holy fuck," I said then, finishing another rum and Coke, "I just made it sound so simple."

She was massaging her temples and staring at the bubbles floating up out of her drink. "Simple, maybe, but still a doozy. I can't even begin to tell you how to solve this one, kiddo."

"Please don't call me 'kiddo.'"

"Sorry." She grabbed my hand then and squeezed my fingers with hers. "But, man, how to get the magic back. How to quit worrying and love the bomb, as it were. Like if you could somehow get back together with him, it would be alright."

We drank in silence for a while. I don't think I'd ever had rum & Coke before and I liked it. At least, by the fourth one or so I liked it. I was feeling drunk but much less unglued when I asked, "Well, if you had to take a wild guess, what would you say I should do?"

She shook her head slowly from side to side. "You gotta relax."

It seemed to take me a long time to blink. "I think this is as relaxed as I get."

"No, I mean, let your guard down. If he wants to fuck you," she put her hand to her mouth suddenly and said almost to herself "oh man, I use the word fuck all the time but when you use it to actually mean *sex!* It just sounds so *rude...*" and then went on "...but anyway, I say let him. Quit holding it in, Daron, just let it all hang out."

"But—"

"But what? If it can't get worse than it is, what do you have to lose? You may as well get laid...?"

My glass was empty again and I decided maybe just Coke was a good idea from here on out. "That's just it. I'm afraid it *can* get worse."

"How?"

The answer to that was nasty and ugly and I didn't want to say it. The downside of opening up to Ziggy was that I was afraid he could and would rip me to shreds from the inside. He could hurt me like no one else. So I said something else and changed the subject. Sort of. "Digger is not going to understand."

"Oh." She took a swig of Coke right from the bottle. "Oh yeah."

"I... wow." A wave of buzzy dizziness passed over me. "Did I tell you I told Bart?"

"No! What did he say?"

"I think he kind of knew already. I told Remo, too."

"Didn't you tell me that already?"

"I don't remember."

"So who knows, then? You, me, Bart, Remo..."

"Matthew."

"Omigod, were you sleeping with Matthew on that tour?" She started laughing, this high-pitched drunken screech, as if it was the most hilarious thing.

"Yes," I said, sure that I was drunk now, if I was just telling her this kind of thing. Inexplicably, I started laughing, too.

"Oh man, I was so nai-*eeve*," she said, between laughs and gulps of Coke from the bottle. She passed the bottle to me and I gulped, too. Nothing like a big caffeine and sugar rush to go with the giddy drunk Carynne was building, I guess. "How embarrassing! Gawd, and I *chased* you..."

When our laughs slowed down to, say, the pace of microwave popcorn when it's almost ready, she poured herself a trickle of water from the bottom of the ice bucket and drank it. "Oh man," she said. "My sides hurt."

"My brain hurts, but I'm used to that."

She stretched in her chair, her flowery print dress clinging to her. "So, you remember last time we had one of these head to head meetings, you told me about you and Ziggy, and now I know about Matthew, too. But did you ever figure out if you're gay or bi?"

I shrugged. "Does it matter?"

"Only in two respects. One, would Digger understand it any better if, you know, it was just like some weird sexual fetish of yours, this thing for men, do you get what I'm saying? as opposed to if it were a lifestyle—a

Yes I Am Gay kind of thing? Do you understand what I mean?"

"Um..."

"Digger strikes me as a guy who has been around the block plenty of times, seen it all, you know? So, I'm sure he's not a prude, you know what I mean? So if this thing with Ziggy was just some 'kink' I think he'd get over it. That's not the same thing as the *oh-my-god my son is a faggot* kind of scene."

"You know that makes a sick amount of sense." I couldn't quite parse why, but it did.

"So, there's two things you have to think about. One is, well, *is it* just some kink for you? Some kind of special thrill? Or are you just plain gay and have to accept it? Because, well, I know Digger might be cool with one but not the other, but, you know, I have to say, I think it'd be kind of twisted of you if that was the way it was, I mean, am I making sense? If you were just some kind of pervert."

"Hang on, hang on." I don't know which made it harder to think, the rum or the Coke. "So why isn't just being gay perverted?"

"Oh come on, Daron, this is the 1980s for gods sake. Gay people have been around forever, but now, you know, there are guys who are like having commitment ceremonies and adopting kids and stuff. It's totally not just like some back alley sex thing, like a peep show or prostitution or something."

I fell silent. I didn't know how to answer the question, or where to fit myself on this line she drew. For me, all sex was a back alley thing—Digger had taught me that from our earliest outings. And what I knew of gay men, I couldn't see myself doing interior decoration and sipping Perrier at art galleries. That seemed to put me pretty squarely on the fuck-addict pervert side, didn't it. But that was exactly the image I was running from when I pulled away from Ziggy in public, when I felt paranoid that people would have one look at us on the stage and think: oh, cocksuckers for sure. Would becoming the opposite help? Could we be like committed partners, could love redeem perversion? "Oh, my head hurts..."

"Lie down." She exhorted me toward one of the double beds and while I made my way to it, she filled a glass with water at the sink. She added ice cubes and said "Quick, Watson, some water. The flames of the mother of all hangovers are beginning to burn."

"What?" I sat up and wished I hadn't, the empty rum and Coke glass on my stomach rolling onto the bedspread. There's something weird about lying on top of a made bed that's not like lying down anywhere else.

Carynne sat down next to me. Some previous occupant of the room had bounced too hard on the bed and the springs sagged dangerously. She gulped water.

I smacked my lips. "OK, yeah, maybe I'm a little thirsty."

I reached for the glass next to me on the bed but as I reached, C. stood up and sent a kind of ripple through the ravaged box spring, and the glass rolled away from me and over the edge, "oh oh."

There was a smash sound as the glass connected with the hard edge of Carynne's Anvil briefcase. "Cheap fucking glasses." I lay back down, sagely deciding I was too impaired to pick up pieces of broken glass without severe blood being shed. "Thirsty," I said.

Carynne flopped down again, bed bouncing ominously, and waved the ice water over my head, melting ice cubes tinkling musically in it. There was a little of her lipstick on the glass.

"Here." She put a hand behind my head and tipped the glass toward my lips. The water was shockingly cold. I gulped and tasted wax and wondered when my heart started beating so hard. I gasped. Carynne's hair hung like an orange love-bead curtain between us and the window. She leaned forward and pressed her unnaturally soft lips against mine. I tasted wax and gasped.

"Is this a bad idea?" she whispered behind the conspiratorial curtain of hair.

"Is what a bad idea?"

She kissed me again and I had a fainting, out-of-body, my-head-exploded kind of blackout moment during it. "Holy shit."

"What."

"Do that again."

This time she explored my mouth with a rum-and-Coke-flavored tongue and it was like lightbulbs were being shot out behind my eyes. "That makes my head explode," I said, when I could.

"Is that good or bad?"

"I'm too drunk to tell."

"That probably means that any sane or well-balanced person would stop right about now."

"I'm sure I'll be upset about it in the morning. After all, I'm the... what did you call me before?"

"I can't remember. I'm sure I meant it, though. Can't we blame it on booze?" Carynne was still, magically, holding the glass of ice. She sucked a cube into her mouth. "Ziggy. We can blame it on Ziggy," she said, around the cube.

"That might even be true." My arms felt like they were on strings being pulled upward as they reached for her. She leaned down again and we passed the ice cube back and forth and I was starting to get used to how soft she was. Her dress came open and she put my hands on her breasts, hanging above me like volume knobs on an old-style control board. I ran my callused fingers over her nipples and she really fucking liked it.

As she was helping me get my jeans down she looked up, serious for a second, and said "As friends, right?"

"Carynne..."

"Friends, right?"

"Right."

The only other relevant things to say at this point are that she made me wear a condom, which I did not protest, the lights-exploding feeling went on even when my eyes were open, and I put off any potential hand-wringing or re-evaluations regarding my actual sexuality until a later date.

Birth, School, Work, Death

I woke up to an ache, not a headache, my thumb. I moved it and the ache oscillated but did not go away. I wondered if I'd whacked it yesterday and didn't notice. I felt it with the other hand—yep. There were bones underneath my skin and beyond that I couldn't tell. I opened my eyes. The goop I'd used yesterday had solidified my hair into pop art and my skin itched. As long as we're cataloguing my discomforts, it was 10:20 in the morning and besides the thumb hurting I think I was mostly awake because I was hungry. I never really ate dinner the day before.

Carynne was in the shower. I dragged myself down to my own room without disturbing her to find Ziggy nowhere in sight, though it looked like he'd slept there, and I got into the shower without investing too much more thought in that.

Add instead to the tally of life's mysteries, why it is that some hotels have terrific water pressure but others are altogether deficient? This place was acceptable, with only minor variations in temperature and pressure as time went on. I'd been in some places where it was scalding one second and freezing the next, but which had hardly enough flow to do any serious rinsing. As my hair grew longer water pressure was becoming a crucial factor in my daily logistics.

I was putting on my sneakers when there was a knock at the door. Carynne stood there wearing purple-tinted sunglasses and yet another flower print dress. "We're all down in my room," she said, "whenever you're ready." For the meeting, she meant.

As we weaved through maid carts up the hallway I tried to think of what to say. Last night, postponing the crisis to a later date had seemed like a good idea. But now I wasn't so sure. I stopped her with a hand on her arm.

"Who's in there?"

"Digger and the guys. I let the road crew sleep in."

"I can't go in there."

She pursed her lips and looked down at me over the tops of the sunglasses. "Daron, you called this meeting."

"I know, but think about it, I'm going to, what, tell Ziggy his coming on to me on the stage freaks me out? In front of my old man?"

"Oh." She rolled her eyes in what I was starting to recognize as an affected expression. "Jeez. Well, you have to tell them something. Or, what, should I go and say I couldn't find you? You've run off somewhere? They all know you spent the night here."

"Oh." I gave a low bark of frustration and a maid popped her head out from the room she was cleaning and gave me a worried look. "Let's go, just back me up in there, okay?"

"Okay."

Her beds were already made and Bart and Chris sat on one, Ziggy lay back against the headboard of the other, his stocking feet crossed. Digger sat in a chair by the window, his head angled toward the floor, "hungover" in the literal sense and I wondered if maybe that's where the word came from, from that tell-tale hunch.

I took the desk chair and turned it around backwards so I could lean my arms and head on the back of it. "Hi," I said. A moment or two of quiet went by as I composed my thoughts. "I'm sorry about last night. I know I was kind of freaked out. I guess we're dealing with stage fright, here."

There was silence for a long minute while everyone thought their own thoughts about that.

Ziggy folded his hands across his stomach. His eyes were on the ceiling when he spoke. "I suppose I could try not to do anything that would spook you." His voice was neutral but I felt or imagined so much more in it. I also felt or imagined Digger staring at us.

"Yeah," I said, my voice a bit phlegmy, "I guess."

"Yeah," Digger said, with the same sort of croak. "Lay off the faggy stuff. I mean, who needs it?"

I imagined I could hear the gears grinding in everyone's heads as they struggled not to stare at him, their eyes trying to turn his direction while their heads stayed rigid. And that was as close to the real issue at hand as anyone would state out loud.

"Hey, listen," he said then. "The seats in that van are killin' my back. I've rented a car for myself."

"Okay," I said, because he paused.

"Not to put too fine a point on it, but maybe we ought to keep you two separated. What do you say, kiddo, ride with me?"

I didn't answer but Carynne flipped the day book shut and said "We leave right after lunch," as if that settled it.

Who Are You

Bart and I had lunch together in the hotel restaurant, where a burger and fries was pricey, but tasty. After wolfing the burger down I sat eating my fries one at a time, munching them from one end to the other. Bart had a turkey club sandwich, with ketchup.

"You know," I said as soon as we sat down. "I really feel okay today."

"Why do you think that is?" he said in his curious and bright analytical voice.

"I don't know. Car' and I got drunk last night. Maybe I just needed to relax."

"Maybe we should get you drunk before you go on stage tonight."

I said "I don't think..." even while I half-considered it.

"I'm kidding." He pulled the toothpick out of one section of club sandwich and scrutinized it. "But you know, Digger's right."

"About what?"

He gave me a 'don't play dumb' look. "It's pretty flippin' obvious that Ziggy's practically chasing you off the stage. Think about it Daron, you used to do all kinds of shit with him and that was when you weren't..." Again, the checking to see who was near us. We were surrounded by banquettes of potted plants, a few balding businessmen in brown suits scattered in the middle distance. "You know."

"I know."

"The damnable thing about it is, that was probably the best show we've done in a long time. Up until the part where you ran off, I mean. Did you see the review in the paper this morning?"

I shook my head. "I only woke up a couple of minutes before the meeting."

"It doesn't matter. You heard the crowd last night. It was a hot show, and I mean hot in the musical, not porno sense. Listen, the Ziggy thing aside, here's something to think about. The idea of a stage persona, I mean. One of the ways people deal with fame is by creating a persona or role that they are on stage. Let the public fall in love with that. But then keep yourself to yourself."

"Where did you hear that?" The fries were hot and salty.

"I think it's something Sting said in an interview. Or maybe it was… no, I'm pretty sure it was him. But it makes sense doesn't it?"

"I guess. But it sounds sort of dishonest. Isn't that what prostitutes say too? And then bad stuff happens to 'Lily Lace' and not to Kathy Jones or whoever. I mean…" I caught myself looking into the distance, instead of at Bart. I focused on him. "I mean, the whole reason I get up there is because it is me, Bart. That's the only time I can really be me."

He digested that thought for a moment and then said "And you haven't been yourself lately."

"That's just it. The real me has been kicked out of the digs by the me I'm trying to get away from. Does that make sense?"

"Well, it explains it, anyway. Do you think Car's going to find you a shrink?"

"Fuck if I know. I don't think this is the kind of thing they can just look up in a book–'Ah yes, I see here, Mr. Marks, you have pseudo-psycho-sexual personality disorder. Take this pill and call me in the morning.'"

He pulled another toothpick out and held it up to the light.

"What are you doing?"

"Checking for splinters. Who was it, some country singer last year, died in a hotel restaurant while on tour from choking on a sliver of the toothpick."

"Jeezus, and you wonder why I'm paranoid?"

"No need to be paranoid," he said, putting the toothpick down gently. "Just careful."

"So tell me how to be careful about this without being paranoid."

He took a bite of sandwich first and then chewed. "You guys can get away with murder up there, if you just do it, if you go over the top with it. I mean, who did we see last year, that concert video, Motley fucking Crue forgodsake. You don't really think for one second that Nikki Sixx and Vince Neil are buggering each other."

"No."

"I bet if we watch Headbangers Ball tonight you'll see twenty images an hour that could be construed as homoerotic. But nobody thinks they really *are*."

"That's why there are all those scantily clad babes in those videos."
I was almost out of fries and was starting to eat those left slower and
slower. "But it isn't really fair to compare us to a metal band. Of the non-
metal bands out there, who do you really get that kind of show from?"

"Well, people used to get it from us."

"And who else? I don't know about you, but I'm getting the distinct
feeling that metal as we know it is on its way out."

"Prince."

"Oh surely you are kidding me. Prince has bisexual written all over
him with a neon magic marker."

"I guess I never thought about it before." Bart moved on to sandwich
quarter number three. "I mean, Purple Rain is all about him getting the
girl..."

"Oh please. Prince is about as sexually unambiguous as David Bowie.
The frills, the hips." I suppressed the urge to flip my wrist.

"OK, you're right. But Daron, come on, think about this, we've got
a singer named Ziggy for gods-flippin-sake who was never sexually unambiguous anyway. But, I just don't worry about what my parents think
when they see him grabbing my leg from the floor in a video."

"Your parents have seen the 'Why The Sky' video?"

He waved the sandwich at me. "I have no idea if they have, but that's
not the point. The point is that if they have, I really don't worry about it."

"But your parents know you have a girlfriend. In fact, if I remember
correctly your past is littered with rampant heterosexuality."

He almost blushed and hid it with a cough. "So you're saying that if
you weren't suffering some sexual ambiguity yourself, it'd be okay. But
because you are, you're afraid people will find out."

"No duh, of course that's what it is!"

"Shit, Daron, follow the logic here, though. The way it was before,
with the two of you hanging all over each other, nobody had a clue, but
now with you running away from him, it's maybe more obvious that
there is Something-With-A-Capital-S going on?"

"Fuck, I hadn't thought of it that way." Scenes of last night's gig were
flashing through my head. "But it's not like I have a choice. I didn't plan
to bug out like that. He comes near me and I just go fucking crazy."

"Let me throw out a crazy suggestion then. Two choices. One is, you build up for yourself a nice, rampantly heterosexual persona, and you let that persona duke it out with Ziggy on stage every night, or, number two, you make a truce with the Z-man and just stay the fuck away from each other on stage. Offstage, too, if that's what it takes."

"You know I hate both those choices."

"Why?"

"Well, for number one, it's the opposite of what I want to do, my whole reason for getting on the stage. Which I said already. Number two, well, I guess I'm just not up to talking with him right now."

"And there's the fact that you'd be fucking miserable standing in the back like some hired guitar flack," he said, just as I was thinking the same thing.

"Yeah, there's that too."

"There's a third option that I know you'll hate even more."

"I know what you're going to say so don't even say it." Coming into the open with it, in the press. "There's a million reasons not to, commercial suicide being only one of them."

"If you say so."

"Fuck on a stick, Bart, what if this doesn't work out?"

He twirled a toothpick in his fingers, unraveling the cellophane top. "Buddy, I am not even going to think about that. If we break up, if the album dies, if Ziggy moves to Tahiti with a supermodel, take it however it comes. Speaking purely from a selfish point of view, Dar', I think I'll always have gigs, even little ones, and I, you know, don't have to worry about being homeless or starving."

"I suppose."

"You'll always have gigs too, if you don't develop some kind of phobia about playing out or something. Or even then, there's studio work. You have the chops for all kinds of shit. And you have connections."

"Is this supposed to be cheering me up?"

"Just being realistic. I think I'm trying to say that the worst case scenario is really not so bad. Well, not taking into account stuff like heartbreak and blows to one's self-esteem, I guess. Do you want my pickle?"

"No." I looked around for a waiter. "Do you think we can get our check?"

"I already signed my room number on it," he said. "Didn't you notice?"

"You're shitting me."

"No, it's already done. Really."

"Christ, I really do live on another planet."

"No lie, bwana."

Life In The Fast Lane

So I rode to Ann Arbor with Digger. Hey, I thought, he's my dad, I ought to be able to spend an hour with him. Right?

We were both still a bit hungover, and opted to keep the radio off. I fell asleep for I don't know how long with my head against the window. When I woke up, we were driving into a heavy overcast. The van was in front of us, the truck behind, and I could see Bart sleeping with his feet up in the back seat. The car's interior was plush, plum-colored, and smelled new. I was thirsty and wondered if I'd been sleeping with my mouth open.

"So this place, it's some kind of a disco."

"Hmm?"

"Wake up, lazybones, I'm talking to you. The Pittsburgh place."

"Carynne mentioned they'd moved us to a bigger venue?"

"That's what I'm telling you, the bigger place is this dance club type thing. Pittsburgh's all converted industrial space, you know." He drummed on the steering wheel as if he wished the radio were on after all. I switched it on to hear the last power chords of the Who's "Baba O'Riley."

"We'll see it when we get there," I said in a resigned voice.

Digger barked out a laugh. "Listen to you, Mister Jaded, tour weary already?"

"I've learned not to get too hopeful or pessimistic about these things." Did I inherit the use of the word "Mister" from him, I wondered? I didn't remember him saying it when I was a kid, and yet it seemed more likely that I'd picked it up from him than vice versa. I was trying to remember if Remo said it, too.

"Yeah, yeah. Look kid, there's a couple of things I gotta tellya. Just speaking as an older individual here, now..."

Meaning what, not speaking as my parent or manager?

"...speaking as someone who has been around the block..."

Which I couldn't help but hear as "The" Block...

"...you've got to accept the fact that there are some things you can't really have wisdom about, can't really be wise about, until you get older. No matter how much talent or skill or smarts you have, you have to accept the fact that there's just shit beyond your understanding."

"Uh huh." I was trying to remember what I'd said that brought this little speech on.

Digger was wearing chinos and what I thought of as an alligator shirt (which would have been brand name Izod? LaCoste? something like that) but was actually a Polo shirt, as in capital P Polo for Ralph Lauren, with a little polo player embroidered over his heart. I kind of wondered when he'd started dressing like this. When I was a kid he was always either in his salesman suit or a pair of faded jeans and a T-shirt. The suits looked basically the same, only better, now, but I wondered when the preppie casual wear came into play. He was still talking.

"I wish there was some way I could just transmit to you the experiences I've built up over the years, you know, without you having to go through them yourself. I mean, I can talk and talk but I can only hope that some smidgen of it all will sink in, enough to get you through come what may."

Digger, whether he'd been drinking or not, used to sometimes get up in front of the guys and pontificate in this kind of low but bombastic way, not unlike he was doing now. So he'd say things like "you know" and "whatevah" but punch it up with phrases like "come what may." I wondered if he knew he did that, if it was some artifact of his own aborted schooling, or what. He'd had two years of college before he was either expelled, dropped out, or took a better opportunity, depending on who you talked to about it and what kind of mood they were in. I was still never clear on how he'd met Claire and ended up married to her, managing her father's shoe store. That might explain the better shoes he wore now, though.

He was still talking.

"So that's why I'm telling you all this now, just hoping it'll help. You know I have your best interest at heart. You know I do. So don't think I'm saying this out of some kind of obligation."

I'm not sure he was aware that he hadn't imparted any actual advice.

"So do you understand what I mean? Or am I wasting my breath?"

"I gotcha," I said, figuring that no, he wasn't aware of it and there was no way I could tell him. It was funny, though, there was a kind of approval in his voice I didn't often hear. Which seemed counter to what I expected, having practically run screaming from the stage the night before—I'd expected to be chewed out about it, in fact.

Then a horrible thought struck me. I'd slept with Carynne, just like he'd told me to. And earned his approval. I suppressed an actual shudder and wished I could go back to sleep. "How far do we have to go?" I asked, hoping I didn't sound too eager to escape.

A while later he said "So I've been thinking about breaking off from WTA."

"What?"

"Technically, you know, I'm managing you guys freelance. I'm not really an agent there. I'm thinking of starting my own agency. Things wouldn't change between us, of course. But I think a couple of other WTA clients might come with me."

"No kidding, like who?"

"Mostly movie talent. The Hollywood connection is where the most dough is. Remo makes a ton just doing quickie film scores, but there's so much more. The real trend is for radio-ready songs to be in sound-tracks now."

"Is that so?" I wondered if that was something he actually knew or if he'd just heard someone say it, or read it in a magazine. It sounded like something I might have heard Remo say, actually, but I wasn't sure. "Nice work if you can get it…"

He drummed his hands on the wheel to Creedence Clearwater Revival. "It's exciting to be a part of it, isn't it?"

"Uh, yeah."

"Hey, has Ziggy done any acting?"

"Haven't the foggiest."

He looked like he was about to say something more about that, but then his mouth kind of went slack, as if he'd just thought of something unbelievable. "You know, you could really be a big part of it all."

"It?"

"Look, I don't want to go into a lot of dry financial detail, but, you know it's going to take a fair chunk of change to start my own company."

"I would bet."

"And well, there's basically three ways to get the money needed."

"Adventure capital, you mean?"

He chuckled and then slapped his knee like I'd told a good one. "Venture capital, kiddo. Venture capital. Well, that's one way, you go to these adventurous investors, who put up a lot of dough, but who... well, let's just say that we also call them 'vulture' capitalists. Then there's taking out a loan from a bank, which of course you gotta pay back, and which takes a lot of convincing to get. And then there's something that is better than both of them put together."

"Which is?"

"Trusted friends and relatives buy into the company. They each own a piece of it. And their collective worth looks good to a bank, so a generous line of credit can be established so cash flow won't run short. It's the best of both worlds."

I think I see where this is going. I would have said it but I didn't trust my voice.

"Whadda ya think? Wanna be a V.P. in my new company?"

"Digger, I'm not really executive material."

"C'mon, that's not what I mean. I mean, have a real piece of the action. Partners." He was nodding his head in time with Led Zeppelin now, his hangover gone or forgotten. "You know the kind of money we're talking about here? I don't mean like the peanuts BNC gave you. I mean, serious money, like ten to a hundred times that. I'm talking about you being set for life from one year's earnings, if we hit it big."

I'm pretty sure at that point I made a non-committal grunt, or some kind of non-committal statement. I am fairly certain I did not say "Yeah, sure," or anything that a reasonable person would construe as endorsement. But since when was Digger reasonable?

That was the end of the discussion, though, as we pulled off the highway and concentrated on following the van closely.

Anyway, maybe it was a good idea—the whole keeping me and Ziggy apart all day and ignoring each other on stage, I mean—because the Ann Arbor show went off without a hitch.

Only the Lonely

Back at the hotel that night, my room was dark and quiet and it looked like the last person to be in here was the maid: the toilet paper folded into a triangle, the beds smooth.

Ziggy'd gone to crash with one of the other guys to stay away from me, but had left some of his clothes scattered around. I watched some cable TV, a bit of the Headbangers Ball (and damned if Bart wasn't right) and paced around.

I packed what I'd taken out of my bag back into it, checked my supply of cash (which I kept in the neck compartment of the Ovation's case—maybe stupid to keep my money with my most expensive possession, but that way I figured I'd be sure not to leave it behind somewhere and I'd be watching to make sure it wasn't stolen).

I took a shower. My skin itched now from being too dried out, all the dry hotel air, and washing too often. In the bathroom was a little bottle of hotel brand lotion and I sat on the bed smearing it on my arms and shoulders. I couldn't help but think, if Zig were here, and we were speaking to one another, he could be putting the lotion on my back. If he had come back to get the rest of his stuff...

And yet I knew I didn't want him to come back.

Hmm. It dawned on me I'd been kind of ignoring the fact that I was horny all night, hyped up from the show (finally!) and wishing I could do something...

Logically speaking, Carynne should have been the person foremost in my mind for that sort of thing, no? But she wasn't, which maybe says something about exactly where on that scale of gay-bi-straight I really fall, or maybe says that I knew, as she'd said, that it was "as friends."

If only we were in a city, and not stuck out here in the burbs. I knew there had to be places men went for sex but didn't know how to find them. Back in Jersey there had been a rest area pull-off from a local highway near our house where men went to get sucked off in their cars by other men. When the police busted some local guys and then closed the area for six months it was in all the newspapers and on TV. I remember Claire expounding her disgust about it. One of the men caught had been a teacher at a local junior high school. I don't know if he lost his job, but I think he did.

I always kind of wondered though, where did those guys go after that? How did they get the word out where the new rendezvous was? How did some place like that get started, anyway? Someone had to tell someone something. Or the Block in Boston, where would the hustlers go if the police set up shop there?

That gave me an idea. I opened the drawer to the nightstand and under the a bright red Gideon Bible was a fat Yellow Pages directory. I flipped through and found a large section on escort services. Huh. Even here in midwestern suburbia there were listings. Pages and pages of them, blondes, brunettes, etc. But most amazing of all, the first in the alphabetical listings: "AAA Gay Dating Service." Jeezus. I suppose if they weren't first in the listings I'd have never noticed them among the many "Exotic Ladies" and "Gentlemen's Companions" ads.

I had two hundred dollars cash in the guitar case by the window. But, I could all too easily imagine Ziggy walking in on me and a hustler. That was probably the biggest reason I didn't pick up the phone. Instead I decided to see who was still up, if anyone. I thought I could hear someone by the elevator. I put on a pair of jeans so I'd have somewhere to put my key and went out into the hall.

Digger, wearing only his pants and an unbuttoned wrinkled dress shirt, was hanging on some woman's arm at the elevator bank and she was giggling. The elevator came and she stepped in and blew him a kiss and then the doors closed. He sighed and turned toward his room and saw me. "Hey, kiddo."

"Hey, old man."

He smelled of cigarettes and booze and perfume. "Hey, kiddo. You want to come in for a nightcap?"

"Uh, naw. Just going to the Coke machine. I'll see you in the morning." And I went to the vending machine, too, even though I hadn't brought any change with me. I heard his door close with a heavy thunk of the lock.

The room was as I had left it. I got in bed and lay in the dark imagining I could hear snatches of songs in the occasional sound of the heating system kicking on or a flushed toilet somewhere else. In the dark I imagined Matthew lying next to me, and that I could roll over, and various things would ensue.

I ended up in the shower again, jerking off, because I knew I'd never get to sleep if I didn't.

Dance Hall Days

It was raining in Pittsburgh when we arrived and seemed much darker than it should have been for mid-afternoon. There was no thunder, just sheets of rain, the water seemingly warm but the gusts of wind cold. My thumb ached.

The venue was a general-admission type club, but a big one, with a clean dance floor and immense rig for lights. Despite the cleanliness of the place the air was stale with cigarette smoke and spilled beer.

We all helped with load in to speed things up as we were in a No Parking Zone and the sanctioned place to park the truck was two blocks away. I hadn't realized it before, but the change in venue made the show earlier, as well. The club promoters were going to put us on at six p.m., then clear the place out after we were done and let the disco crowd in. They did the same thing with live shows the Citi Club in Boston and it didn't really affect me one way or the other.

The backstage area was a basic unoccupied office kind of space that was literally behind the stage, a short hallway with one big room on one side, and two small rooms on the other, one of which was also a store-room for broken, unused, or out-of-fashion lights. We moved ourselves happily into the big room and I once again began to think of my life as a long parade of secondhand couches. These had sheets over them as if they might be too hideous too contemplate. The walls were painted completely black with occasional glittery graffitoes, band names mostly, and some bumper stickers.

A club employee wearing a bunch of laminates around his neck stuck his head in to tell Carynne that someone had dropped the ball on catering and what did we want. She told him to come back in five minutes. There was plenty of stuff around, pizza shops, a pinball arcade, etc. and I suggested they ought to give us all the bottled water and beer we could drink and a hundred extra bucks and we'd fend for ourselves on food. The PA had been rented for the occasion and took longer to debug than usual. Digger stayed with us while Carynne went to the hotel to get our rooms set up. In other words, things were in their usual logistical frenzy of preparation.

And eventually it was time to go on.

I had not forgotten what it was like to play to a dancing, jumping crowd, with people pressed close against the foot of the stage, as much sweat and smoke and heat coming from them as there was from us. The air was humid with rain and the air of people. With my eyes closed I could sense them, and I played notes out into them like a beauty queen throwing kisses. Every now and then Ziggy would catch my eye and kind of do a little shuffle-dance, but I'd look away, into the sea of faces. With the smaller size stage here I spent all my time right up at the front, while Intellibeams pierced fake fog like rays of god light, and police lights twirled above the dance floor. My thumb hurt a little but not enough to do anything about. The crowd was going proverbially wild and I wondered what radio stations here played us. The truce between me and Ziggy held and the show went without major mishap.

When we came off stage, Christian poured half a bottle of spring water over his head and then put his wet hand on my shoulder (which was almost equally wet with sweat), and said "Thank the lord above, praise the lord" in a voice that was supposed to sound Southern preacher but came out a bit like a Richard Nixon impression. Then he added in his own voice, "I knew it wouldn't last."

"Knew what wouldn't last?" As if I didn't know.

"I think you just needed to get back in touch with the audience, Boss."

"Yeah, now if only I can get back in touch with you and Bart, we'll be in business again."

"Me and Bart can take care of ourselves," he said and took a series of long gulps from the bottle.

Bart was changing his shirt. "What do I have to take care of now?" he called as his head emerged from the neckhole of the clean shirt.

"Nothin'" Chris replied and left me to do my own changing and such.

Our hotel was nearby, and not long after nine o'clock we were back in the one room with a suite, sitting around telling the same stupid jokes as always. Carynne was checking messages on the phone, Digger and Chris had gotten into a cribbage game. I set about changing my strings even though Colin said he'd do it for me. I just felt better doing it my-self somehow. Someday maybe I'd have somebody like Matthew along just to take care of the guitars. But not yet. I got the Ovation strung and would play a little, then have to tighten the strings, then play a little, then tighten again.

Colin, who was sitting next to me as if he might jump in and help if needed ("C'mon man, you're paying me to do something besides sit with my thumb up my ass...") finally asked me, "What is that thing you play?"

"This?" I played through a little bit of the riff I was using and laughed. "It's probably one of the first songs I ever wrote." It was a lot of open chords and fingerpicking, a kind of Steve Howe sort of thing. It had no words and hence no title in my mind, and it kind of went with the occasional spatter of rain on the window.

"It's cool," he said, tapping his fingers on his knees. "Pretty."

Bart, who'd heard the tune more times than anyone with the exception of myself (and maybe Remo), put in "Yeah, but it's got no ending."

I stopped playing and tuned the strings up again. For some reason the G always goes flat faster than any of the others. "What does it need an ending for?"

Colin looked at me askance. "Why doesn't it have an ending?"

"Because I was like eleven when I wrote it and could never decide where it was supposed to go," I answered.

"Well, it's cool anyway," he said.

I started the tune again. There was a little strangled cry from behind me and Ziggy (it had to be Ziggy) wrapped his hands around my face from behind and tilted my head up so I was looking into his crazed face. "I can't take it anymore! Play something else, please."

Bart laughed. "No, c'mon Zig, tell us how you really feel."

"Alright, jeezus." I switched to "Here Comes the Sun" which I seemed to be stuck on lately.

"You know *hundreds* of songs, I'd think a little variety would be a natural thing..." Ziggy was saying from where he stood behind me on the couch.

I started to put the Ovation in its case but Bart motioned for it, so I passed it to him while I started restringing the Strat. He started playing Paul Simon tunes and I kind of sang along while I worked. Ziggy and Kevin got into another round of musician/light bulb jokes. Everything kind of came to a sudden halt when we were trying a rendition of "Me & Julio" and an argument over the lyrics broke out.

Chris: "It's 'When the copper found out he began to shout at the start of the investigation.'"

Bart: "No, no, it's 'when papa found out he began to shout and he started the investigation.'"

Chris: "But that doesn't make sense. The 'mama pajama' ran to the 'police station,' hence 'the copper' and that makes more sense with 'investigation.'"

Bart: "You're wrong. It's 'Mama' and 'Papa.' That makes sense."

I chimed in. "Come on, none of it makes sense. It's just a fun song. I mean, what about the verse about the radical priest and stuff?"

Digger was shuffling the cards and I was surprised that he jumped into the argument. "I think Christian here has a point. I don't think that's the way the song goes, but it might be better that way. Then again I don't think Paul Simon really wanted people thinking the song was anything but nonsense, given the implications." He put the deck down on the coffee table. I think my mouth hung open a little—this wasn't the kind of analysis I expected from Digger.

Chris cut the cards. "What implications?"

"It's got to be either sex or drugs, don't you think? I mean, what was it that the mama saw him and Julio doing down there in the schoolyard?" He dealt cards to himself and Chris and then looked up for consensus. "Don't you think?"

"Drugs, it's got to be drugs," Chris said. "I mean, it was the sixties."

Actually, it was the early seventies, but I didn't say that.

Digger arranged the cards in his hand. "Yeah, that's what he assumes you're going to think. But me, I think Paul Simon's a faggot anyway."

OK, so maybe it was what I expected after all. Carynne hung up the phone and glanced at me with a did-I-miss-something? look. I turned my eyes studiously to the tuning machines and said nothing. The moment probably would have just passed if Ziggy hadn't said "Now hold on, what makes you say that? Isn't he married?"

"If I remember correctly Carrie Fisher was his second wife," Carynne said with a wave like *hello-I'm-here-too*.

"You mean Princess Leia?" Bart said.

"Yeah."

Digger just grunted. "Like being married means something. Even having kids, that doesn't mean a guy don't bend over in the park. A course, that's why he got rid of Garfunkle. Because Garfunkle was even faggier."

Ziggy threw up his hands in resignation and I sat there tuning and tuning and pretending the whole thing never happened. It's not like it was the first time I'd ever heard Digger say something like that. I'd probably heard the word faggot (or some variation thereof) come out of his mouth more times than I'd heard him say my name. That thought began to depress me and I wished the guitar were strung already so I could play something to change the subject or at least distract myself.

The subject changed anyway, as it always did, though, and people went on to talk about other stuff like nothing had happened. Because nothing did happen. People saying crap like that is normal, right? Especially when Digger is talking. Thing is, it was starting to bother me, and

I think it was bothering everyone, but no one really knew what to say about it. Or at least, I didn't.

A while later I went back to my room, and turned on the TV.

I still got a little rush whenever I turned to MTV and saw us or heard us mentioned. Why the Sky had just made their top 20 video countdown, according to Digger who'd talked to Mills earlier in the day. I had to watch maybe ten minutes before it came on.

They had flown us to Arizona to film it, driven us out into the desert where they could get lots of footage of us miming our parts while standing on top of weird rock formations. In the video they had time lapse segments of the sun setting into the mountains, and of clouds streaming through the sky. It had been hot and dry in the desert, and we'd had to do the main bulk of the filming at the literal crack of dawn before it go too hot each day, but looking at the finished product, I think it was probably worth it. The movement of the clouds was mesmerizing.

I think I was asleep when the knock came on the door.

I was surprised to see Ziggy standing there. He gave one of those feigned nonchalance type shrugs. "You want to get something to eat?"

"What are you thinking?"

"I'm thinking wander around and see what's good. It's only like eleven, and you didn't eat a thing at the club."

I nodded, he was right.

"Come on," he said with that shrug again, "we've got nothing better to do."

"Yeah, alright." I zipped my leather jacket up.

Voices Carry

Outside rain was still coming down, but we walked along from awning to awning. We came to a used record shop that was open until midnight and browsed a while, and then one of the clerks recognized Ziggy and we signed a copy of the vinyl album from the original Charles River pressing.

I was following Ziggy who was following his nose and not saying much. We passed through a convenience store where he picked up some Raisinets ("for later") and looked in the windows of several different eateries. We were pretty damp by the time he took us into a barbecue place, but my mind wasn't really on the weather. We placed our orders at a call window and a kind of American Indian-looking guy, with dark skin and short black hair, told us to sit down. We took a space in a booth with orange plastic chairs and a yellow Formica table that looked like it might have been cribbed from an out-of-business Burger King.

"So, how do you feel?" Ziggy said as soon as we sat down.

"I think I'm okay." I played with the calluses on my left hand with my left thumb.

"Did it really help for me to stay away from you?" He looked earnest, leaning over the table so far he was almost looking up at me instead of across. "These past two shows?"

"I hate to say it but it did. I think."

"Because I made you nervous."

"I guess."

"Am I making you nervous now?" He was using his down-to-Earth voice.

"Not yet." The black-haired guy put drinks in paper cups down on the table without looking at us and rushed away. There was a line at the call window now and the seats were filling up with rain-dampened college students. Some kind of event was letting out, I guessed.

He leaned forward even more so he could talk quietly and still be heard by me. "You know that's not what I want."

"What's not."

"I'm not trying to make you nervous. I'm trying..." He blushed suddenly and sat back. Then he leaned forward and said closer to my ear. "I'm trying to make you want me again." He slid back in the seat, and slumped, his legs wide and his shoulders bent.

I sipped my lemonade (the kind that came from a bubbling clear plastic machine). Finally I said to him, "Why?"

He chewed his bottom lip while he studied the pattern of scrapes in the table's surface. "You know why."

"Because... " Now I leaned forward, though over the sound of the cooks shouting to each other and people laughing and talking I doubted anyone could make out what we were saying to each other. "Because you want me? Is that all? Why me, Zig?"

Someone in a greasy apron put two cardboard boats of fries down in front of us. "I don't think this is the best place to talk about it," Ziggy said, salting his fries with the plastic shaker.

You'd think it would be me who would have been the antsy, nervous one, talking about this stuff in public. "You brought it up."

He grimaced. "I did. I'm sorry." He fingered the edge of his fry boat but didn't say any more. Well, until he said, so quiet I barely heard it myself, "And I really, really am sorry about Chicago. Truce?"

"Don't chase me off the stage and we'll be fine," I said.

Two styrofoam plates of brontosaurus-size ribs appeared on the table. Ziggy retrieved plastic silverware for us both, two knives apiece because he wasn't confident that one knife could withstand the meat. But as it turned out, the meat was as soft as wet tissue paper and fell right off the bone.

(*Readers of the DGC website funded this bonus chapter from Ziggy's point of view, telling the story of how the band went to Arizona to film "Why the Sky." We'll pause in Daron's narrative now, to let Ziggy have his say. More bonus scenes can be found on the Daron's Guitar Chronicles website.*)

147. Ziggy's Arizona Chronicle

He has no idea.

He really doesn't.

He's so used to fading into the background that he has no clue how beautiful he is. Daron, I mean. He had no concept of himself as attractive.

This puzzles me. At first I thought it was an act, false modesty. But as I got to know him I began to realize, he not only doesn't think of himself as attractive, he doesn't even really have a good sense of what he looks like to others. This is a guy who will walk around all day with his shirt buttoned wrong and never look in a mirror to figure out he's still got stage glitter in his hair from the show the night before.

This really hits home when we're in Arizona to film the Why the Sky video. We're in the make-up trailer, and he's getting his face done while I'm getting my hair done, in adjacent chairs. And he is arguing with the stylist.

I come to the poor woman's rescue. "Dar', just let her do her job."

"But I don't want to look done up for this."

"That's the point. She's going to put make-up on you so that no one can tell it's there."

"Then what's the point of it?"

The stylist and I exchange looks, and I think of what to say. "That's the thing. Because of the lights and the way the camera works, you'll look all washed out and weird if they don't put something on you."

He looks at me like he thinks I'm kidding, and I see him go through a thought process. I am seeing this all too often, weighing whether to believe me or not.

He decides to believe me this time. "Okay."

The guy trimming my hair pokes me with his thumb. "What about you? Want me to change anything?"

"Yes," I say. "Change everything."

I've been trying to figure out when I started to lose him or if maybe I never had him at all. Thinking back, it's more likely the latter. He doesn't even remember the first time we met.

It was a party on the Cape, with a bonfire on the beach, and he was sitting on a log playing guitar with Bart, but Bart was only playing half the time, and chatting up some girl the other half of the time.

OK, I'll admit, I was chatting up a girl myself, a different girl from the one who'd brought me to the party in the first place, who had gone off with some preppie guy supposedly to try to score more drugs. I wasn't much interested in drugs then and I was pretty sure it wasn't drugs they were scoring anyway. It ended up with a bunch of couples all making out around the fire, except for him, just playing the guitar and sometimes singing softly to himself.

In case you've never tried it, sex on the beach is actually pretty hazardous unless you like abrasion and sand in places it really shouldn't go. So I didn't stay down there long. The girl and I went up to the house and found an unoccupied bed, but in my ears it was like I could still hear him.

I figured I'd never see him again. I forgot the girl's name immediately, but I didn't forget his.

Sometimes I want him so much, I think maybe it's more than I've ever wanted anyone in my entire life.

He's standing on a butte in Arizona, with a hot dry wind blowing his hair back and the sunset painting the whole landscape with umber and gold, staring at his shoe. He has no idea how much the camera loves him. He isn't even aware that the camera is on. He's in his own little world and I really wonder what he's thinking about.

I hope he's thinking about me, but he's probably thinking about music.

Some days, I feel like my one goal in life is to get his attention.

Lately, though, when I get it, it's usually for the wrong reason. That night, we're back at the hotel where they've put us and the crew. It's nothing special, but the suite is spacious and some of the tech crew have gone out and brought back booze, and we're sitting around shooting the shit. Daron's got a guitar in his lap but he's not playing at the moment, just lying there, staring at the ceiling, slumped on the couch. But the conversation flows around him.

It eventually turns to the usual subjects, which is to say, women, and as the all-male crew gets drunker, we end up talking about sexual exploits. One of the camera crew tells a hilarious story about losing his virginity to an older woman, which for some reason rubs me the wrong way, and the next thing you know I'm being challenged to tell my own.

"How old were you? Was she older, too?" the guy says.

"Yeah, she was older. I was fourteen," I say.

"Fourteen!" Bart sounds surprised.

"Why, how old were you?"

Bart is pretty hard to shock, and I realize his exclamation wasn't shock at all but something else when his apple cheeks redden. "Oh, it's just, I was fourteen, too."

Camera guy shakes his head. "That's why you guys are the rock stars, I guess."

Bart shrugs. "She was sixteen, does that count as an older woman? We were in an all state high school band together."

"Two years? Eh, maybe. At that age, everyone out of high school is ancient," I say.

"So how old was she?" Camera guy asks.

I realize that I have no idea. "Old."

"Like, old old? Or just old."

"I dunno, like twenty five maybe?"

"Holy crap, talk about robbing the cradle…!"

"Well, I lied and told her I was eighteen." My turn to shrug. "Maybe she was only like 22, 23. Hard to say. At the time it didn't seem like a big deal." What had mattered most to me was that she was old enough to decide for herself what she wanted.

"Did she believe you?" one of the other video guys asks.

"I guess so. Like I said, we didn't make a big deal out of the age thing. She didn't even know I was a virgin."

"Dude, why?"

"You think I wanted her to think I was an eighteen year old and still a virgin?" I shake my head. "Besides, if she knew she was my first, it could get complicated. I was just in it for the sex."

Nods all around. I don't even have to get into the whole thing about how I thought it was better to lie about my age to get laid than to pressure girls my own age into doing something they weren't ready to do.

Daron leaves the room before anyone can get around to asking him about his first time, mumbling something about jet lag and a headache.

I go into his room a little later and hand him a bottle of Gatorade I bought out of the machine by the lobby. "It's the altitude and the dryness, or so they tell me," I say. "This'll help. Drink it." He does what I say.

If only he always would.

Okay, while we're on the subject of first times, I have a kind of confession to make.

I really fucked up my first time with him.

Not that I regret it, don't get me wrong. That was some of the best sex I've ever had, with anyone, of any gender or age. He'd probably say the same.

But it's complicated. He actually is the first guy I went all the way with. But I played that up too much maybe, and so if I ever tell him the whole truth, it'll come out like a lie. I let him think I was a lot less experienced than I was and now that he's figuring that out… he's slow on the uptake, you know, but he's not stupid.

I played "doctor" with friends when I was a kid, both boys and girls. I jerked my best friend off when we were twelve, at a sleepover (and then he was too chicken to do me back).

I've watched a lot of gay porn. And I know I've got a reputation now as reckless. But I wasn't so reckless that I ran out and tried to suck or get sucked in a Times Square theater on my eighteenth birthday. The word about AIDS was just starting to spread then. Or I should say, the fear about AIDS. It made me not just steer clear of sex with men. I steered clear of gay men's culture as a whole. I didn't really start looking into it until after Daron and I got going.

And then I'm not even sure why I did, other than Boston had a pretty vibrant gay men's scene then. Bookstores, clubs, bars, gay-owned cafés, newspapers. I started soaking it up; it was like discovering a new cuisine.

But like I said, I don't know why I bothered. He may be gay, but he's not *culturally* gay, if you know what I mean. I guess it's like the difference between being Israeli and Jewish or something? He's homosexual, but he doesn't fit any mold of "gay man" out there.

And of course I live to break the molds. But he's pretty much texbook "straight-acting, straight-seeming." It's hard to tell how much of that is he's suppressing something, and how much is just that his cultural role models are so different. His role models are people like Eddie Van Halen. And Remo Cutler.

I dont know why I ever thought it could work with me and a guy like that.

☆ ☆ ☆

Arizona is another planet. Mars, maybe, since everything is all rocky and desert-like and reddish.

After I put Daron to bed with his glass of water, I went out the back way from the hotel to see what there was to be seen. I got in a cab and started asking questions—cabbies always know where the hot places are. He dropped me off at a nightclub with loud music and a line outside.

I didn't get into much trouble. No one recognized me with the new hair, and the number of people who tried to speak Spanish to me told me I didn't look here the way I do back in Boston.

In Boston, I read as "ethnic" when I'm not just plain passing for white. "Ethnic" could be Greek or Italian, I've learned, whereas in New

York I'm more often mistaken for Puerto Rican, or mestizo. No one knows what the fuck I am.

And I like it that way.

I came back to the hotel around four in the morning, having had my dick sucked (badly, but can't be choosy all the time… and she was pretty) and having lost a few hours to some pill in combination with some drink(s).

Here's where I'm supposed to say I would rather have spent the night with him, right? Except that would be a lie. I like my fun. But I wouldn't mind spending the *next* night with him, you know?

"There's no hope for this. We're just going to stick you in sunglasses."

The stylist's voice is too loud in my ears. My head feels tender to the touch. Even I can see in the mirror my eyes are bloodshot to hell, though. They've already tried industrial-strength Visine and it was all I could do to keep from screaming when they put it in. "Fine."

The director is wringing his hands. I mean, literally like grabbing himself. "Oh, if only we'd done those lip sync shots yesterday," he is saying, pretty much to himself. Like what he's thinking is ack, rock stars, why did it have to be rock stars? Get used to it, buddy.

"We've still got tomorrow," Daron points out.

"True." The director takes a clipboard from the skinny female PA standing next to him and looks it over. Daron takes it from HIM and scribbles something on it and hands it back. "Yeah, you're right."

"I want some sunglasses anyway," I announce. "The sun here is fucking killer."

Another PA, this one male and in need of a shave, hands me a pair. I put them on and slink out of the trailer, waiting for the Tylenol to kick in.

Daron comes up to me a little while later, with a bottle of Gatorade. "This'll help," he says. "Drink it."

"My head hurts," I say. "I mean, like, hurts."

He looks at me like he has no idea what I mean, but then I think maybe he does, because he reaches out and runs his fingers very very very gently through my hair.

It feels good. I lean toward him.

He presses his fingers against my scalp, both hands now. We're sitting on a low rock wall at the edge of the parking lot, and the sun is lethally bright, but he's massaging my head. I see him do these little exercises all the time with his fingers, like he's playing invisible pianos, and it gives him such a light touch.

I want him to touch me like that all over, but I'll settle for this right now. My jaw relaxes. Time stops moving, but his fingers don't.

And then someone is calling us to get in a Jeep to head up to the butte again, and he pulls away before I can say *thank you*.

That night, no shenanigans, because we're going to shoot at sunrise. It'll be our final day of filming, and he and me and Bart decide to stay up all night instead of trying to sleep for like 4 hours before the wake-up call.

The two of them are playing guitars, and then after a while Bart switches to a little Indian drum someone picked up as a souvenir along the way. And I start singing along, not like *singing* singing, you know, just kind of joining in.

There's no audience here, not even the rest of the crew, just the three of us. Even Christian's asleep already.

Daron starts up the riff of a song we worked on with Jordan, one of the ones we didn't end up putting on the record, one that didn't really quite come together, but which goes around and around and around now, and I'm making up lyrics as we go, about flowers and rocks and clouds, and dancing and love and, like, kittens and stuff.

When we wind down, Bart's laughing, and Daron has a goofy, self-deprecating grin on his face, and all I want to do is kiss him.

No really, just kiss him. Which would lead to me wanting other things, but I'm not kissing him so let's not go there.

The moment passes, and he starts playing something else, something I don't know, but he only has to wind around it twice maybe before I start to make a melody on top, quiet and sweet. He's picking individual strings, and it reminds me of a music box, and I hum and *la-la-la* a counter-melody.

Bart falls asleep with the drum in his lap, and Daron and I just keep going along. And the next thing I know he's singing with me, harmonizing, this song with no words at all, but the melody is as clear as words in my head, and his too, I guess.

Can't be explained in words, maybe. What that's like. Making music with somebody like that, with no idea where it's going, just in the moment.

Okay. I suppose it's like sex in that way.

We aren't even looking at each other, and we don't have to be. When our eyes do finally meet, we bring the song to an end.

There are no words. We have nothing to say to each other that isn't hurtful. So we don't say anything. By telepathic agreement, we say nothing. He slips the guitar into the case, and then sits in the silence.

Or almost silence. Bart snorts in his sleep and breaks the spell.

"Maybe that's a good idea after all," Daron says.

He goes to bed alone. I stay up and write lyrics to the song, wondering if I'm even going to have the guts to show them to him later, or if that's just going to be one more thing we'll fight about.

Not that I'll give in, of course.

I finish the song and the wakeup call is going to come in under an hour. I take a shower and lie in bed damp, watching TV. The Candlelight video comes on and I watch it, the golden light and screaming people and his fingers crawling up the neck of his guitar… I can't even remember which city we were in when they filmed the footage. San Diego?

If it was San Diego, I suddenly realize, then it was before. Before him and me. Before I knew what his mouth tasted like.

His mouth, but not his sweat. There's a moment in the video where we're pressed so close together, I get his hair in my mouth.

I can't wait to get the taste of Christmas out of my mouth. We'll be on the road soon. And you know how tours are. Things happen. I fell into his arms once. Maybe this time he'll fall into mine.

One Of These Nights

The wake up call came at ten, and we motorvated ourselves to pack up what we'd scattered and get dressed and get out. Digger hit the road for New York, and the rest of us to Philadelphia.

I drove the first leg, wearing what I still thought of as Matthew's sunglasses and playing a 90 minute tape I'd made mostly to horrify the guys, a mixed tape of stuff I knew that I, and they, had listened to a lot of not so many years ago: Toto, Journey, Hall & Oates, stuff that was never going to have a retro-revival and which was not aging well. Bart shrieked when "Hold The Line" came on and said we ought to do a cover of it. "C'mon, I know you know it," he said to me, and was right. I refrained from making any promises. On the B-side I had E.L.O., Supertramp, a little George Harrison solo stuff.

Today was another five hour trip, not counting pit stops. We arrived at the Philly hotel at three in the afternoon and I was a bit bleary from having napped the last hour or so. So my eyes weren't the best-focused they've ever been when I walked into the lobby. Which would explain why when Jonathan jumped out of a chair and started shuffle-running toward me my first thought was—whoa, psycho killer. But that impression didn't last as I did then recognize him. Much handshaking and back slapping ensued and this only slowed down the check-in process slightly.

"Jeezusfuckingchrist, it's good to see you," I said as we walked to the elevators together. I meant it, too.

"So you mind if I hang out?" His hair, dirty blond and overgrown a bit in the front curtained his eyes as he shrugged.

"Not at all. Stick around. We're off to meet the crew and check next. I haven't seen what the plan is for dinner, show time, et cetera yet."

"Whatever. I've got nothing better to do."

"So this is pleasure, not business?"

"Technically I'm here to do a short piece on the band that's opening for you. But I only live like an hour and a half from here, I figured I'd catch up with you guys. If a story comes out of it, well..." He pushed the button in the mirrored elevator lobby. "You won't mind, would you?"

"Did we already have a conversation about where you're from?"

"I don't remember now..."

"Because you live not terribly far from near where I grew up, if I remember rightly."

"Maybe we did have this conversation before."

So Mister Freelance Journalist became attached to our retinue once again. During the less-noisy part of our soundcheck he interviewed the other band, then sat and listened while we played full volume. I hit the riff to "Hold The Line" and Bart laughed so hard he couldn't even join in.

"Are you alright?" came Kevin's voice through the monitor. (He'd been in the truck during the earlier AOR hits fest and didn't get the joke.)

Bart regained his composure and we ran through a couple of things until the other band started looking edgy and then we quit and gave them the stage. I decided not to eat much before the show and go out with J. after. I spent most of the time playing on the new strings to get them worked in.

OK, how to describe the show: mostly uneventful, pretty good over all. Maybe it's a bad sign that I was getting used to being kind of hyper-sensitive and downright stiff on stage, and playing predictably. I could make it through, and the crowd clapped for an encore, and we did Candlelight of course, and then we were done. My mind was already wondering where Jonathan was taking me, as he'd insisted that he pick the place but wouldn't tell me where. He also insisted he'd pay for it, which I thought was kind of weird, but I was willing to play along.

His car was a beat up hatchback, the back seat covered with half-read newspapers, books and magazines, empty tape cases, fast food wrappers, etc. He told me the front seat had been like that too but he'd cleaned to make room for a passenger. We drove to the Four Seasons hotel where he let a valet take the charming vehicle and then into the lobby we went.

"You've always struck me as a fast food kind of guy, and forgive me if that's a mistaken prejudice," he said as we walked over a carpet so soft and thick I felt like I was walking across wet sand.

"I eat what there is," I said, my hands in the pockets of my jeans and wondering if my still-damp-from-the-shower hair looked ridiculous among the crystal chandeliers and claw-footed chairs we walked by. "And we've been living on Denny's."

"Are you ready for a change of pace?"

"You bet." I followed him up a shallow set of stairs and past a fountain to what was clearly the entrance to a restaurant: the little lit podium and fresh-faced hostess gave it away. We had reservations even though there was no one in there at that hour and she did not even give my high top sneakers or wet hair a glance. Not that Jonathan himself was terribly well-dressed. He always dressed like every bit-part "writer" character on a TV sitcom I'd ever seen, purposefully so, I think, right down to the jacket with suede elbow patches.

Most of the fancy restaurants I had eaten in had been during the last two years, some with Bart who took me places his parents used to take him when they'd lived in MA, and some with Digger like the fancy place he'd taken me and Carynne on Christmas Day. So I knew at least part of the drill, like what a crumb squeegee was and what it was for. But we were the last customers into this place and it was like we were eating in the mansion of some billionaire recluse whose entire staff were turned out to serve us. I can't even remember the name of the thing I drank, but it was a before-dinner kind of drink, and then we had a wine that perfectly matched the food, and I won't even try to describe the food because it will just sound ridiculous when I botch the list of exotic ingredients and try to convey the artfully sculpted prettiness of the dishes.

This was food so good it made me... giddy.

And the dishes came out at just a leisurely enough pace that we were able to pack away huge quantities of food without being overstuffed until the end, which was chocolatey and beautiful and hallucination-inducing.

By hallucination I mean the persistent feeling I was having that this whole meal, the witty banter, the friendly jokes, were all part of some grand scheme seduction. I recklessly licked my dessert dish and Jonathan laughed, betraying nothing.

And it turned out he was actually staying at this hotel, despite living only one and a half hours drive away, and we went up to his room to continue our chat about how MTV UnPlugged was both the perfect savior for MTV and its antithesis, and speculating about what Jools Holland was up to these days, and other ancillary industry bullshit that made me feel close to this guy even though I didn't know him from a hole in the wall.

We lay side by side on the bed and channel surfed and saw the Why the Sky video, which I would have shut off if he'd wanted to, but he seemed to really really want to see it, and then at some point I began to feel myself fading. And that's when I said "J-" (the nickname I'd come to call him in the course of the evening) "can I ask you something?"

"What?"

"What made you become a rock journalist?"

He laughed and answered immediately. "The urge to spend late nights hanging around with people I worship and idolize, what else?"

"You really mean that."

"You're living proof."

"I can't quite wrap my brain around that."

"What, that I'd make a profession out of it?"

"No, that you think of me as someone to worship or idolize."

"Get used to it, D-" (which became his nickname for me) "because it's just going to snowball from here. I got on the bandwagon early, I mean really really early."

"That's right, you saw us in Providence, the previous incarnation."

He nodded.

"Jeezus, J." We were both looking a little drunk, I think. His nose got red like a cartoon wino's. "You know, you don't have to bribe me with lavish luxury meals to get me to spend time with you."

"I know," he said, "but I wanted to."

"Next time you'll let me pay."

"If you say so. It's just such a luxury to actually get to spend time with someone I like, you know? I mean, I had to spend like two weeks touring Europe with Sting and it was such a hardship. I mean, Sting's I nice guy, but I don't know, I wouldn't invite him to the beach house for a week. And so often it's like, oh, twenty minutes here and then, poof, gone. Like I was supposed to spend three days with R.E.M. last December and it eventually boiled down to a single interview given in the limo on the way to the airport."

I yawned. "What are you doing tomorrow? Come with us to DC. It's only, what, two, three more hours from here?"

"Can't," he said. "Deadlines."

"Ah." Now was my moment to leave, I felt, if I didn't want to possibly end up in some kind of awkward situation. Right now I did not even want the awkwardness of finding out if the situation would be awkward or not. "I think you better put me in a cab."

"You could stay here." Bing! Another drop in the bucket that said, awkward situation to be avoided.

"They'll worry," I said.

He nodded and made as if to use the phone. Then he sat down on the edge of the king sized bed and said "Can I ask you something?"

"Sounds like you already are."

"Something kind of personal. Off the record." Bing!

"You can ask but I can't promise I'll answer."

His face was serious, the most grave I'd ever seen it. His voice was quiet and I used the clicker to mute the TV. "What happened between you and Ziggy?"

Ice clogged my veins, then a hot flash ran over my skin. I had a pang of this morning's heartbreak feeling. "It's that obvious, is it?"

He shrugged. "Not to everyone certainly. But I've seen you perform so many times, and like what they got in the Candlelight video, pretty explosive. Now it's like... it's not like that."

I could only nod in agreement.

"Is this 'creative differences?'"

"I guess you could say that. I'm not saying that to be coy, either." I was trying to be real matter-of-fact about it. The last thing I wanted to do was cry on J's shoulder. "If I could neatly describe my relationship with the Z, well, maybe it wouldn't be such a mess."

"Ah." He nodded like he understood. J. kept up the light but analytical tone, thank God. "Do you think there's a bit of the classic singer/guitarist conflict in here, or is it something else?"

My turn to shrug. "I don't know if I believe in the 'classic' situation. I mean, Plant and Page, Daltrey and Townshend, we're talking about pretty unique guys here."

"Full of idiosyncrasies and unknown variables. That's true. Yet it feels like there's something of a pattern in rock and roll conflicts."

"Spoken like a Brown student," I said, sitting up more in the bed and swinging my legs over the side next to him. "Ziggy and I are on some kind of rollercoaster." The idea that maybe I could tell J more flashed through my mind, and then the thought that this could potentially be very bad careerwise followed it. But half-truths could lead to wild speculation, too, so maybe I should just be straightforward about us... off the record. "How much do you know about me and the Z?"

He hunched where he sat and looked at me sideways. "Are you asking what I know, or what I suppose?"

I held out my hands: whichever. "You can probably make some pretty wild guesses and you'd probably even be right about some of them."

"Aha." His head came up suddenly and he pressed his lips together like he was quashing a smile. "Speaking purely speculatively then, I think either you and he weren't involved before, but once you got involved your stage presence changed, or it's the other way around, you were involved, and now that the relationship has gone cold, it's reflected on the stage. One or the other, I can't tell."

"Christ," I said and rubbed my eyes. "I hope you're the only person for whom it's that, like, obvious."

"Well, I'm not the..." but he broke off and said "So which is it?"

"I hate to answer like this, but it's kind of both and kind of neither. Like I said, if it were so simple, we'd have fixed it." I brushed hair out of my eyes. "But you were saying?"

"Oh, just I'm not your average observer. I mean, most people look at the Candlelight video and are just not going to think it's homoerotic."

I was thinking back to the conversation Bart and I had had on this topic. In some way I felt almost prepared for this discussion and no panic welled up. "But you did."

"No. Only after meeting you and him, then I started to wonder."

"Did he tell you anything?"

"Not in so many words, but, well, did you read the article?"

"Um." I tried to remember. "Not all of it."

"Oh." He chewed his lip then, worried, a mannerism I hadn't seen on him before.. "I tried to soft-shoe it, as it were, just give his and your words verbatim and not try to draw to much attention to the whole issue of, shall we say, sexual ambiguity. Or… or make people think I was trying to… agh. I think you better read it."

"I better?"

"Just so we'll be on the same page." He couldn't help but snort at the pun there, then he paused as I looked at him blankly. "Oh, I have in my briefcase."

So there was no getting around it. "Okay. I'm not too drunk to read."

He hopped off the bed and pulled several issues of Spin from his bag and flipped through them. He handed me the one that had us on the cover.

That odd shot that looked like it was taken when we were just goofing around, not posing. Ziggy's eyeliner looked more exotic than ever. Like war paint. I flipped the pages. We were closer to the front than I remembered.

I hate the way my publicity photos look, the way most people hate how their voices sound on tape. I had forgotten Ziggy was shirtless in his and I suddenly wondered why he was holding a guitar in it. Not playing it, just sort of hugging it. There was also a shot from the Candlelight video, the three of us on stage, but it was focused on the silhouette of the crowd. I liked that one.

Here's something you may not know. Those sections of interviews where they print Q and A? They're never the way the conversation really went. They edit out the dumb stuff, and the diversions, and put it all into a logical order. I read the edited down version of that conversation Jonathan and I had in a hotel bar one night and he'd made sense out of it. A kind of sense, that is.

I realized suddenly that he was nervous. And the longer I sat there staring at the page, saying nothing, the more nervous he got.

I finally closed the magazine and said quietly, "You can kind of connect the dots to make the picture here."

He said nothing.

"That is, if you know what the dots are." I raised my head.

"I wanted to be… true to you, without being too obvious," he said, sitting on the bed across from me. "I didn't know that there was something to be obvious about, either, you know? I just wrote what I saw. What I heard."

"Yeah." I had to stretch and I rubbed my forehead. It was not lost on me that neither of us had exactly said what it was that we were talking about, but I said: "The secret is safe with you, right?"

He held up his hand, thumb and pinky touching. "Promise. Exciting a story as it would make, it'd mean I'd never get to hang out like this with you again, wouldn't it?" Something about his face made me think he was making a larger point about friendship.

"Come with us to DC."

He grimaced. "Man, I wish I could. I…" He looked like he was getting ready to blow off some serious commitment.

I wondered if I could pay him back for whatever money he'd lose if he blew a freelance article assignment or something. Then I decided that would be a horrible idea and make us both feel weird. So instead, I said, "Please?"

He looked at me with a sober expression. "I'll make a phone call in the morning, see if I can rearrange a little… no promises, but maybe I can work it out."

I smiled, feeling like a weight had been lifted. "Awesome."

He seemed lighter, too. "You want that cab now?"

"Yeah, I better."

The doorman hailed me a cab from downstairs and the cabbie was fortunately able to figure out which hotel I meant when I couldn't quite remember the name ("kind of a weird name, some guy's name… or two guys maybe…") and dropped me off at the Adam's Mark Hotel.

I sat down in the lobby where J had been sitting when we'd come in. I didn't want to go upstairs just yet. I sat there in the piped in lobby music (the Four Seasons had been blissfully Muzak-free) and thought. So, was J coming on to me, or not? I didn't get that vibe, yet he definitely had this urge to be close to me, to be "intimate" but I wasn't sure that meant in a sexual way.

I was coming to see something Remo had described about people who can be fanatical about you. It's hard to tell, he'd said, what it is that inspires some people to go to the ends of the Earth for you, and they can make powerful allies in the biz, but they can also be kind of creepy and obsessed and such. Not that I thought J was creepy at all. Far from it. And Remo had also told me to take friends in the biz wherever I found them.

I hoped J could come to DC with us.

Hooked On Classics

We were a three-vehicle caravan still. Digger headed off for New York in his rental but Jonathan's hatchback joined us. Bart and I both rode with him, which was fun. J was very easy to get along with and I got the feeling Bart genuinely liked him, too.

The drive to DC was so short in comparison to what we'd been doing each day that we were shocked to arrive so early in the day and find our rooms not ready. Everyone milled around with little heaps of luggage except me—I tagged along behind Carynne as she sought out the manager. Carynne went for the jugular when she found him and we only waited maybe fifteen minutes in the lobby before he gave her keys. (Digger would have been proud.) As she accepted the keys and switched her expression from tangled annoyance to California smile, she saw me out of the corner of her eye. She pressed a key into my hand.

"So, tell me, is Señor McCabe rooming with us?"

"I, ouch. I don't know."

She rolled her eyes and blew a piece of nonexistent hair out of them. When she marched up to the group she passed out keys as usual and then said casually but loudly to Jonathan, "We've got plenty of bed space if you want to crash with us. I don't mind if the Boss doesn't mind."

I flapped my mouth and held up my hands like whatevah, no-biggie. J had left his stuff in his car anyway—we could sort it out later.

Even stranger than the arriving-early break from routine, we weren't playing a show tonight. (In fact, it was a miracle that Carynne had set up as tight and regular a schedule as she had.) The idea was to come down here rather than stick around Philly an extra day, and do some publicity and maybe sightsee if we wanted to. On the map it didn't look like we'd come that far south, but here summer was beginning to happen already and Carynne and me and Jonathan and Bart had lunch in an outdoor cafe and I got my face sunburned while sitting there.

Carynne opened her day book while we were waiting for the check. "Did I tell you everything about today's schedule?"

"Unless anything changed since we've been on the road, I think we went over everything pretty carefully before we left," I said, shading my forehead with my hand.

Bart sat forward. "Remind me."

Carynne sucked on the end of a pen while she told him about the two interviews we had for today, one for a newspaper, and one on-air radio station gig. "What songs do you think you'll play?"

"Whoa," Bart said, "Play?"

She turned her eyes on me. "You didn't tell them?"

"I... I didn't really think about it. Is this the one where they want us to do an in studio 'unplugged' kind of thing?"

"Dar', I don't have an acoustic bass."

I winced. "You can play the guitar, though."

"A little rehearsal would have been nice."

I looked at him, still wincing. When we'd set this all up I wouldn't have dreamed we'd ever need to rehearse anything, but that was before my own bout with stage fright or whatever the hell I was having. "Why don't you play bongos?" I suggested. "Chris has some. Just the three of us do it. Didn't the station say something like they only wanted two of us to talk anyway?"

Carynne squinted in the bright sun at her notes. "Yeah."

"It'll be fine," I said, watching traffic go by and ignoring the pursed-lips look of doubt and skepticism that Bart was giving me. Hey, everyone had said to lighten up and stop worrying so much, and I was, wasn't I?

First came the interview for some entertainment rag, which Ziggy and I did in the hotel lobby. It was almost a rote interview, how did you meet, what's it like being on a major label, who are your influences. It'd be a one page feature running alongside weekly clubdate ads and our publicity photo, I knew. I'm not sure what everyone else was doing while we were doing that. Jonathan and Bart reappeared to go with us and Carynne to the radio station at "drive time" i.e. rush hour. I brought the Miller and Bart brought a set of bongos.

In the van on the way over (Carynne drove) Ziggy asked "So what should we play?"

"It won't be more than two songs," Carynne said.

Ziggy pressed his hands against the ceiling of the van and stretched his shoulders. "One old, one new?"

"'Walking In Time' works good acoustic," Carynne suggested, with a glance at me in the rearview.

"How about 'Walking' and 'Windfall' then?" I said as we came to a halt in traffic—the disadvantage of doing a drive time interview, I guess. Maybe we should have taken the subway.

"They're both kind of depressing, though," Ziggy said. "We should pick one fun one."

"Just which of our songs do you consider fun?" I asked. "We're just not going to compare to, say, They Might Be Giants or The Dead Milkmen."

"Hmm, good point."

Carynne added another data point. "This is a pretty heavy AOR station, guys, not alternative at all. Two serious songs'd probably do them just fine."

We arrived with enough time to get whisked through a heavily bumperstickered business office into a studio, shake hands with disk jockey, situate mics, and get stools and cups of water for everyone, before we were on the air.

The disk jockey's name was Mike, who on air referred to himself as Mick Blabber. During the mic-situating, I convinced Bart to do the talking along with Ziggy while they miked up my guitar. The walls of the studio were lined with shelves of LPs and directly behind the dj was a rack of about sixty compact discs. Stacked up all around the control board were blue and gray cartridge tapes. We all put headphones on which meant that when the dj hit his mic the only indication we had that we were on the air was a white light that came on next to the studio door.

The light looked like maybe it had said "On Air" or something else once but the letters had been scratched off over the years by bored and destructive engineers. Through the glass windows we could see Carynne talking with staff members.

And then the song (Bob Seger's "Katmandu") was ending and Mike was speaking, a stream of smooth patter, his name, call letters, relevant stuff about weather and traffic and then "I have with me here in the studio the members of Moondog Three, playing tomorrow night at the Palazzo. A show I believe is sold out, but we, we of course, have some tickets to give away, and we'll give some away in just a little bit but first let's say hi to the boys."

"Hi," we chorused.

"There are three of them here folks, but, tell me the name of the group is Moondog Three but there's really four of you."

"That's right," Bart said, leaning in to his mic. "We left the drummer home."

"Hiiii, Christian," Ziggy said.

"So what's the three refer to?" Mike said, facing us across the little counter top separated him from us.

It doesn't mean anything, I was thinking, but had no mic to speak with. Bart and Ziggy looked at each other. I started to play the "thinking music" from Jeopardy on the Miller.

"Whoa, kids, didn't mean to stump you." Mike looked like he was in his mid-thirties and liked to overeat. Someone once told me that the only people who stay in radio are those too funny-looking to be in television. Maybe. He gave me a wink and a nod like—yeah, keep up that playing to fill the space.

Ziggy spoke up. "There's a bunch of different answers, but if we told you, then we'd have to kill you."

"Oh, a mystery then. Anyway, we've got here today Ziggy..." Squinting at his notes.

"Yo."

"Bart..."

"That would be me."

"And Daron."

I played a little bullfighter-ish Spanish riff.

Mike had this way of saying one thing into the mic while seeming to say something else to us with gestures and facial expressions. "So you've got a new record coming out, what, in a few months?" is what his mouth said while he seemed to be asking us if we'd be ready to play a song soon. I nodded a lot.

Ziggy told him about the new record while I plucked out part of Wonderland. There was some more essentially content-less banter which I couldn't add to, so I played more in the background, little riffs here and there.

"Yeah wow! This guy's great, he's like your own personal soundtrack," said Mike to Ziggy, at which point I started an improvisation on the Darth Vader music from Star Wars and everyone cracked up. "Why don't you fellas play us a song."

"OK, alright, this one's from the new record," Ziggy said, making eye contact with me—okay?—"live and unadulterated..."

"Oh no, no adults here," added Mike.

"... and we call it Windfall."

Bart counted off and then we were doing it. First just Bart and I playing the intro, and then, Ziggy coming in singing, breathy and sweet and in a different voice than the way he usually sang it. He let himself improvise on the melody like a jazz singer, and I forgot all about the On Air light being on or what it meant. Here were the three of us, playing, sitting in stools like we could be sitting on a park bench somewhere, with a couple of interested people standing around listening.

And so it was, just like that, that I did it for the first time in what, months? I forgot. I forgot to worry about things and forgot to wonder what anyone was thinking and simply played. And two verses later as the solo came up I came back to myself and realized the solo was really not going to work without severe improv work, which was too much to hand to a drive time audience, and I made it into the ending instead.

Mike and other studio personnel clapped.

"No applause," Bart said "Just throw money."

After the interview they took us into another studio and recorded us saying things like "When I'm in Dee-cee, I listen to..." individually and as a group. And we signed some stuff for their prize vault, and for the staff, and shook hands with the program director and then we were back in the van and back onto the roadways.

"Great job you guys," Carynne said from the driver's seat.

"That was cool." Bart held the bongos in his lap like he wanted to keep playing them. "Did we get a tape?"

Jonathan held up a cassette. "They taped it from the prod studio."

"I bet Chris taped it, too," I said. We had the radio tuned to the station and they were playing a Nomad tune, "Missing." No one seemed to notice my brief return to sanity during "Windfall" and I felt better not mentioning it. The next song to come on the radio was Dire Straits "Telegraph Road"—a song I hadn't listened to in a long time but was pretty sure I had brought on tape with me.

"Is this on Love Over Gold or Making Movies?" I asked the general air.

"Love Over Gold," Bart answered. He was sitting in the seat behind me, drumming without seeming to realize he was doing it, on the back of the seat instead of on the bongos in his lap. He sat forward suddenly. "Hey, you know what we could do tonight?"

"What."

"We could... see a show." He said it like it was a truly strange and novel suggestion, and maybe a bit lewd. And maybe it would be if you consider it voyeurism for performers to watch other performers succeed or fail.

Jonathan laughed. "I'd think you'd want to rest your ears one night at least."

"Eh? Did you say something?" Bart answered, cupping his ear.

"We should have asked at the radio station if they could get us in anywhere, what shows are going on," Jonathan continued. "Ah well."

"Let's see what Chris & crew are up to," I suggested. "Maybe they've picked up the newspaper."

Jonathan turned partway around from where he sat in the front seat.

"If you could see anyone, anyone at all, tonight, who would it be? Any-one. A genie gives you this wish, and you just have to think of who. Dead or alive. Who?"

Ziggy winced. "Only a reporter would come up with a question like that."

Jonathan. "Off the record, I assure you."

"Jeezus. I have to think about it," Ziggy said.

Bart hesitated only a moment. "Spinal Tap."

The sound of "Missing," Remo's subtle guitar propelling the melody along, still echoed in my ears. So I lied when I told Jonathan that it was a toss up between the 1968 Beatles and the 1971 Bowie.

You're All I've Got Tonight

Back at the hotel the others were feeling dinnerish and plans were tossed about for going here, doing that, seeing this... while people visited each other's rooms and got dressed and so on.

I changed my shirt and hustled Jonathan to an elevator before anyone noticed we were gone. Once we were on the street and moving toward the Metro I said "Sorry to be so James Bond but I had to get away from them for a while."

"Understandable," he said and nodded. "So where are we going?"

Hmm, so I was in the proverbial driver's seat, even though we took public transit. I didn't know much about DC but the guidance of some freebie papers (one of them perhaps the one we'd be appearing in) got us to a college-y area and I was sure we could find amusement and food here.

"Reminds me of the Hill," Jonathan said as we weaved through Walk-manned women and men, past bookstores, record shops, a Native American trinkets store, the front of a cafe.

"Only bigger," I replied. The interesting part of College Hill in Providence was essentially three blocks long, with nothing on the side streets to speak of. "What school's here?"

"Georgetown is the main one, plus there are some others." His path took him closer to me and I swear he started to reach for my hand, but maybe that was my imagination. "Do you ever think about going back to school?"

"Not for music, I don't. That's for sure."

"But, for a regular bachelor's degree?"

As evening came on, summery heat rose up from the sidewalk and I had the urge to lie down on it. "I don't see what would be the point."

"I don't know about that. Did you have good grades in school?"

"Good enough, I guess. I wasn't an overachiever, let's put it that way. But come on, Jonathan, can you picture me now, reading a lot of books and writing term papers and stuff?"

His hands were in the pockets of his faded jacket. "No, I guess not. I guess I'm having trouble thinking that it's possible to go through life without a college education, but that's because I have one, I guess."

I laughed. "And people say I think too much? Hah! But think, J, if I had gone to college, I'd only be what, a junior now?"

"Something like that."

"Besides, a music school education isn't like a regular college. Shit, if anything I'd know even less about the world than I do now."

"What do you mean?"

"I mean, come on, J. If I've got four classes in a semester, it's four classes that have to do with music. Conducting, theory, advanced composition, orchestra, even at a diddly school like the Conservatory, it's music music music. Composers of the romantic era. Wind ensemble. Ear training." I shook my head suddenly, like I was trying to wake myself up from one of those dreams where you find yourself in a classroom taking a test, but it's not a class you've ever taken and for some reason the test is in Swahili or something. "I mean, did I really need to learn conducting? Could I have spent that time better reading Moby Dick or running white rats through a maze? I don't know."

"I'm trying to imagine you as a conductor."

I patted at the air in four-four and growled out a few loudening bars of Ride of the Valkyrie, my gestures becoming more emphatic until I almost poked him in the nose as we walked. "I got a B and got to keep the baton."

"You think you'll ever use any of that stuff?"

"The baton?"

"The classes, the stuff you had to learn."

I shrugged. "I might end up writing movie soundtracks. Everyone else does. And then there's stuff like Paul McCartney composing for the London Philharmonic. Which seems downright silly to me, but, hey, maybe when I'm pushing fifty it'll seem like a great idea. And at least I'll actually know what I'm doing." Then I decided I was being an ass. "Well, partly anyway. I mean, I was only there eighteen fucking months before I booked out of there."

He slowed down a bit. "So where are we going?"

We were coming to the end of the interesting-looking stores. "Wherever I damn well feel like it," I said. "And tonight I'm paying for dinner."

The Low Spark of High-Heeled Boys

We ended up at this funky, candle-lit (too dark, actually) place with a large vegetarian selection and ringlet-haired waitresses wearing patchouli.

The important thing about the dinner I should relay is not anything to do with the food or what we talked about or anything like that, of course, but the fact that I FINALLY realized that, hey, if I played my cards right the possibility existed that I might be able to sleep with someone I genuinely liked and knew the name of.

Besides Carynne and Ziggy, there'd been one other in that category—Matthew—and I hadn't exactly handled the end of that terribly well, but it had been okay, and I didn't regret much.

The possibility of doing something I wouldn't regret was exciting in and of itself. I hadn't really decided one way or the other which was worse, being a "pervert" who fucked men for a sick thrill, or accepting a label that came with a completely different kind of baggage, even if I could be "proud" of it some day.

But with J sitting there, all smiley and warm and witty and so goddamned intimate with his questions and his answers, I thought maybe it was best to leave off theorizing until after I'd done some more field research.

Having a realization and making a decision on a course of action are two different things.

In fact, making a decision to make a decision, and actually making the decision, are two different things.

In other words, I didn't know for sure if I wanted to or not, but I wanted the possibility, and enjoyed not knowing, for once.

The result was a long and lovely evening, where we talked and laughed and told things about our varied and sordid pasts, and ate and drank and drew things out as long as possible, such that it was close to midnight when we went back to the hotel, and sat around in the bar until maybe one a.m. and then...

And then I flashed to the possibility that maybe I still hadn't drunk quite enough for me to be the leader here, and that I didn't really know one way or the other what *Jonathan* wanted.

At the moment when this occurred to me, we were sitting at the actual bar, elbows on the wood, with our noses deep in snifters of something, I don't remember now if it was cognac or whiskey. Something rich and dark and complicated, and J's eyelashes looked light in comparison, a wheat-colored piece of his hair touching the outside rim of his glass while he inhaled, eyes closed. It seemed like he'd sit that way forever unless I made the first move toward seducing him.

And then I thought, whoa, what if he doesn't want to be seduced?

My tongue burned with liquid smoke and I suppressed the urge to cough. The bartender, who I guessed to be about my age and bored, was ignoring us, his eyes on a silent television from where he rested at an inside corner, not even pretending to polish glasses. I imagined the scene from his point of view and couldn't guess what he might think. Decadent rock and roll types, maybe. So I tried to imagine it from J's point of view. What did he see when he looked at me? What did he want? I imagined myself successfully seducing him and then finding out later that he hadn't wanted that.

My own nose in my drink, I closed my eyes, and thought,

Jeezuschrist, Daron, he's spent every waking moment with you for the past two days. How much more of a hint do you need?

I opened my eyes. J was looking at me.

I cleared my throat and said in a low voice. "I have to ask you something."

"What?"

My lips pressed slightly together as I got ready to open my mouth. The bartender chose this moment to stop ignoring us and asked if we needed anything else. "We're fine," I said, "just leaving." He slid me the bill and I signed my room number on it. J raised an eyebrow and slipped what was left in his glass down his throat.

Upstairs, in the room, alone, I tried again. "I have to ask you something."

"So ask." He sat across from me on the other bed, the light from the table lamp making a cone of light on our legs.

"This is going to sound funny, possibly. But, well, it depends on how you take it." I shook my head. "I know, that didn't make any sense since you don't know yet what I'm going to say."

"You're getting deep." He moved to sit beside me on the bed.

"Damn right I am. So promise me you'll be quiet and listen to this whole thing before you speak, before you answer, okay? For my own peace of mind."

"Anything for you, D."

I did not dwell on the implications of that statement. "Okay, here goes. I really want to ask you something, but I want to clarify it first. Well, first the question is, um, how would you feel about, ah shit how to put this..." I held up my hand to keep him from breaking in. "I want to ask you if I should be seducing you. But,"—that sounded loud—"I don't want you to think that my asking you is necessarily a first step to actually seducing, if you don't want to be. So I want to ask you how you'd feel about it, but without that actually being a start to me doing so. I mean, I know that flirting and all that stuff's a game, and that it's important, but I want to kind of call time out for a second, and have the fact that I'm calling a time out not be a factor in influencing your feelings." Jeezus, the more I talked the less sense it sounded like it made. The fumes had gone to my head for sure.

He had an open-mouthed smile on his face and he looked up, looked down, looked up. "Can I speak now?"

"Oh, um, yeah."

"You know, you're one of the sweetest guys I've ever met."

"You're making me blush."

"You started blushing long before this, D."

"Yeah, well."

We sat there looking at each other for a few long moments, while I suppressed the urge to take him by the hand and start sucking his fingers or something equally corny but hard to keep from doing.

And then I heard the chunk of Ziggy's card key in the lock. Don't ask me why it is that I could keep myself from licking J's palm, but I couldn't stop myself from standing up and taking a few steps away from him when the door opened.

The bleached lock of Ziggy's hair shone goldly in the hallway light under blacker strands that hung down like limp fingers. He came to a halt with his eyes on us, like I somehow knew he would. "I'm not interrupting anything, am I?"

See, that's Ziggy in a nutshell—always asking you a question that you can't answer. If I answered it "yes" or if I answered "no" it'd still sound wrong. And saying nothing would be just as bad.

Fortunately, Jonathan was quicker on the uptake than me, and he said something I wouldn't have expected. "We were just wondering where you were."

Ziggy smiled and gave me a sideways look. "Oh yeah?"

J leaned back on the still-made bed. "Yeah, we went all over the city tonight but we got to wondering what everyone else did. See anything fun?"

Ziggy sat down on a corner of the bed and started pulling his boots off. "Bunch of us went down to some club, I forget the name already. But it was kind of dull so I went down the street to a dance club." He shrugged. He kicked the loose boot off one foot and it hit the carpet with a thud. The second one followed and he lay back, looking relaxed.

There was a knock at the door then and I opened it to find Bart standing there. "I wondered if you guys were here."

"Nobody but us in here, nobody but us," Ziggy sang.

I don't need to describe, probably, another night partying on the road. Yeah, sure, J and I could have probably found another place to go if we had really been sure that we wanted to. But there was no way I was going to come around with that question again now, and he didn't do anything else to indicate one way or the other, and well, there were other pleasures to be had, too, passing a joint and drinking and jamming with Bart on two guitars. In fact, that's the part of the evening I enjoyed most, though I remember it the least, Bart and I sitting in chairs by the window, trading licks and playing songs, some of ours, some of other folks', and singing quietly, and sometimes just picking a couple of chords and going with them until our fingers were too tired to keep it up any more.

J watched and listened with an open kind of joy on his face that made me hopeful he wasn't disappointed, either.

Electric Avenue

A knock on the door woke me up and I was surprised to find myself alone in the room. I had slept in the bed nearer the bathroom, as always, and a heap of bedding in one corner of the room seemed to indicate J had crashed here last night, too. I was still in most of my clothes and my eyes felt scratchy, but otherwise I was in fairly good repair.

Carynne was at the door, looking a little tired, her smile a little thin. "Good morning."

"What time is it?" I asked.

"One thirty. Jonathan said to say goodbye for him. He had to get back and didn't want to wake you."

"Nice of him." I wondered if he'd woken her up to tell her that. Probably not, he was a pretty considerate sort of guy. The bedding in the corner was neatly folded with a pillow on top, a pile of similarly folded newspapers on the table next to it. "So to what do I owe the pleasure."

"Just making sure everyone's prepped to go over to the hall at four."

"I don't know how we'd do it without you."

"Ah, you could do it without me, you just wouldn't have as much fun." She turned like she was going to go, but I said:

"Yeah, Car', but do you have enough fun?"

She rolled her eyes over her shoulder at me. "If I have any more fun, I'll have to give it up," she said, and winked.

I don't know what the wink was for, but as long as she was happy...

Echoes of last night's jam session were bouncing around the empty cave of my skull when we went to soundcheck. Me and Chris and Bart did a half-way convincing rendition of Hold The Line, with Bart singing falsetto since Ziggy didn't know the words and in all seriousness it was better that he not know them.

Actually, Bart didn't know them terribly well either. The engineers got a good laugh out of it, anyway. Chris had been having some trouble keeping the bridge tight in Why The Sky so we went over that a couple of times tweaking levels and kidding him that his big china crash was making him deaf.

And Ziggy was still ignoring me onstage and off. He gave me a wide berth on stage, playing mostly to the front row and staying in his own little orbit, not interacting with Bart or Chris either. I built my own sphere on my side of the stage, between my rack and the invisible line where Ziggy's territory started. The show went fine, no major problems, and I even managed to enjoy myself quite a bit. I never "forgot," but hey, maybe that was one of those things that was supposed to get more rare as you got older. I'd have to ask Remo about it sometime. I couldn't ever remember Remo seeming like he wasn't 100% there and on top of things, but maybe there was a time when he'd blank out the way I used to, the way I still longed to. I'd have to ask when I saw him next.

After the show I sat in a folding chair back stage, sweat drying on my face and plastering my hair to my forehead, and looked at my hands not shake. When I didn't play myself into a frenzy or a rapturous blank, I realized, the post-show high was different. Not bad, just different, more like the calm haze of pot than the buzz of booze. I sat there while other people packed up stuff around me, and laughed and goofed around. Chris had taken to dousing himself with bottled water after every show and that degenerated into a water fight among him, Colin and Kevin. Some time later it was time to go, and we did, back to the hotel again to wash up and do back-to-the-hotel kind of things.

And as the glow of the show left me and I combed out my wet hair, my thoughts drifted to what I was going to do tonight. I didn't have to do anything. I could lie around, watch TV, order room service, and go to sleep. But if the performance high I had tonight was like pot, the feeling I had now was like the munchies.

Hmm.

I picked out a pair of good jeans, put on my boots, moussed my hair back slightly. Black T-shirt, the weather was too warm for a jacket, even this late at night. J, helpful to that last, had left behind several newspapers, one of which had the information I needed. I pointed myself walking toward where I wanted to go.

Every city where I'd bothered to look so far had someplace like it, a block, a neighborhood, even if only one club or bookstore, but a place that felt to me like a little piece of Greenwich village transplanted. DC was no exception, as I'd seen while walking around the night before with J.

So there I was, looking at the way boys looked at one another, and looking for my chance to join that dance myself.

I had my choice, late night bookstore, restaurant & bar, disco, or just lean against a tree in the park until the right kind of eye contact came along. With the summery warmth coming out of the pavement and the breeze soft, I opted for the park, my eyes up as I criss crossed the blue lit paths instead of on my feet or the ground in front of me.

When he came along, he smiled. There was so little talking involved that we sounded like we knew each other well. I didn't for one moment doubt who wanted what. He lived nearby, in a brick townhouse with hard wood floors and ethnic-looking rugs.

There are maybe two things worth remarking on at this point. One, I discovered the shock of truly liking the first touch of cold lube.

Two, some time after that — moment, minutes, I don't know — in the embrace of a stranger and sinking into his rhythm, I lost myself at last.

White Room

I returned to the hotel dazed and sleepy, the colors and lights of the lobby seeming too bright while the sounds of clerks on the phone, the elevators dinging, seemed muffled and distant. In the hallway to my room the seams in the carpet interested me more than the pattern and I decided I was tired.

The suite was dark and empty, the beds squarely made. I took off my boots and jeans and sat in my usual place, on the edge of the bed by the phone, not quite ready to lie down yet. I pulled the Ovation out of its case and played for a bit, my mind looping on a sexual rhythm and a trance of no thought, just the notes through my fingers like water. The trance lasted until my thumb began to ache and I was putting the guitar to bed when I heard the door lock engage and Carynne's high-pitched giggle.

Ziggy opened the door with Carynne draped over one of his shoulders like a fringed cape. "Oh, hey, Daron," he said like he hadn't expected to see me but was now trying to act like he had. "Whoa..." He boosted her up a little and she tilted toward me and waved, her eyes half-closed. "I, uh, I think I better get her to her room."

I nodded. The door swung shut on the sound of the two of them giggling now. I climbed into bed and switched on the TV. After two videos and a slew of commercials had gone by, I decided it was unlikely Ziggy was coming right back, and killed the set and the lights, and lay down.

Being as tired as I was, with so little sleep, I would have thought I'd go out like a light. But the quiet and calm I'd found with the Ovation in my hands mere minutes ago was gone, and voices chattered around in my head, keeping me awake like someone trying to talk to me.

I was trying to tell myself not to worry about Carynne, she was a big girl and could take care of herself. If even half the things she'd said about her escapades on previous tours were true then a drunken night with the Z wouldn't bother her. But did it bother me?

The more I tried not to think about it, the more I thought. My over-tired muscles no longer wanted to lie comfortably and I turned over, listening to the sounds around me as if they might distract me from the voice in my head. The sound of the city outside was like the rushing sound inside an airplane, but quieter. What makes a city sound like that from rooms in high rise hotels? The occasional slow surf-breaking sound of a car going down the avenue, the HVAC hum in the building's bones.

But there's another sound, a background whisper, the hiss of an amp left on, the sound of alleys and buildings sliding past each other like continents on the move? I could also hear the muffled sounds of a banjo—the Beverly Hillbillies in reruns on a television in some other room, another insomniac trying to numb his brain. I couldn't tell if he was above me or below me.

The sheets were soft and the pillow firm as I slid from side to side searching for sleepiness. The mini-bar refrigerator kicked on and added its trickle and buzz to the soundtrack. I found myself wondering the stupidest things, like if she'd do the same things for him as she had for me, like if he made the same faces when he came with a woman as with me. The banjo was jangly like my nerves and I wished I was unconscious—a good thing probably that none of our crew was into recreational sleeping pills because I'd have been popping them like M&Ms.

That's what killed Hendrix, you know. Not insomnia, taking too many pills for the insomnia.

The word insomnia has too peaceful a sound to it, like a monk's chant—in-som-ni-yah. I tried to remember the name of the guy Carynne had brought to my birthday party and couldn't.

The refrigerator shut off with a stalled-engine stutter; a car alarm complained in the distance. The unlocated television switched to "I Love Lucy" and I wished I wasn't alone.

Breakfast In America

Ziggy woke me up in the morning looking too fresh and happy to be believed. I could smell his hair gel as I forced myself into a sitting position, my head heavy with undersleptness. "Come on, boss," he said, tugging on my foot through the blanket. "It's five hours to Chapel Hill and Bizzy says we've got to be off the stage by ten."

"I'm up," I said. The only people who say "I'm up" are the groggy, ever notice that?

I could have been packing instead of laying there thrashing last night, I realized, which of course made me feel just great about myself, too. Ziggy swept his toiletries into his backpack and was pretty much ready to go, and out he went. I packed and got dressed with the curtains still drawn against the morning sun.

I should explain about tour nicknames, shouldn't I.

This is one of those things that spontaneously happens, somehow along the way people pick up nicknames which generally last only until the tour ends. I couldn't tell you when we started called Carynne "Bizzy (because she's a busy bee) or Kevin "Puck." Bart had gone from being Yoo Hoo to being Boo Hoo when we couldn't find any for sale, which became Boo Boo sometime later. Chris easily became Christ. In fact, I might have been the only one not to pick up any specific nickname, at first because everyone was too worried about sending me off the deep end, and later everyone picked up J's habit of calling me D, which led to Christian saying things like "Dee doo ron ron, dee doo ron ron, you want to drive first or should I?"

I told him to take first shift and I moved to the back. Carynne, her darkest sunglasses on and a bottle of spring water in her hand, climbed into the passenger seat. No one seemed very talkative this morning. I went back to sleep.

At our first pit stop, a kind of tourist-trap-ish place with mountains of pecan brittle and commemorative salt and pepper shakers strategically placed between the entrance and the rest rooms, I stepped up to Carynne in the cashier's line. "How are you?"

She looked at me over the tops of her sunglasses. "Fine. You?"

"Tired out."

"Me too," she said and looked down at the packs of gum in her hand. Even for a tired, hung over Bizzy this seemed too curt.

I had planned to make some kind of stupid joke about Ziggy, but the tightness of her lips and the way she sort of shook the gum in her hand in silent encouragement for the cashier to hurry, made me forget whatever I was going to say. It wouldn't have been funny anyway.

So today Carynne was ignoring me, but Ziggy wasn't. Back in the van he wanted to debate the relative merits of Boston ska like Bim Skala Bim and the Mighty Mighty Bosstones versus British two tone groups of a couple of years ago.

"You don't seriously think that Allston ska is going to break mainstream," I said. "How can you compare international hit machines like The English Beat to the Bosstones?"

"Bosstones just did a Miller Light commercial," said Christian, from the driver's seat.

"No, really?" Ziggy sat forward, his dark eyes sparkling in Southern sunlight. "How'd they get that gig?"

Chris shrugged. "Just heard about it from some of the other guys in the Mile. Don't know who they had to blow, if that's what you mean."

"See?" Ziggy said to me.

"What's to see? New England ska just isn't the same phenomenon as the rude boy Brit pop thing."

And so it went for several more miles. Chris got tired of the tapes he had brought and we played Name That Tune with the radio, which, in the South, was a bit different than playing it up North. Chris and I could go head to head on classic rock, but when it came to genuine "oldies" I could slaughter them all. Thank Remo for that.

Burning Down the House

We had lunch in a Denny's and about four o'clock reached the Chapel Hill city limits.

The venue was a bar, but unlike the usual night club set up where we'd play late, this place was having some kind of to do with their local city council about noise and liquor licensing, and so had to have us off stage by ten.

That left us two hours to set up before the doors opened and not much time to do much else.

The owner himself, a kind of ex-hippie-ish looking guy with no

Southern accent named Carl, came out and apologized for all the trouble and assured us there would be a good crowd no matter what and thanked us for coming. I don't know if it was that Carynne was still suffering from last night, or just that he was so darned nice, but she didn't get on his case about the fact that he didn't even have a real sound technician there and the backstage area was the size of a closet. ("Just like home," Chris said as we put our stuff down on a pile of beer cases.)

The sound wasn't great but would do. We didn't even really have time to get to know the opening band before they had to be on stage and we were in the back waiting. The dressing room wasn't at all shielded for sound and so was a bit like being in the garage where a garage band was practicing. I wasn't sure what to make of the fact that most of the guys in the band seemed to be pushing thirty, but the music sounded like any bunch of well-meaning teenagers. At least they were having fun. We traded smiles as they came off the stage.

And then we were in what passed for dark in the smoky room, waiting for the lights to come up with an opening drumbeat, searching the dimness for the glint of familiar eyes. Carynne stood by the sound board under a yellow light that made her red hair glow. People were pressed close to the edge of the low stage, looking up, expectant, fresh-faced, eager. I smiled to one girl who bobbed up and down like she had to pee but her eyes were glued on Bart. A fan.

Christian clicked off the count with touches of his sticks and then we were into it. The first riff sang out and I imagined I could see the sound ripple through the crowd, people's faces and postures and looks changing subtly from the front of the room to the back as the music swept by, cheers of recognition and happiness and excitement going up. Ziggy came in with a little vocal run up to his first note and in the back of my brain I thought—hey, nice.

As we played I began to have that illusion that the sound was actually coming from my fingers and strings and not from the amps and PA, a direct stream of volume from somewhere in my midsection. In "You Know" for the chorus just before the break I switched to playing up the neck, up the octave, and Bart followed me. It came out sweet and then Christian hit the china crash and into the bridge we went. I was already playing high so I kept the solo up there, working my way slowly down to a bitter groove on the bottom string by the end. As I laid down the riff I dropped lower and lower until I was on my knees, the tall crowd against the low stage looking down on me, a private audience of twenty, while cheers went up.

When I came up, the chorus back in full force now, Ziggy shuffled backwards up to me, and we worked that same groove to the floor, back to back, sinking lower and lower, until we were both on the ground. He pulled away and I fell back, lying on the black surface of the stage looking up into coffee can gels and ripping out the surge of the closing riffs. He was somewhere on the other side of the small stage now, weaving around Bart or something. I waited until the song was over to get up.

As he put his mic back into its stand, he gave me a quirk of his face and lips that might have been a grimace. He introduced Why the Sky and then we were playing. Of course, as soon as I thought too much about enjoying myself, I tensed up, and WTS fell into a bit of a rote feel, but that was soothing in its own way, not quite trance-like but automatic enough to let my mind wander. In the back of the club where there was slightly more room I could make out the dim shapes of people swaying, the I'm-still-watching dance. Puck was at the sound board, his face lit from below by a flashlight. He saw me looking and gave me a heads up but I shook my head, no-just-looking.

I stayed that way through a couple of songs until Bart started teasing me with little licks—in "Rain" he kept pulling a little phrase out of Why the Sky and slipping it in. My fingers were ahead of my conscious mind going along with him on it—nice—before I could really plan it out. The quote worked and I wondered why I'd never thought of that before. We were probably the only two people noticing it, but who cared. We looked at each other across the stage like tennis players passing a volley back and forth. He nodded his head in time and rocked from one high-topped sneaker to the other, his bowtie askew.

And then Ziggy was there in my line of sight, right up in my face, singing hard enough to spit, and we kind of went back and forth, pushing each other with the force of our sound. He broke off when my solo came up, though, moving off to do an interpretive dance or something while I looked back into the ring of faces at the stage's edge and gave them what they were listening for.

It seemed like a long set, yet when we went back to the dressing room/beer closet, the clock showed 9:20. "And we're supposed to be cleared out by ten?" I said. "Why don't we do 'The Right Hand' into 'Candlelight?'"

"We haven't rehearsed it," said Christian in a devil's-advocate-type voice which pretty much guaranteed that he'd try it.

"So? C'mon."

"The Right Hand" opens with guitar only. There wasn't any good way to get the word back to the sound board so I just went out there and plugged in amid cheers of approval, and let the sound of the crowd die down slightly before I began the fingerpicking that opened the song. I'd named it "The Right Hand" before Ziggy or I had written any words to it, only because it was all right handed picking. The resulting song was a bittersweet ballad about the forenamed hand not knowing what the left was doing. That theme came up in more than one of our songs and I tried not to think about the potential for pop psychology analyses of what that meant.

Some plain pure emotional part of me gave a little skip of happiness when, as the song reached its peak, Ziggy crawled on his stomach toward me, then lay curled at my feet as he trailed off and I picked up the melody as hands of audience members reached toward us. I hung over him, playing, playing, until he got back to his feet and turned his attention elsewhere. We're doing it, I thought, it's working, we're doing it, and I'm not even having an anxiety attack. I wasn't blanked out, either, I wasn't wild. I was awake and present and working hard and tossing my head until sweat flew from my hair onto his bare back.

"The Right Hand" ends loud but mournful which made a nice lead in to "Candlelight." North Carolina was lighter country, apparently, and people held up little flames as we rolled into the song they knew best. Now, almost by tacit agreement, all three of us faced front, solemn as a choir as we gave the show a finish, no playing back and forth, no grandstanding. Such a simple song in a way, doing it like this gave it a certain dignity and gravity I don't think we always brought to it.

And then the show was really over and I was sitting on a backstage milk crate feeling a little dizzy and like I wanted to drink a gallon of water but didn't have the energy to lift a bottle to my mouth. The concrete was cool against my back through my soaked shirt. I pulled the shirt off and sat with it balled in my hands while people shuffled back and forth in front of me.

Bart cuffed me on the head as he went by, saying only 'Yeah" in an emphatic way and then hurrying on.

I knew what he meant.

Hey Hey, What Can I Do

Energy came back to me slowly and I got up to find Colin had already dismantled my rig and carefully stowed the guitars in their cases. He was working with Chris and Kevin on getting the drum kit apart. "Thanks, man," I told him.

"No sweat," he replied handing me a cymbal stand. "You're paying me, after all."

I put on a dry shirt and my denim jacket and looked around for Carynne to find out what she thought of the show. I was hoping to hear some effusive praise, actually. But the only people I could see were the crew and Chris at the kit, and Bart with one elbow on the bar talking to the tall girl from the front row who'd been glued to him earlier. I went and got the water I'd been wanting and sat back down on my crate to wait.

The truck was mostly loaded and the bar cleared of patrons by the time I got up again and went into the men's room. Three scuffed black doors demarked multiply painted stalls, facing three urinals and three sinks. A pretty big men's room for a small bar. Maybe they drink and/or piss more in the South. I went to the farthest urinal and began to unzip.

The sound of a whimper came from one of the stalls behind me, whether a sound of pain or pleasure was hard to tell. I thought it was a woman's voice. I took my piss, figuring if people couldn't wait until they got home, it wasn't really my business. The sound of motion, clothes rustling rhythmically, could be heard while I tinkled. I didn't linger.

Now Bart and fan were nowhere to be seen and I wondered if it was perhaps the two of them in the men's room. I joined the others sitting on the back of the truck and sharing a joint. Ziggy came out a little while later, in dry clothes and carrying his backpack of wet things. "Where's Bizzy?" he said.

We shrugged. "Probably talking to the owner," I said, realizing I should have looked for her in the office. Whatever.

She appeared some time after that, looking worn out and faded by the heat, her hair limp and her eyes closed. "Where's Bart?" she asked.

"Went off with a groupie," Chris said. "He said not to wait up for him."

"Figures," she said and motioned us to the van with a languid sweep of her arm.

Her tiredness sort of pervaded everybody and exhilarated as we might have been, we kept quiet on the drive to the motel. This was a place with doors that opened to the outside, a yellow light outside each door surrounded by a small swarm of bugs. The doors were red on the outside and beige on the inside. After we were settled I knocked on Carynne's door, feeling slightly hungry and still wanting to ask her about the show.

"I knew it was you," she said, opening the door. She was wearing a bathrobe and her wet hair had the furrowed look of the just-combed. "Oh god." She sat down on one bed, put her feet up and looked at the ceiling while she lit a clove cigarette.

"I thought you were quitting," I said, sitting on the other bed.

"Yeah," she replied, watching the smoke she blew.

"So how'd you know it was going to be me at the door?"

She shrugged. "Maybe I was just hoping it would be you."

"I wanted to ask your opinion on tonight's show."

"What did you think?"

"You first."

She pursed her lips. "Seemed okay."

"Compared to the other shows this tour?"

"It was hard to tell what was going on from the back."

"Pardon me for asking," I said, taking my jacket off, "but are you on the rag or something?"

Now she looked at me, the sourness in her face threatening to crumble into something else. "Or something."

Was it the look in her eye, or just a good guess that made me think the "something" was the illustrious Mr. Z? "Don't tell me."

"If you don't want me to, I won't. But I could sure use some advice." Her voice softened and she flicked ash into the plastic ashtray on her stomach. It had the name of the hotel embossed in it in white letters and discolored places along the edges where other cigarettes had burned too long.

"It's Ziggy, isn't it."

"Yeah."

I gave half a laugh. "And here I thought you'd be helping me with him, not the other way around."

"You're not jealous? Please say you're not."

I did laugh. "No, I'm not. I mean, not really," I amended, thinking about my thoughts of the other night. "Is that what's been worrying you?"

"Partly." She took a contemplative drag and the cigarette crackled spicily. "You're sure?"

"I'm sure." I realized there was a difference between jealousy and envy, and maybe the other night I envied them both a little. But looking at the bags under her eyes, I didn't now. "So what's the other part?"

"Oh," she said with feigned nonchalance. "You know how he can be."

I didn't say anything and her face hardened and she looked at me.

"I've been avoiding you all day," she said. "Not because of the jealousy thing, but because I kept hoping I could put off saying this."

"Saying what?"

"I think I have to go home."

"You mean leave the tour."

She nodded.

"Because of him?"

She nodded again.

"I need more details, Car'. Help me out on this."

"Oh, fuck," she said as she started to cry. "It isn't even that big a deal, you know, I mean, it isn't like I've never done anything crazy or wild before. But it's like the more I want him the more scared I am of him."

"Why."

"Come on, Daron, you know what he's like."

"Master of mind games?" I leaned toward her but there wasn't any way I could really comfort her without getting on her bed, and that seemed like a mistake right now.

"It's like, oh, I don't know, maybe I am even getting a little obsessed with him, like... " She gave a little gurgle of frustration. "You're like the one person I know who might understand this so I'm going to try to give you the explanation."

"Okay."

"Sex with him is very, very intense."

"Yes, it is." And what a strange thing it was to be able to say that out loud. Not that I had a huge basis for comparison, but still.

She went on in a shaky voice. "It's like, he pushes me. He pushes my buttons. And I like it when he does that. At the time I get off on it, too, you know, the thrill of it, but later I feel ashamed and dirty, like how could I let him do that?"

I couldn't quite imagine what she was talking about, but I figured she might tell me if I kept my mouth shut.

"He… it's like he knows me somehow, knows the sick corners, and he gives me what's there. So I'm totally obsessed with him for knowing me so well, totally wanting and needing that, and yet totally scared of it, too, totally scared of what he's capable of talking me into."

Nope, I couldn't guess. I resorted to asking. "Like what?"

She crossed her arms over her chest and spoke with her chin down, the cigarette burning down between her fingers. "He… won't use a condom, Daron, and once we start, he'll just keep going and going, even if I start to struggle like I want him to stop or pull out, he'll just fuck and fuck and fuck until all my resistance breaks down and then I'm like somehow totally fucking grateful when he does pull out and come all over me."

"Oh jeezus. What if he gets you pregnant?"

"I'm on the fucking pill, stupid. Don't tell me you aren't scared of AIDS though."

I said nothing.

"Oh jeezus yourself, Daron! When was the last time you were tested?"

I said nothing.

"Oh fuck," she said again and hid her eyes with the hand that was cigarette free. Then she took a long drag and sat up. "What would you do in my position? I don't even know if it's me he's interested in, or if I'm just convenient. Like he'd do this to whoever was at hand. I'm like totally obsessed with him, though, too. That's why I have to leave. I mean, what am I supposed to do, reason with him? Ignore him?"

I looked at my hands, at the callouses on my fingertips that looked yellower than the rest of my skin. "I've tried reasoning with him, and I've tried ignoring him. It can be done, Car'. If you want to keep up with him..."

"I don't. I have a boyfriend, Daron. I don't want a rock singer for a relationship anyway. I'm not looking to get anything out of this; I'm just looking to get out of it."

"So why'd you start sleeping with him in the first place?"

She blew smoke in an exasperated stream. "Call me weak. Temptation. Oh come on, you know how he can be when he turns on the charm. Irresistible."

"When, when did it start?"

She bit her lip in a guilty look. "The night after you and I did."

"Do you think that's why...?" Now for some reason I felt guilty, too. "Was that you two in the men's room?"

"Yes." She didn't blush or anything. "Do you want more details or is that sordid enough for you?"

"I'm convinced."

"He didn't even come. He just got me off again and again like I was some kind of insatiable slut. No wonder I'm confused. I spend years fucking rock stars who think of nothing but their own squirt and kind of resenting them for it, you know? And along comes one who's different..."

I held up my hands. "Stop. Don't even try to unravel it. This is Ziggy's specialty—making you think you're the one who's guilty, like he's totally doing it for you, so you'll come begging back to him." I couldn't, at that moment, remember just how he'd done the same to me, yet as I said it it sounded so fucking right.

"You want to know what's sick? Here I am complaining to you about him, and just thinking about it's making me horny." She ground out the cigarette with a growl.

"Have you really, really tried to say 'no' to him?" I asked, a little timidly.

She put the ash tray down and crossed her arms. "Not exactly."

"Not exactly?"

"It's... it's hard to say no when I want him so much," she said. "And I'm kind of afraid that if I do say no outright either he'll stop completely and leave me high and dry, or maybe worse, that he won't stop at all, and then we're talking a really awkward situation if he actually rapes me. Which I don't think he'd do. There's too much at stake. But... fuck."

"This is my fault," I said. "He's only paying so much attention to you because he's not allowed to chase me anymore."

"Whoa whoa," she said, waving he hands. "Didn't you just say that's what he's good at? Making you blame yourself?"

"Oh. Yeah."

"This isn't your fault, D, and it's not mine, either. There's only one answer. I've got to get away from him," she said finally. "For my own sanity. I've got to get back to reality."

Yeah, reality.

Reality was dinner and a midnight blow job at a truck stop off the interstate. Yeah, I was worried about being shot up by rednecks, but I wasn't. I would have rather found somebody like Mr. DC Townhouse, but you take what you can get.

So Far Away

Carynne left in the morning for Boston, telling the others she had a family emergency to take care of, and I played along, taking charge of the day book and delegating Kevin to be Bad Ass if we needed any tough talking or arguing down the way. We had a six hour drive to Athens ahead of us, and after dropping her at the airport, we got underway.

The plan was to arrive at the motel at night, head over to the venue mid-afternoon the next day, play that night and then stay over a second night in the same place. Then there would be a ten hour drive to New Orleans, same plan, drive all day, arrive late, sleep over, show the next day, sleep over, then go on, eleven hours to a place in Texas between Austin and San Antonio. The Texas leg would be the longest haul yet since Boston to Cleveland, but we'd stay three nights there, one night before the Austin show, one night before the San Antonio show, and then one before the two-day drive to Boulder

Did I mention how fucking big the West is?

In the South and in the West there's a lot more of nothing than there is in the Northeast. The whole scale of the land and the journey changed as we adjusted ourselves to the longer trips, longer silences in the van, and fewer tempting places to make pit stops. With only four of us in the van it was righteously roomy and we took turns sleeping. I found myself not wanting to talk at all while driving, just gunning down the road on an endless set of rhythmless dashed lines. The mountains were sometimes beautiful. The sun was sometimes too hot. When we did talk, it was often to play some kind of game. Halfway to Athens we got onto a kick of trying to come up with combinations of two of more artists with common words in their names that went something like this:

Bart: The Grateful Dead Milkmen.
Ziggy: The Grateful Dead Kennedys.
Chris: The Grateful Dead Can Dance.
Me: The Rolling Stone Roses
Chris: *Bzzt,* thank you for playing, but it'd have to be Stones, plural, with an 's.'

Bart: I don't know, I think it scans.
Ziggy: Do solo artists count too, or only band names?
Me: Solo artists, too. That way you get Philip Glass Tiger.
Bart: Ouch.
Ziggy: The Pointer Sisters of Mercy.
Chris: Iggy Pop Will Eat Itself.
Me: How about the Richard Thompson Twins.
Ziggy: But what maps to Moondog Three?
Me: Let's not think about that shall we?

And so on.

And I wasn't about to confront Ziggy about Carynne. That just seemed stupid, like she was my kid sister or something and me, what would I do about it? She said it herself, she was a big girl and made her own choices. I had to respect that and acting like she needed to be protected wasn't the way to respect her.

Plus I didn't want to disturb what little equilibrium we'd gotten back before we had a chance to play again. I kept my trap shut and hoped the next show would be good.

One of These Nights

We arrived in Athens close to ten o'clock, too late to see anything that night but the little restaurant and bar adjacent to the motel. The only thing any of us knew about Athens was that this was where REM, the B52s, and Love Tractor were from.

As it turned out, the clerk working the night shift was a Love Tractor fan and I sat in the lobby talking to him until well after midnight. I was staggered by the number of clubs and music halls in this one town, college town or no. I didn't think I could name as many places in Boston. We were booked into a place called the Atomic Music Hall. I wrote the kid's name down (Jim Calandra) and told him we'd put him on the guest list. He seemed to appreciate that and said to call him at the desk if we needed anything.

With Carynne gone we needed one fewer room, so I dropped it from our reservation and thought maybe tomorrow I'd call ahead to confirm our other ones and drop it on those, too. This, however, landed Ziggy and I back together, like the rest of the band decided to see what would happen… or maybe they really hadn't noticed exactly who was rooming with whom recently. Whatever.

Zig and I stayed up until two or three watching cable (they had a real cable feed at this place, not a pared down "hotel" service), passing the clicker back and forth when ever one of us would get up to piss or something. We could watch a minimum of four channels at once, following a movie, a rerun, a documentary, and MTV at the same time, switching every time a commercial came on or something got dull. I must have fallen asleep before he did since when I woke up some time later all the lights and the TV had been turned off, which I didn't remember either of us doing.

In other words, we didn't talk, we didn't fight, we didn't antagonize each other, and we sure as hell didn't fuck.

No blood was shed; I considered it a good night.

So, Athens. I was pleasantly surprised to find a lively downtown area near the club, warm but not hot weather, sun and outdoor cafes, free newspapers—most of the comforts of home and then some. The six of us stuck together for the most part, doing some used record shopping, wandering around what was kind of considered hallowed ground for indie rock.

I mailed postcards to Remo and Digger, and thought about sending one to Car' but wasn't sure that would be in good taste. She had apologized ten million times for leaving and had several times changed her mind about it, arguing with herself that she wanted nothing more in the world than to be doing this, but in the end had gone. ("I'm a big girl and this is my problem to deal with," she said at one point. "So I'm choosing to deal with it later." I supported that choice.)

Ziggy seemed unaffected by her absence. He came up to me while we were sitting around backstage, shortly before we went on, and said, with a fake punch to my arm, "Hey, let's make it good tonight."

How could it not be? We had a crowd who knew all the old songs and had learned half the words to the new ones before we were done. I had a strong feeling bootleg tapes were being made but I didn't care. We were on, and I made it through another night without an anxiety attack or mishap. After the show someone told me one of the guys in Love Tractor was there and wanted to know if we'd be sticking around for a few days and if we could jam. (It was too bad we had to be on the road in the morning because those guys can really play.)

After the show the town was still awake and Bart and Ziggy and I had dinner in a brew pub. Toward the end, Bart went off to the men's room, and Ziggy leaned in close to me. "How are you?"

"Fine."

"You seem a little more relaxed."

"It's easier with Digger not around," I said, not sure if I was tossing that off as an excuse or if it was partly true. The feeling was less one of something being wrong than there being a lack of something at all, like it had all been a mirage that disappeared the closer you came to it.

Disappeared. I looked at him and I felt nothing. Not an ache, not a pang. It was an odd feeling. It was like somewhere along the way, I'd had my fill of him. I'd stopped needing him like a drug.

As we left the restaurant I detached myself from the two of them and headed off on my own. I ended up at a gay bar/dance club called Boneshakers and tried hard not to think of whether the awful pun was intended.

And of course I thought of Z. and C. while I got down in the men's room with a new friend and a rubber dispensed not from a machine but from a basket on the bar next to the tip jar. If anyone recognized me, they didn't say anything, probably pegged me for a UGA student, and I was back at the motel watching cable by 2am.

Games People Play

In the morning Christian woke me up banging on the door and hollering. The clock on the night table read 10:00 AM and I sat up with my heart pounding, wondering what had gone wrong. I opened the door. "Jeezus, what happened?"

"Aren't we supposed to be on the road? It's eleven hours to New Orleans without stopping." He looked at his wrist where there was no watch but the meaning of the gesture was not lost on me. He was fully dressed, hair blown dry and wearing a black T-shirt and jeans.

I rubbed my eyes. "Shit, I guess I'm supposed to be in charge now, aren't I."

"That's right, boss."

"OK, right. I gotta make some phone calls and take a shower or you really won't want to be cooped up with me for the entire day." The sunlight was bright and I covered my eyes with my hand. "I guess, make sure the crew's up?"

"You got it, boss." He went to the next door and I let ours shut before opening my eyes again.

Ziggy was sitting up in the bed when I turned around. "Oh, I'm tired," he singsonged. "Has it only been two weeks? It feels like forever."

"I'm getting in the shower," I told him. "Go back to sleep."

But once I was in the shower I heard him running the water in the bathroom, shaving, brushing his teeth or whatever, whistling. Then his voice over the rush of the water. "You have fun last night?"

"Yeah. Good crowd," I said, ducking my head under the water.

Then his head appeared on the far side of the curtain. "Where did you get off to after dinner?"

"Slumming," I said, looking at him with one unsoapy eye. "What about you?"

He grinned and said only "Daron, I do believe you're learning how to live. You're going to like New Orleans."

"Yeah?" My face was in the stream now and he waited until I stepped back from the spray to talk again.

"It's a great city for music." He had that tone of voice, that slinky sound, that made it sound like he meant something else. "Can I show you around?"

"Sure." I watched his head disappear and then heard the door open and shut. I finished rinsing and shut off the water.

I wasn't unaware of the fact that since Carynne had left my interactions with him had been really on-the-surface friendly, like everything was cool. We were acting more friendly to each other than we'd been in a while, in fact. But maybe that was just it, "acting" friendly. Were we friends now? Did ex-lovers, co-workers, and/or one-time crushes count as friends? Wait, did I say ex-lovers, and is that what I meant?

I couldn't pursue that line of thought without driving myself into a black mood. The show last night had been good. So what if I wasn't hitting that rapturous losing myself feeling every night—if I enjoyed myself, if I gave myself to working hard and getting the job done and it all worked, well, that was all I could ask for, wasn't it?

I felt older thinking like that. And I didn't know if that should worry me or not.

Take Me to the River

Within an hour we were on our way to Louisiana. Carynne had left me some specific notes about our route through Alabama and Mississippi, where to stop for food and such. Don't Fuck Around she had penciled in block letters on the page with the route outlined and although I didn't figure she meant it literally we spent the minimum amount of time necessary to do what we had to in rest stops and at roadside restaurants.

There really are Denny's in every conceivable corner of this nation. We'd all gotten to the point where we knew what day of the week was for which soup and I was weirdly looking forward to the next vegetable beef day.

Eleven hours is a long fucking drive. I almost wanted to spend more of it driving than riding because I seemed not to get as bored, although I got more tired. In my head I'd do these little calculations, like, if we drove from Boston to New York, how many times could we have gone back and forth in eleven hours? That was to New York, back to Boston, and almost all the way back to New York again. That was driving between Philadelphia and my old house more than seven times.

I had no idea what to expect when we pulled up to our hotel in New Orleans past midnight. Some cities would have been shuttered up by then and we'd be lucky to have one sleepy, overnight clerk check us in.

Not here. A whole bunch of brass-buttoned door men and bell hops (all black, I noticed) stood like an idle army around the driveway and in the lobby, some of them coming alive as we pulled up, while others waited in reserve (in case there should be a mad midnight rush to check in?). The lobby was lively with people in everything from elegant formal wear to tacky French Quarter T-shirts, cameras around their necks. A fountain bubbled, people laughed, and what I thought at first was piped-in Muzak turned out to be a jazz combo of piano, stand up bass, and drums in one potted-plant-secluded corner of the open air bar.

I made Kevin handle check-in while I hovered around the three bell guys handling the bags and instruments. Every now and then one of them would catch me looking and tip his hat at me and smile. Then they started asking me questions, where were we playing, how long we were staying, that kind of stuff, and I told them and they seemed to genuinely care about the answers, chiding me for not spending more time in the city and telling me I'd be back soon once I'd had a taste.

This banter continued right up the elevator and into our rooms while they set our bags down where indicated. We had three rooms at the end of a hall, one bigger than the others and two connecting on either side. I tipped the three of them out of my pocket cash and then went to the wide window in the suite. It looked over some kind of low shopping mall on the Mississippi River. Boats were pulled up to a pier there, some kind of pleasure river boats, their railings lit with tiny white bulbs. I could see people walking along the plaza and down the main street parallel to the river. The sound of cars reached me.

Midnight appeared to be a fine hour for New Orleans.

Ziggy and Bart both came up to the window.

"That's pretty," Ziggy said.

"No lie, bwana," Bart added. "Should we go out? What time do we have to be up?"

I yawned but felt more tired than sleepy. "We don't have to be any-where until tomorrow afternoon."

Ziggy. "Let's go then."

Bart was already headed for the door. "Where are we going?"

"In this town, you don't have to go anywhere. Let's just have a look around." Ziggy dug into his backpack and pulled out a blank tank top. He traded his T-shirt for it and ran his hands through his hair.

I was in high tops, jeans, and a T-shirt and had no intention of changing. We collected the other three but once we got moving into the French Quarter we only loosely tried to stay together. Our hotel was at the western edge of the quarter and we started at that end of the infamous Bourbon Street and walked east.

Bart stuck close by me as we went past shops selling mardi gras masks, tchotchke, and T-shirts, T-shirts, T-shirts. We passed bars with live jazz, reggae, karaoke, country and western, R&B, you name it pouring out their open doors into the street. I'd never heard so much live music crammed into so few blocks before.

Neatly groomed young men, both white and black, with flyers in their hands, invited us into place after place with promises of "no cover." The hand-painted signs hung in most doorways that read "two drink minimum per set" kept us watching from the middle of the street with large groups of other tourists. There were people walking everywhere, in both directions, carrying drinks in plastic cups, laughing, looking at each other.

Bourbon Street reminded me more than anywhere else I'd been yet of the Jersey Shore, of the way people walked up and down the boardwalk at the Shore, not really doing anything other than walking and enjoying themselves by being there. Of course, you couldn't carry booze on the boardwalk, and you had to imagine all the pinball arcades replaced with female impersonator strip shows, the ice cream stands with Hurricanes-in-cups stands, and the games of chance replaced with live music venues one next to the other. However, the vibe was similar, and the T-shirt shops were about the same, tacky and densely placed enough to make you wonder if they really could all stay in business.

As in the lobby of the hotel, people here were in everything from tuxes to bermuda shorts. Brightly painted mule carts went by filled with wide-eyed families. Hey, shouldn't those kids be in bed? It's one a.m.! Nobody seemed to mind. Bart eventually declared himself thirsty and pulled me into a place where they were playing real jazz, and we sat at a little table and bought club soda and root beer for four bucks each and sat through the rest of the set sipping slowly and me thinking, jeez, what a life. The musicians played hot and yet it was clear they were playing for themselves—most of the glassy-eyed tourists in here wouldn't have known good jazz if it bit them on the proverbial ass.

These guys were mostly young, not wizened Mississippi blues guys but mid-thirties, some black, some white, trading licks and having fun. I wondered how many sets they had to do a night, or per week, to get by. When they were done, a different band set up and we moved on.

We hooked back up with Ziggy in a weird, crowded little shop where they sold voodoo paraphernalia, occult supplies and tourist trap stuff like good luck charms and Voodoo Queen post cards. Ziggy was buying some of the post cards and haggling over the price of a Mexican prayer candle. I put a hand on his shoulder then, shaking my head like I couldn't possibly have heard right. "Were you speaking Spanish?"

"*Claro que si,*" he said, in what sounded to me like a natural accent. "You bet."

"I didn't know you spoke Spanish."

He looked at me sideways. "I guess there are a lot of things you don't know about me, huh."

I suddenly felt as if he were several feet away instead of right there, leaning on the counter next to me. "I guess..." I began but didn't finish. He was so far away and I felt cold even in the pressed heat and crowd of the shop. I did not move.

He turned back to the clerk (who had agreed on his price), took the brown paper bag and handed over green cash. Then he jerked his head my way and I followed him out of the store.

We walked a few more blocks, not talking, and the crowd thinned a bit. But I could see more lights and people ahead of us, and hear the throb of dance music. We passed a corner diner that kept late hours and some locals sitting on the curb in the dark sharing a cigarette. "How you doing?" Ziggy asked me as we walked.

"Fine I guess." A general answer for a general question.

"Good." He gestured with his paper bag. "The Quarter is basically a big rectangle, with the river on the South side. Our hotel is at one end, the touristy end. The other end," he pointed ahead of us, "is the gay end."

"How do you know all this?"

"Came here once a couple of years ago with some friends. Crazy friends, we drove here in a car with like almost no money, driving for days, just determined we'd get here and once we did we'd have a great time."

"And?"

"And we did. Have a great time."

Now most of the pedestrians were men, some with appraising eyes, some in pairs, in hooded sweatshirts with the sleeves cut out, in dapper jeans tucked into black boots, in mesh shirts double-dotted with dark nipples, shirtless (their shirts tucked into a back pocket or tied around their heads bandana style).

They were mostly white and I wondered if they were tourists or locals. Maybe by being in the gay part of town gay tourists became like locals and anyone not gay, whether from here or elsewhere, became a tourist by default. I felt like a tourist, and looking at the way Ziggy swept his eyes back and forth over the crowds of men spilling out the doorways of two big club/bars on either side of us I got the feeling he felt like one, too, which surprised me. Men were leaning over a second floor balcony, sometimes whistling to other men on the street, waving to guys they knew or commenting on passerby, but they were mostly silent, the silence I associated with DC park benches and East Village bars, the silence of waiting. Generic disco pulsed in the background.

"I think I'm going to head back the other way," I said in a low voice.

"You sure? I thought you said we didn't have to be up early." He did not look at me, his eyes continuing to scan.

"You don't have to come back with me."

His gaze passed through mine then for an instant. "I was wondering if I should ask you something."

"What?"

"Do you think you'll be up when I get back?" He was now looking behind me, as if making eye contact with someone back there. He took a step toward them, and me. Then another, until we were almost touching shoulders. "I've been meaning to ... I mean, it's been a while since we gave it a try, you know."

The ever elusive "it" again. "Does that mean we should?"

He looked at me now, our faces close. "You sound bitter."

"So do you." I didn't really have anything I was burning to say to him and yet I wasn't going to just walk away. "Let's not start this again."

"Start which."

"Fighting." I stuck my hands into my pockets to keep from making fists. "We don't have to argue."

He closed his eyes and made his voice soft, almost plaintive. "Please just be there when I get back."

"How long will you be?"

"Not long," he said, looking past me again. "Not long."

Don't Fear the Reaper

I walked down Bourbon the other way, not tempted to stop and now vaguely wondering when I'd lost Bart. I didn't see any of the others and felt a pang of guilt over Carynne; she'd have liked it here. When I got back to the room I called her, only thinking after I'd dialed that perhaps it was a bit late.

"Hello?" She sounded awake but puzzled.

"It's your boss," I said, holding the phone on my shoulder while I sat on the edge of the bed and untied my shoes. "We're in New Orleans."

"Omigod, isn't it fabulous? Did you just get there or have you seen anything yet?"

I told her we'd seen Bourbon Street and met the world's friendliest bell hops. "Everyone else is still out. I'm thinking of going to sleep."

"I tell you, if that gig at UT-Austin hadn't come through, I would have left you there for another day. I went for Spring break a couple of years ago. If you feel like blowing a lot of money on a humongously good meal..."

"Don't tell me. It'll ruin us for the rest of the trip. You know we've eaten in six Denny's thus far?" I carried the phone to the window and watched fog forming over the river.

"I guess that's one thing I don't miss."

"I haven't eaten so much grilled cheese since I was like eleven years old."

In the background I could hear something, the radio maybe. "So how's everybody."

"Good."

"Our friend isn't too freaked out by my leaving?"

"Our friend is at the far end of Bourbon making mincemeat out of the local bar scene and haggling with Voodoo priests." I wondered if she smiled at that. Maybe not, since the next thing she said turned her voice serious.

"I should tell you something."

"What."

"I went and got tested today."

"Oh." I didn't know if it was rude to ask or what. We were both silent for a few moments.

"I won't get the results back for like two weeks."

Oh. "Jeezus."

"Yeah. I'm not too worried, though."

"Why not?"

"Jeezus, Daron, listen to you. I did it just for my peace of mind, you know? And yours, I guess. You ought to be more worried than me, I think."

"Thanks, that's just what I needed to hear."

"No, but seriously, I figure I can't change the past and I don't regret the things I've done. Yet. Say-la-vee, no use being all worked up about it. What about you?"

"What about me." I probably don't have to say I didn't like this line of questioning.

"Are you worried?"

"If you mean about AIDS, I guess…? I don't know." This really wasn't what I expected to talk about. And there I was saying I-don't-know again, dammit. "I guess you could say I'm concerned, but not worried. Not yet."

"Oh shit, I just got worried."

"Why?"

"About you. Here I was all resigned to take whatever may come my way, but oh man, I don't even want to think about you. Oh jeezus Daron, I don't want you to die."

"Hang on a second, I think we're getting a little premature about this." How the hell did we get on the subject of death? "Other than with him, I haven't really slept with very many people, you know." I was already backtracking in my mind: I'd used a condom that time—in Athens was it? Yeah. DC, too. But not for oral sex… I had that same sinking-anxious uninformed feeling I had when I went to do my taxes, which did not strike me as a funny coincidence at the time. "I really don't think I'm about to die. And I haven't really been around that much. Really."

"Yeah, but what about him?"

"That's hard to tell. I have no idea." Once upon a time he'd let me think I was the first guy he'd ever had sex with. I still didn't know if I actually was. Other times, like tonight, you'd think he'd been here a hundred times, not just once. "I think he talks a bigger game than he plays," I finally said. "But it's mostly talk. He saves the actual fucking around for people like us."

"Well, that's good." Her voice had a kind of forced cheerfulness that made me feel a little desperate.

I decided to change the subject from death to broken hearts; how's that for an improvement? "I wish you'd stayed."

She said nothing.

"Something's different when we're all guys here. Too much testosterone or something. We're sick of talking to each other."

"Already? Christ, read a book or something," she teased. "I wish I was there, too."

"It seems kind of stupid that you left, now, doesn't it."

"I guess."

Outside the window, the fog bank was building and drifting toward the hotel. "I mean, couldn't we have talked to him, figured things out?"

I heard her click her tongue. "Hey, I said I wasn't going to regret anything I did, and that includes leaving."

"You're right, I'm sorry. I'm a lunkhead. But you could fly out and meet us in San Fran like Digger's doing. Or in Boulder. The other guys think you had some kind of emergency—we could act like it was fixed."

"You're tempting me."

"Tell Digger I said we'd pick up the tab. I'm the boss, remember."

"That you are," she said with a little laugh. "That you are."

Instant Karma

I had just hung up the phone and was exploring the extra-large bathtub in the suite's bathroom—it had some kind of jets—when I heard the door open. Ziggy came in and threw himself down on the king-size bed.

"Tired?" I said as I came in, my voice neutral.

He threw his arm over his eyes. "Yeah. But kind of wired, too. It's this place. Talk about a party town."

I sat next to him on the bed and crossed my legs. "I just got off the phone with Bizzy."

"Oh, yeah?" His eyes were still hidden under his arm.

"Yeah. I told her I wanted her to come back."

"I thought she had some kind of family emergency..."

I pulled his arm down and looked into his eyes, anger sudden and rough in my veins. "Don't give me that bullshit. You know she left because of you."

He furrowed his brows in mock disbelief.

"Why?" I held him down, my hands on his shoulders, my legs under me. "What possessed you to fuck with her like that, huh?"

His lips pressed into a thin line. "So it's all my fault, eh? Come on, Daron, you know she flirted with me. It's not like a forced her into anything."

I let him go with a grunt of exasperation. Even Car' had said that, I couldn't argue with that. And I couldn't bring myself to wave the safe sex issue in his face. "She was our road manager," I said lamely, glossing over the fact, for the moment, that I'd slept with her, too.

"Is it my professionalism that's at issue here?" He turned over onto his stomach, crossed his feet in the air. "Just who are we allowed to get to know biblically and who aren't we, then, huh boss? I don't remember anything in the contract about this."

I stood up but did not pace, no matter how much I wanted to.

"I mean," he continued, rolling onto his side and holding up his fingers to tick off items, "it would seem that fans and groupies should be allowable, right? And how about total strangers, that's a nice option. Let's see, who else do we ever see? Hmm, local sound engineers, club managers, bartenders? Are they on the list or off?"

"I didn't say..."

"How about members of the press?" His eyes glittered black.

I was shoving my hands into my pockets again. "I did not sleep with Jonathan."

"I don't believe you."

"What are you trying to say, that because I might have slept with a reporter it's okay for you to sleep with our road manager?" I was breathing faster, and my words came out in a rush before I could really think about them. Danger, Will Robinson. I tried to breathe deep, but it was too late for that. If I'd been on edge lately, now I was positively teetering.

"I didn't say anything of the kind. I'm trying to point out that it's useless to try to make a rule against sex with a person based on professional relations." He looked down and blinked his thick black lashes a few times, then looked up at me through them. "Case in point..."

And I did it. I stepped off the edge. "I never should have slept with you." I gritted my teeth against the word "never." There was no stopping me, no rationalizing, no going back.

His mask crumbled and tears, possibly real ones, sprang into his eyes. "Oh that hurts," he said, as if to himself, as if he hadn't meant to speak aloud. "Oh my god."

"Look at yourself," I said. "Ziggy, you hurt people. You totally messed with Carynne's head and made her fucking run away because she couldn't trust being with you. And I'm supposed to trust you now?"

"Christ, I'm sorry," he said, not looking at me. "But I was jealous, okay? I'm not used to that." Tears ran down his face, leaving gray trails of eyeliner pencil. "I'm not used to caring one way or the other. But it was like... I mean, we were finally beginning to work again, and then he came along..."

"And you took it out on her...?"

"No! I like her. I was lonely. I had no idea she thought it was too much. It wasn't meant to hurt anyone."

"Anyone except me." I had that urge again, to hit him across the face, like that would change anything. Could it change his feelings for me? Would it make him hate me? Of course, the last time I'd tried to really hit him I'd ended up with a sprained thumb.

Violence was no answer, not when words could do just as much damage. Maybe more.

I took another step backward to put some space between us anyway, before I asked, "So, why did you want me to be here when you got back?"

For a moment it looked like he was going to get up and walk out. Like he was going to leave me hanging, or chasing after him for the answer.

Instead, he clutched his head in his hands. "Things have been better, haven't they? With you and me." He was positively whining. "The shows have been pretty good…"

"Because we've been ignoring each other."

"Do we have to keep doing that? Onstage and off?"

"I think it's a good idea not to fuck with it." Or each other, I didn't add.

He blew air through his lips and turned full-on puppy dog eyes on me. "I've missed you, okay? I didn't come here to fight with you."

"You mean that now that you don't have her around, you've decided to see if you can get some from me. Am I right?"

"It's not like that," he said, frowning. "It's not like that at all."

"Then what is it? It's not as if you love me." I shocked even myself by saying it.

His answer was immediate. "I never should have said that."

So I stared at him, daring him to fill the silence.

"I don't know why I said that. At the time, I thought…. Shit." He was working out the puzzle in his head just as I was. If he meant it then, then he was being a manipulative shit now, and if he meant it now, he had been a manipulative shit then. "I mean, you were so gun shy…"

"And this is going to make me less gun shy, now? My neck is sore from you jerking my chain so fucking much."

Things got worse from there. There was name calling. There were accusations. Once the fight got going, maybe we were fighting for the sake of fighting. I don't know. Nothing we said mattered anymore. We were so far off the map of reality that there was no telling what was truth or lies from either of us.

It ended with me sitting on the rug hugging my knees and saying, "I don't even know whose fault it is. I don't even care anymore who loved who or when. I just want it to stop. I just want you out of my face. I've had it with you jerking me around and screwing with the others. Next time it won't be Carynne who leaves the tour. It'll be you or me, do you hear me? The bullshit stops now, Zig, or it's all over."

He didn't say anything to that, just twisted his face into a wounded look, and walked out.

I had the feeling the evening with me had not gone as he had planned.

And I'd never felt so shitty after winning a fight.

Walk Away

I lay for a long time on top of the bedspread with my clothes on, thinking, thinking. I couldn't even remember half of what we had just said, which was unusual. Usually I could play back a traumatic exchange like a movie. In fact, I was usually helpless to stop the endless replays. But it was all fucked up now. I wasn't even sure which of us had said what. Meltdown. All I remembered was that I'd given him an ultimatum. Stop the bullshit or I'm pulling the plug.

I thought about the little truce we'd had, keeping out of each other's way, like that was supposed to restore my confidence and get me playing better. I had been playing better, acting better... what was going to happen now? As for how I felt about him, though, that seemed clear for the first time in a long time. I was no longer obsessed with him. I didn't even feel much like friends at that moment.

I was still not sleeping. I got undressed, brushed my teeth, washed my face. I got into the bed. The sound of nighttime hotel seemed loud, the faraway roar of air conditioning, a radio or television on MTV in the next room. That was probably Bart.

I got back into my clothes and knocked on Bart and Christian's door. Bart opened it. "What's up?"

"Me. Can't sleep. Oh, man."

He opened the door wider and I went in. This was a standard rectangular two-double-bed kind of room. Chris was nowhere in sight. Bart got back under the covers where he'd been sitting with all his clothes on. His socks didn't match, one black, one blue. I went to the window, this one faced away from the Quarter, onto a wide street with other hotels across the way. "Ziggy and I had a fight."

"I know, I could hear you were yelling." He muted the TV and looked at me. "So, what's the update?"

I sat down in the chair by the window so I faced him. "It's pretty much a state of mutual angst right now. I don't think we even really like each other very much anymore. I'm not sure what to do now."

Bart shrugged. He looked like he needed a hair cut. "What's to do? Is there some kind of decision to make here?"

"Not that I can see."

"I mean, is it a question of whether we stay together? Or finish the tour? Or is it a case of you trying to figure out how to make up with him? Or with each other enough to keep going?"

"I can't even answer that." My hands formed the fists they'd been trying to all night.

"Maybe getting some sleep would be the best thing. I'm sure it won't look so bad in the morning."

"I tried sleeping."

"Well, at least quit thinking about it. Lie down over here." He unmuted the TV and I found myself watching/listening to Kate Bush trilling through some chastely sexy melody. Late night was really the only time MTV was watchable, the only time anything interesting came on. "Why The Sky was just on a little while ago," he said as I settled onto the bed next to him. "Looks like it'll be in the top twenty countdown of the week."

"No kidding."

"You should give Mills a call in the morning and see if he knows anything."

"I should call Digger, too. I haven't talked to him since he went back to New York."

And then we didn't say much other than side comments about videos and commercials that came on. My jaw relaxed and my fists unclenched and my burn settled to a simmer. Eventually I was too tired to be angry anymore and luckily I fell asleep before my tiredness could become depression.

I Still Haven't Found What I'm Looking For

In the morning I woke up in Bart's room—actually it wasn't morning, it was just past noon, and Bart was elsewhere and Chris was blow drying his hair in the bathroom. My body felt as hot and wrinkly as the clothes I had slept in. In fact, I had slept with my card key in the back pocket of my jeans. Carynne had designated today as a laundry day in the schedule and it was just as well. The suite had been made up, cleaned and straightened; there was no way to tell if Ziggy had slept there or not. He was not there now.

In the shower I tried to think about what I'd say to him when I saw him again. I tried to imagine apologizing, but I couldn't really think of what I'd be apologizing for, exactly.

I tried to imagine him apologizing, crawling on the shag carpet toward me like the way he did on stage, admitting his crimes and begging forgiveness while the city of New Orleans glittered and shone in the window behind me...

Seemed unlikely.

The crew of two and Chris decided to go ahead to the venue and set up. Bart asked if I wanted to go into the Quarter to get lunch. I decided to stay in and have room service. Another black staff member, in a chef-type jacket, arrived some time later with food on a rolling table. I'll say one thing about the food—even for room service and me being in a bad mood, the gumbo was so good I didn't think I'd ever be able to order it at Denny's again. I was playing with the garnish and looking out the window at the river when Bart came back.

"Uh oh," he said when he saw me staring out the window.

"No sign of him yet," I answered, to confirm his suspicions. "You don't think we should actually worry, do you?"

"No use worrying about what we can't change." He ate the pickle I had left on the room service tray. "Did you call Mills yet?"

I hadn't. I went to the phone by the bed and dialed—it had been a while since I'd been the one to call him, but I still had the number memorized. When it rang several times I opened the day book to check that today was a weekday. Then a male voice I didn't know picked up and cheerfully confirmed I'd reached the right office. Mills came on a few moments later.

The conversation went about like this:

"Daron, my favorite moondog! How are you."

"Fine."

"I was wondering when we were going to hear from you. It's been what, a week since we've had any word."

"Oh?"

"Yeah, Digger was calling in every day for a while there." Snapping his fingers. "But I guess he's back in New York now, isn't he. Sounded like the Northeast went well. It's too early to see a sales spike if there is one but, hoo, radio play has been through the roof."

"That's great."

"I don't know if you've heard yet but 'Why The Sky' is going to be like number 15 or 13 or something on the MTV countdown." Yelling to someone else. "Cheryl! What number—? Ah never mind. Anyway, how's the South? Any problems?"

"No, not really."

"Where are you now? Georgia?"

"New Orleans."

"Ah, Jazz Fest City. You'll like it there. But it's corrupt as hell, you know, old money, that sort of thing. Hey listen, I'm kind of in the middle of something here. Did you need something? Is there something Cheryl can help you with?"

"Uh, no, just checking in."

"Great. Fantastic. Plans are in the works for the summer dates already. Have a great time in Georgia. Call Cheryl if you need anything."

"Yeah, okay, bye."

I didn't remember anyone named Cheryl in his office. I filled Bart in on the side of the conversation he couldn't hear, then called Digger and had to leave him a message. "Was there anyone else I was supposed to call?"

"Yeah, call Michelle and tell her I miss her."

"Are you joking?" I got up and began picking through my bag, looking for the right shirt to wear later, tossing out flyers and other crap I'd picked up at previous shows. "I mean, I know you're joking, but about which part?"

He stretched out on the bed watching me dig through my stuff. "Of course I don't mean for you to call her."

"But do you miss her?"

"Of course I do."

"You make it sound like missing her's an obligation."

"I don't mean it that way," but he looked at the ceiling when he said it. "I wouldn't still be with her after all these years if there wasn't something there. And no, I don't miss her less now than I did when we'd first met."

"That's cool. I was just, I don't know, wondering if everything was okay."

"Why, because you're a general worry wart, or was there something specific?" He pursed his lips at me. "And don't wear your Bigger Thomas shirt tonight. I'm already wearing mine."

"Okay, jeez. I'll quit beating around the bush. Does Michelle know... I mean, how does she handle you sleeping around?"

"Oh is *that* what's bothering you." He sat up and laughed a little.

I held up a black T-shirt with bright red letters that said "Cartoon Factory," a Boston band we'd played with a few times. He shook his head and went on. "You don't have to keep it a secret, if that's what you're worried about."

"I'm not worried." I pulled out a blue shirt with black leopard spots on it—Ziggy's. I held it up tentatively for his approval.

He rolled his eyes and he looked at me like I was crazy to even contemplate wearing that. "She knows."

I tossed the shirt over my shoulder and rummaged deeper into my duffel bag. "Does she sleep with other guys while you're gone?"

He gave a half-shrug that could have been I-don't-know or It-doesn't-matter. "She could if she wanted to. She hasn't yet, though."

"She'd tell you?" I had another black shirt in my hands, balled between them as I looked at his face.

"Yeah. And I tell her. Not the gory details of course. It doesn't make sense to do it any other way. It'd be like, I don't know, if I worked in a bakery and she tried to get me to promise not to eat any cookies at work."

"Cookies," I repeated.

"Yeah."

I held up the shirt. I couldn't remember what band it had come from. It read, "It's Only Fun When Someone Loses An Eye."

We Will Rock You

We waited around a bit more, but Ziggy didn't reappear at the hotel.

Bart wrote a note and left it on the bed with the name and address of the club just in case, and we took a cab up there. Tipitina's was like an oversized honky tonk, rustic wood, minimally fancy lights, you could picture women in hoop skirts and men in string ties stomping their feet in there. But up in the second floor balcony there were photographs of people on the stage, a staggering array of Stevie Ray Vaughn, REM, Coco Taylor, Talking Heads. My estimation of the place went up. The backstage area was roomy, like an efficiency apartment attached to the club with separate rooms and a little kitchen.

The parade of old couches continued.

In New Orleans, as I was learning, everything was done to excess. Every shot was a double, every meal was enough for a family of four, and we had two opening bands instead of one. There was a healthy crew running sound, four or five guys, with one board to the side of the stage for monitors and one out in the club for PA. Like the bellhops, the crew were all super friendly. Unlike the bellhops these guys were all white, the fact of which made me wonder what percentage of roadies and techies everywhere in the country were white. It was an uncomfortable thought.

Everyone was more or less waiting for us when we got there and after dumping our stuff in the living room-like area of backstage we got right up on the stage and plugged in.

I was standing there with the Ovation on when the head sound guy lifted himself onto the stage from the floor, his back to me so he sat there for a moment swinging his legs before he stood all the way up. Kevin came from behind me and said "This is Kevin."

"No relation," the sound guy said shaking my hand. He had some gray in his beard but otherwise looked like late-20s, T-shirt, jeans, keys on his belt loop. He wore combat boots with the laces tied loose. "Pleased to meet you." He pointed out other staff members where they were in the club, Nick behind the monitor board, Jimmy on the floor, and "Carleton Edward Hill the Third, but we just call him Ray" up on the balcony aiming some lights. Ray waved.

Kevin, our Kevin, twitched his face at me (what's up) and said "Ziggy didn't come with you?"

"Nope." I gave a shrug. "You want to wait for him?"

Shrugs all around. "It's up to you," The other Kevin said. "The other bands'll wait."

"I hate making 'em wait," I said. "I always hated waiting around. Let's do what we can and if you really think you need him later, once he gets here we can do a quickie."

"Suits me," he said, and walked away, boots solid on the wooden stage.

Chris got on his stool and I found out they'd already done all the drum setting already, which was nice since that's the most boring part of a soundcheck, and we got down to me and Bart. We played Kevin, their Kevin, various sections, loud ones, soft ones. To my ears the hall sounded mellow, which would change when there were people in it, but for now, mellow.

"Why doesn't one of you get up there are fake some vocals," their Kevin suggested.

"Don't look at me," Bart said when I looked at him.

"Yeah, yeah," I said, stepping up to the center mic. "Okay, fine, let's see, let's do Walking. What you're about to hear is my imitation of our absent vocalist, to try for maximum simulation effect."

"Check," said Kevin.

Right. Walking In Time was one of the easiest songs to sing I'd ever written probably. It was a blues tune, basically, with predictable, gut-satisfying chord changes and an easy chorus. I remembered Carynne singing it backstage at the Orpheum in her Janis Joplin voice. We didn't do the song very often anymore—it didn't fit in the set the way it used to. When Ziggy sang it, he sang it with venom, laying full blame on each character in the song. I riffed through the opening and sang:

People, keep walking in time
Walking in line
Walk, walk, walk, walk, walk, right into my life...

Whenever I try to imitate Ziggy's singing voice I think I end up sounding like Steven Tyler of Aerosmith. I've heard myself on tape and although Bart denies it, that's what my voice sounds like to me. With the down & dirty blues guitar I laid onto this song, even more so. All three of us liked this bluesy stuff because there was so much room to put in our own little fills, pass stuff around. There was a lot of breathing space between the lyrics, between very short verses that were barely more than one line each:

Sister,
don't you lie to me
cause I can see
gotta move (move, move, move...) on your own two feet

I could see Ray's head nodding from his perch in the balcony, the orange dot of a cigarette in his hand. My tongue felt big and loose in my mouth while I formed the words, singing them louder... back into the chorus,

People,
keep walking in time
walking in line
walking right out of my life.

My voice matched the little riff my fingers had just invented and I
stuck with that: out of my life, out of my life... trying the notes on the
words different ways, up the scale, down the scale, putting the em-
PHAsis on a different sylLABle. And then I felt Bart nudging at me
with notes and I let him take the solo, and I turned to face Chris and we
finished off in our typical ham-it-up windmill-the-arms arena-rock type
rolling-cymbal ending, which wasn't at all apropos for a bluesy tune
like that, but so what.

The echoes disappeared into the room and all three of us laughed.
Colin laughed too from the behind the side board and we left the stage
to the other bands and crew.

Same Old Song and Dance

Our Kevin clapped me on the shoulder as I went one way and he went
the other. I came around the back of the stage to the stairs that led up to
the backstage kitchenette, and stopped short.

Ziggy was sitting on the steps, his hands hanging between his knees
and his lower lip hidden in his teeth. He blinked heavily-lined eyes at
me and stared. I stared back. Bart and Chris, who had been behind me at
some point, were as disappeared as mafia informers.

"Hey," he finally said.

"Hey." My hands migrated to my pockets and I rocked on my heels
slightly as they dug in. I didn't have anything to say about last night and
I fished for something else. "You're late."

He thinned his lips and nodded contritely, eyes down. "I fucked up."
There was, as usual, no way to tell whether he referred to what was spoken or what was un-.

And I was getting good at that game. "Nobody's perfect," I said as I climbed past him and left him on the stairs.

Another One Bites the Dust

We each did a pretty good job of avoiding the other after that.

At one point all of us were sitting around sharing beer and stronger substances with the openings bands (you guessed it, they were ultra-friendly) and having a wide-ranging group conversation, but that didn't really count as speaking to each other. Ziggy was discussing hair coloring with the keyboard player from one of the bands whose hair was a long, wavy, unnatural orange. I contented myself with a lively argument over the roots of modern surf punk. ("Come on, do you think it's a coincidence that "pogo" and "gogo" rhyme?") And then the first band went on, and Bart and Chris went out to watch. I moved myself to one of the side rooms to put my eyeliner on.

I sat in a chair in front of a mirror with the pencil in my hand and couldn't bring myself to touch the tip to my skin. I pulled my hair out of its tie and let it fall around my shoulders. It was longer in the back than on the sides and too straight to do much but lie flat. I stuck it behind my ears and brought the pencil up to my eye again.

My heart just wasn't in it, I guess, and I gave up without putting any on. I left my hair down and put on the "Loses An Eye" T-shirt. After I put my boots on, I tied my sneakers together by the laces and left the pair looped over the arm of a couch. I checked my strings and tuning, played a little on the Ovation with what sound was coming from the stage, a kind of funked up blues with a jangly guitar on top. I could go out and watch from the balcony, I realized, but didn't feel the urge. Someone in the kitchen talked over the music, I didn't know who. It didn't much matter.

But eventually the moment came when we four were assembled to go on stage, standing in the little living room waiting for Ray's signal, looking at each other and not talking. Ziggy, who preferred to be the last one onto the stage, spun in place and sneered at the painting hanging on the wall above the couch as if it were a mirror. Bart and I exchanged meaningless looks. And then I was going down the stairs with the Ovation in one hand and the banister in the other.

The club seemed bigger when full of people, as if it had expanded to fit them all. For some reason I kept thinking I'd see a familiar face if I looked hard enough, a strange illusion that persisted throughout the show as I'd scan the crowd in quiet moments, a deja vu-like feeling that was irksome rather than comforting.

Anyway, we played. The energy of the soundcheck was gone and this was serious work. Welcome felt strong but peaked too early, leaving the crowd sitting back and waiting for something more. We'd moved Why the Sky up in the set and I was unsteady through it, feeling uncomfortable and out of the groove. Bart crossed to my side of the stage after the bridge, and didn't try to say anything or give me any meaningful looks, just stood by me, playing. We faced each other and played in unison, he nodding his head in time and me trying to watch his face and not his fingers. When the song ended he went back to his side. Work work work. Ziggy and I continued to ignore each other.

During the encore of Candlelight I started to get an idea for a song, just a vague concept really. I didn't know what the song was about, only that the chorus would have the words "You Know" featured—two little words that carry so many different intentions.

And then we were done and I was sitting with one foot on the couch backstage with my chin on my knee and my sneakers hanging on the other knee, and staring into space. Bart sat down next to me and I said "One step forward, two steps back."

"What makes you say that?"

Someone with keys jangling from a beltloop brushed past us. "A few months ago, we would have said that was a terrible show. But now I'm like patting myself on the back for getting through it."

"It wasn't that bad," he said, emphasis on "bad."

"I hope no one was shooting video."

"It wasn't that bad," he repeated, emphasis on "that."

I looked him in the face. "Wasn't it?"

He shook his head. "I bet if you did see video of it, you wouldn't think it was so bad. Crowd ate it up."

"This is stupid."

"What's stupid?"

I didn't know. I felt tired. My post-show high had almost instantly become a post-high hangover. I stifled a yawn.

"Oh, come on, don't make the pouty face," Bart said, standing up and yanking on my arm to try to get me up, too. "Let's go. There's plenty of fun to be had in this town at this time of night. Let's go out and have some."

I made some lame sound of protest and he cackled, suddenly energetic. "Jeezus Christ, Daron, at least try to be cheered up, will you? Did you ever wonder why your hair is always damp?"

"What?" I brushed my cheek with my hand, dislodging stray bits of hair that had pasted themselves there with sweat.

He shifted from one foot to the other. "Why your hair is always damp."

"I don't..."

"It's because of that stupid gray cloud around your head all the time." He was grinning and it occurred to me that Bart's own post-show high had not worn off. "Put on your shoes. We're going out and that's final."

Pretzel Logic

Bourbon Street was the same as last night, with people wandering through the bright neon-lit humidity looking as much at each other as at the store fronts and bars. Music poured out of every doorway and was sort of soothing after a while, the booming bass of one place fading into the cajun wheedle of the next as we walked, Bart bright-eyed like a fever victim and me, well, me just me.

We didn't talk, but we didn't *not* talk, if you know what I mean. My brain felt busy even though I wasn't really thinking about anything in particular, repeating loops of free floating anxiety and loose ends. The usual. We were away from Ziggy and that suited me. One piece of logic had lodged itself in my mind which I clung to a little—if I couldn't predict what he'd do, and he often did the exact opposite of what I expected, then if I expected him to make me miserable... well, then maybe he wouldn't. It didn't seem likely, but hey.

I followed Bart down a side street and we went up another street lined with two- and three- storey buildings, store fronts on the ground floor and the balconies of townhouses above. The people were fewer here but still numerous. A leathery-faced black man in a loose leisure suit and hat stood on one corner in a darkened doorway playing the tenor sax, another hat at his feet with a few scattered coins and bills in it. He looked like something out of a postcard; you could cast him as an extra to play the part of "New Orleans Jazzman" on a sitcom. A little voice in my head said, jeezus, did he intend to grow up to be a stereotype? And another voice answered, hey, stereotypes have to come from somewhere. I was too distracted by my discomfort over that whole concept to listen to what he was playing.

Bart wasn't exactly wandering aimlessly and he led us to an Italian restaurant someone had told him about during the course of the day, and he sat me down and got us some fabulously fresh-baked bread, and menus. My thoughts: shit, this bread is too perfect, like you can hardly imagine bread more exactly perfect. The crust, the texture, the smell, the flavor. It is The Bread. Just like that guy was The Jazz Man. These thoughts were giving me a chill, like there was something Twilight Zone about the whole thing, like we'd gone from the real world into some kind of marketing weenie's dream, where everything was Exactly As Advertised. Better than sliced bread, you might say.

And who were we in the marketing weenie's dream? Hot, new, up and coming, different... I was wishing I'd never read the Spin article or any of the propaganda BNC's media machine put out. So what if it was true? Did the hype's being true make us any less of a cliche than that sax player on the street?

"Bart," I said softly, my eyes on the dimly lit wall in the restaurant's distance and my calloused fingers digging slightly into the white cloth. "I think I'm having a crisis of faith."

He stopped in mid-chew and one eyebrow dipped low on his face. "What sort of crisis of faith."

"I mean, crisis of faith."

"As in, not sure what you believe in any more."

"Uh, no, more like sure that what I believe in is crap."

"Oh." He took a swig of water from a tall, elegantly curved glass. "Care to share with the class?"

I nodded while I waited for words to bubble up. My eyes stayed fixed in the distance. The restaurant was all off-white plaster and stucco on the inside, with painted figures on the ceiling and vaguely Mediterranean sconces, rounded doorways, a grape vine motif that popped up in wrought iron decorations and plaster friezes. White-shirted waitstaff flitted back and forth in my blurry vision.

"Well?"

"You know that guy playing the sax?"

"On Royal Street? Yeah." Bart broke off another piece of uber-world bread and buttered it.

"He was like, I don't know, so stereotypical."

"Daron, there's a difference between typical and stereotypical."

"But neither of those words has a happy connotation, does it."

He bit down on the bread and made a little mmm sound as he chewed. "You're going to say you're afraid to end up like that guy, busking on the street corner."

"No."

"You're going to say you wish you were busking on the corner instead of doing what you're doing."

"No."

"You're going to..."

"Will you let me explain already? Jeezus." His face came in to focus at last. "I'm not kidding around here."

"You did use the word crisis."

"Yeah. I did." I looked at him sitting there, eating the world's best bread and for some reason I couldn't help but smile. He smiled, too, like he'd been hiding it by chewing. Then he started to laugh, through his nose, silently, but I saw his shoulders shake. And that started me to laughing a little bit, too. "What's so funny?" I said, but I was already shaking my head.

"Eat your bread," he said, putting a hunk onto my plate. "I can't handle a crisis on an empty stomach."

"Okay, alright." I didn't butter my bread. I poured a green puddle of olive oil onto my plate and dipped it. If the bread was perfect, I was crazy to let a crisis get in the way of my enjoying it. If typical things were always this good, there'd be a lot less to complain about in the world. "I'll tell you later," I said with bread in my own mouth. "I'll tell you some other time."

"Well, okay." He gave me a that's-my-boy kind of pat on the side of the arm and neither he nor I mentioned that particular crisis again.

You May Be Right

After Bart and I ate, we sat around in the mostly-empty restaurant in no hurry to leave. Late night patrons still laughed loud at the bar in the back and waitstaff drifted back and forth with new bunches of fresh flowers for the tables and filled salt shakers.

Now that I was full, and probably better grounded, I brought my mind back to more concrete problems. "I don't even want to see him right now."

"Ziggy, you mean."

"Who else."

My mop-topped bass player of a best friend shrugged. "Sleep in my room again. We can shuffle everybody, or, I don't care, three of us can stay in the one. You're really angry at him, huh."

"Angry's not the right word." I pushed a half-eaten serving of liquored-up custard around on its enormous dish with a spoon. "I think I'd just feel better if I didn't see or speak to or deal with him for a while."

"Okay, boss. That's probably easier to arrange than um, I don't know, counseling or something."

I barked out a laugh. "That's a good one, inter-band counseling, like marriage counseling or something. God, I bet there even is such a thing in LA."

Bart cleared his throat. "You want to hear my current Grand Bart Theory on the situation?"

"Sure."

"I think you'd be getting along fine, or well, if not fine, a lot better, if you weren't always butting heads over creative issues."

I was shaking my head. "That's backwards."

"Is it? It's a chicken and egg problem, I think."

"Then there's no telling which came first, is there." I put my spoon down. "I just think we should give it some time to cool off."

"Well, let's try to get back before he does, then." Bart stood up. "I'm on the job, boss."

"Yeah, yeah." I was stuffed and sleepy and tired of angst and feeling the decadence of the city, so we hailed a cab to take us the half mile back to our hotel where we were once again greeted by the nighttime army of bell hops. Bart rubbed his stomach in a slow circle as the elevator took us up and smiled to himself. Chris was happy to move into the suite ("Last one back can have the couch, hey?") and I moved some of my crap into Bart's room.

He was brushing his teeth and I was getting under the covers when I thought to check the day book. The wake up call would come in too few hours, then it would be eleven more on the road until we reached the next hotel outside of Austin. It was gonna be my first time in Texas and I didn't look forward to it.

No More Words

Of all the parts of the country I'd been in, Texas was the strangest-feeling yet. We were due to stay three nights in a motel on the edge of Austin, the first night to sleep off the drive, the second night after the Spring Weekend concert at University of Texas, and the third night after the show in San Antonio which was maybe two hours drive from there.

My whole feeling about Texas was that beady-eyed big-hatted men were watching me through binoculars with shotguns in their laps. Maybe I'd had the feeling from as soon as we'd come into the South, and the longer we stayed down here, the stronger the feeling got. Austin was supposed to be a funky town, college-y, artsy, yadda yadda, but where we were staying was fairly suburban. After the let-it-all-hang-out attitude of New Orleans, I didn't feel confident about anything here, not even how to read the cultural signals that might have led me to a few moments re-lief and blind bliss in the hands (or mouth) of a stranger.

Most of what I remember of Texas is the numbing act, me and Ziggy avoiding each other, and when we couldn't avoid each other, the false smiles, the forced camaraderie, even the act on stage, the pretend enthu-siasm for one another's moves and mime-like mugging and grimacing.

That first night in Austin, I rushed from the stage after the last tune, drenched from the oven-like heat and drained from the huge, pumped, frat-boy crowd, and puked twice and then cried with my head against the cool porcelain of the toilet backstage.

Christian declared it heatstroke, made me drink half a Gatorade, and I made it back up there to fake my way through a rote encore.

Back at the hotel, Chris's big-brother mode continued, and the two of us sat up in the hotel lobby drinking vending machine sodas and talking until almost morning. The upshot of this was I felt marginally better and Christian felt I was maybe a little more cracked than he had previously given me credit for. ("But a talented motherfucker," as he put it, "and that gets you a lot of slack in my book.")

The next afternoon I learned something that surprised me, which was that Kevin was a kickass harmonica player. And while I felt paranoid about going out, we sat by the pool with a guitar and harmonica and Bart on the hand drums playing the blues until we were sunburned.

San Antonio had a more civilized venue, an airconditioned music hall. I remembered to drink plenty of water and my stomach behaved. But the show was more of my imaginary marketing weenie's dream world, me playing the part and stumbling around, waiting for it to be over.

That night, while not sleeping and listening to the sound of the motel breathing and the whisk of cars on the highway, the night before we hit the road for Colorado, something began to sink in. *Waiting for it to be over.*

The tour had four more dates, but they were distant, and spread out over the course of almost ten days: Boulder, San Francisco, Eugene, and Seattle. There were 1200 miles between Boulder and San Francisco, and about a thousand between Boulder and here. Days and days of driving and being trapped with him and waiting for it to be over.

I must have made some noise of frustration or despair because Bart said from the other bed, "Are you okay?"

"I can't keep this up."

He knew what I was talking about—every one of us did. If the fakery wasn't fucking obvious to the audience that was only because they believed in the dream world illusion we took on. "So talk to him, have a fight, or something. If you do nothing, it won't change."

"It won't work though." I sat up, holding my head in the dark. "I've tried. I can't talk to him or fight with him. Because he's like not real. It's like we're not even speaking the same language. It's like we can't even keep track of what's wrong, it's so wrong."

"Well, fuck. I can't stand it anymore, either."

I heard cloth rustling and his voice moving. He clicked on the light by the window and was pulling on a pair of shorts.

"What are you doing."

He didn't answer but he put his glasses on and went out the door.

"Oh fuck." Then I was looking for my jeans and putting them on and trying to follow him.

When I got out into the hall, he was standing in front of Ziggy's door with his hands on his hips, looking at his own bare feet.

"Did you knock?"

He looked at me and I could see that he hadn't.

"What are you waiting for."

"I'm trying to think of what I'm going to say," he said, holding one arm by the elbow and frowning.

"See what I mean?" I said, my eyelids feeling heavy.

"Shit," he said, and we went back to bed.

Blister in the Sun

Here's what I remember about us leaving Texas: a brutal sun sent light and heat through us like arrows and the black top of the parking lot almost audibly sizzled while we loaded up. My sneakers felt tacky on the bottom and made me do this little marching band step from one foot to the other. Everyone wore sunglasses. My sunburn itched; the top of my head was hot like the dashboard. Baked.

Colin jumped out of the back of the truck and his breath went *whoooo* out of him as he landed. He brushed his hands together in a little crash-cymbal motion, like they were dusty and it was time to go. No one spoke.

Bart put the brown paper bag of bottled water and road snacks into the back seat of the van. Even a white T-shirt felt hot. We stood in the burning sun as long as possible to avoid getting in the oven of the van. No one would meet my eyes, or was that the sunglasses creating that effect? Ziggy's legs were golden brown under tight black bike shorts. I would wear nothing but jeans no matter how hot it was.

And then in the van, Christian cranked the AC, so that it blew hot soggy wind at us for several miles, until it got going. The seat was hot even through denim and Ziggy sat on his hands to keep from burning the backs of his legs. Closing my eyes behind my sunglasses, I wondered if anyone could tell they were closed.

That's what I remember.

That and Christian saying, "What's the difference between an accordion and a trampoline."

And Bart answering from shotgun, "People take their shoes off before they jump on a trampoline."

Long Distance Runaround

We had voted to drive straight through. (Nobody else had liked Texas much either, apparently.) We could always pull off at a motel in the night, we figured, if no one was up to driving. Carynne had mapped us a route that clipped through a corner of New Mexico, 969 miles to be exact from parking lot to parking lot. This was the expensive part of the trip, with lots of overhead and little income. In the planning stages of the tour we'd come close to deciding not to cross the Mississippi. But, I don't know, somehow we ended up going for it.

If the drive to Cleveland had felt long at almost six hours with two pit stops, imagine this, twenty hours. As I stood pissing in a rest area northwest of San Antonio, I calculated that would be ten pit stops at minimum. I felt like a dog, pissing every so often to mark my trail. Jeezus.

If I hadn't already been numb, the miles would have made me numb. Bart and Chris would sometimes banter with each other as if Ziggy and I weren't there. Z wasn't saying much and neither was I. I rode one stretch in the truck with Kevin and it was a minor relief. But to keep on going we had to rotate drivers and riders and eventually me and Z. would be in the van again. No one suggested we two take the truck, which was just as well. And regardless of any angst I might have been experiencing, while Ziggy drove the van, I fell asleep.

When I woke up Chris was saying, "What's the difference between a raccoon and a violist squished in the road?"

And Bart answered, "The raccoon was on his way to a gig. And don't you dare start in with bassoon player jokes, asshole."

In New Mexico we stopped at a roadside diner to piss, rotate, and eat. The placemats were paper maps of New Mexico with illustrations of various tourist attractions, none of which were particularly near to our route. It was night, and I'd slept some, and I had no idea if it was before or after midnight, nor did it occur to me to wonder. Besides the placemats, the place featured more variations of the "Western" omelet than I'd previously seen, and you could get a side dish of rice and beans as well as fries or toast. In all other respects, though, we could have been in any of a hundred diners anywhere in America and I was finding it hard sometimes, eating grilled cheese or standing at the urinal, to remember where we were or where we were going.

After a while I almost forgot that there would be an end to the trip. By the middle of the next day I was settling in to traveling as if it were itself the main activity, as if we'd be doing this forever.

I had to pee one and a half times as often as the van needed gas.

Around sunrise Bart asked, "How many drummers does it take to change a light bulb?" and was greeted by total silence. (We all knew the answer: none, they have machines that do that now.)

Go West

I was driving in the late morning the next day, my sunglasses greasy from being worn so long and the Rocky Mountains trundling along on our left like the world's longest skyline, when we pulled into Boulder, Colorado.

There were no tall buildings here, as if the mountains used up all the tallness. Office buildings were three storeys at most, and spread out long with gleaming mirror windows as they were in suburban industrial parks everywhere. Strip malls. Houses with redwood decks. Kinko's. Taco Bell. The sunlight seemed brighter, sharper, than it had in Texas, like the dry air was too thin to slow it down (which I suppose in a way it was). Otherwise, being a mile above sea level didn't seem to make much difference.

When we had settled into yet another room with two double beds, a TV, and a desk, Bart lay back on the bed and said "Are you okay?"

"Just dazed from the drive."

"You've said maybe two words the past two days. Just checking."

"Nothing to say." I lay back on my own bed and we both contemplated the coffee cake crumb-style plaster in the ceiling. "I'm sorry."

"What are you apologizing for?"

"Because this sucks, and I know it sucks for everyone, not just me."

"Nobody said this was going to be fun."

"Yes they did. *We did,* we always thought this would be fun, didn't we?"

"Is that why we're doing this? Fun?"

"Stop. Stop right there. Don't get into wondering why we do anything or you'll end up like me."

"I think you need a nap."

"You're probably right."

I woke up sometime later still on my back on top of the bedspread, stiff and weirdly cold and alone in the room.

The message light was blinking and I called the desk. A perky clerk told me to call Digger, and then gave me a phone number and a name, Dave, to call, here in Boulder. I recognized the number from the day book as the venue. I called and asked for Dave.

" 'lo."

"Yeah, this is Kevin Kilmer," I lied, "from Moondog Three. We got a message you called? What time would you like us there?"

"Uh, yeah, one sec." There was the crackle of him shifting the phone from one ear to the other. "Yeah, well."

"Is there some kind of problem?"

"I sincerely hope not. Um, look. We're having some problems here, technical problems, and I thought you should be aware of them before you got here."

"What kind of problems?"

"We blew a power transformer and it's dark."

"Dark."

"The power company said it might be a while before they can get somebody down here. We've got an emergency generator running, but it's only really got enough juice for like office lights and phones and stuff. I've got somebody trying to get another generator online, but it's looking iffy right now, getting one this late in the day."

I glanced at the clock. It was 4:30. "Should we come down there, anyway?"

"Yeah, I guess. If we do get power back, I guess you'd better be set up."

Yeah, I guess. "We'll be there in a little while."

If it was already 4:30 and this guy was this blasé about how soon we arrived he was either on 'ludes or he was naturally very laid back.

I tried to hang on to some of that laid-back-ness when I got on the phone with Digger. "Hey, kiddo!" he said, sounding just like himself. "Long time."

"We've done nothing but drive for two solid days," I replied, and sounded more defensive than I should have. Old habits.

"So hey, I've got some financial stuff I want to go over with you in San Fran. Moondog Three as a multimedia property."

" 'Scuse?"

"I got all kinda opportunities shaking up here, kid. I'd wait until you got home but there are some things I want to move on right away."

"Like what?"

"It's better if I go over everything when I get there."

Yeah, I guess. I gritted my teeth a little, after we said goodbye. So here's something that's really urgent but, oh, I won't tell you what it is right now... There was no use arguing, but I would have liked at least some hint. Well, I had more immediate things to worry about, like no electricty at the venue. I went to gather the troops.

Rocky Mountain Way

I don't know if this is going to make any sense, but Boulder, Colorado is the one place that's not California that I had ever been that was the most like California.

The people, first of all, lots of brightly colored clothing and sun-bleached hair, guys slumped in surfer attitude, girls chipper in that LA way. Then, the food, bean sprouts and avocado and tofu everywhere (even at the steak and ale type pub where Chris and I would later eat). I wondered if there were a lot of Californians living there the way there were a lot of New Yorkers in Florida. And Dave wasn't the only ultra-laid back person we met either.

We arrived at the theater with the Rockies casting sunset shadows into the valley. Boulder is also very pretty, I have to give it that. Growing up around New York, big mountains are something you see reproduced in panoramic photos, framed and hung on walls. To have that view out your window every day, would you get bored of it? I didn't think so, but what do I know.

The theater where we were playing was in the college neighborhood, instantly identifiable by the used record shops, poster stores, and cheap eateries along its main street. It's like college towns are almost as thematic and defined as Chinatowns or Little Italies or something.

The power situation had not resolved itself by the time we arrived and me and Kevin and Dave sat down in Dave's little paperwork-heaped office to discuss our options.

"The power company assures me we'll be back up tomorrow, but with a crew here now they say it's going to be several more hours before we go up tonight. The doors are set to open at 7:30 for an 8 p.m. show. We could try to push the time back, cut the opening band, say, and open the doors at 9:30 and have you play at ten. But there's no guarantee that we'll be back on the air, so to speak, by then."

"Could we play acoustic?" I asked.

"Yeah, but it's the lights that are the real problem. We don't even have enough juice in the generator to run the house lights, and it's a fire code violation if we can't light the exits and aisles. It's lights." Dave sat in a rolling office chair that looked like it was as old as he was. "If we could reschedule the show for tomorrow, would you guys be able to do that?"

"We'd rather not," Kevin said with a glance at me.

"There's nowhere else we can move to?" I leaned against Dave's desk, careful not to upset the precarious heaps of paper. "No other space?" In Boston, often clubs and theaters shared an owner and venues were often switched at the last minute to accommodate lagging or skyrocketing ticket sales.

Dave shook his head. "No place we can get a permit for anyway. Like there's campus spaces at CU, but not gettable on such short notice."

"Can I make a phone call?" I stood up straight, planning to go to the pay phone in the lobby, but he pointed at the heavy black rotary phone on his desk and then left the room to give me some privacy, I guess.

I tried to get through to Carynne to ask her how important the interviews were, or if they could be moved later, but I got her answering machine. So I tried Digger.

"Digger Marks," he said in his professional voice.

"What are you doing still in the office? Isn't it like eight there now?" I said, in that same giving-shit tone that Remo always used.

"Seven," he said. "How the hell are you?"

"We're okay, but we've got a problem."

"Yeah?"

I explained the delay and the San Francisco media situation.

"I dunno, kiddo. If it's all print media…"

"It is."

"I'm sure they can reschedule. It's up to you."

"Hm."

"So hey, I have some news for you."

"Yeah?"

"Galani Gilliman is signing on."

"Excuse me?"

"The supermodel? Going to be a DMA client."

Digger Marks Agency? "Oh. Great."

"I think I'm going to need an LA office though."

"Well, that's great, old man."

I found the rest of the guys on the loading dock. Colin and Ziggy were laughing and red-faced sitting on the tailgate and I could see they each had red welts on their right forearms. "Rock, paper, scissors," they said in unison and each threw out a hand.

"Damn!" Colin held out a flat hand to Ziggy's scissors. Ziggy licked his forefinger, held Colin's arm by the wrist, and slapped it hard. Then they both laughed again.

"We have a decision to make," I said. "And I'd like your input." I outlined the choices, cancel, or do it tomorrow and do a buttload of driving afterward.

"Buttload of driving," Bart said, raising his hand like a school kid.

"Driving," Chris concurred.

"Buttload," Ziggy said and he and Colin laughed again.

"Alright, driving it is. I'll tell Dave we're going to clear out and come back tomorrow."

Kevin stayed with the others and Bart followed me this time, down the darkened hallway to the lit office. Dave wasn't there, but another guy with blonde tips in his hair and a goatee was. "Have you seen Dave?" I asked.

"I was going to ask you the same," he said. "Hey, you're Daron the Moondog."

"Just Daron," I told him and we shook hands. "This is Bart."

"Cool. Jason. I play guitar for Stumblefish. We were supposed to open for you guys." He shrugged and looked down like *aw-shucks*. His T-shirt was so thin and faded I couldn't make out what it used to say. "I guess the gig's off, though."

"We were thinking we'd stick around and just do it tomorrow," I told him. "That's what we came to tell Dave."

"Alright!" It sounded like *aw-rye*. "We can do that. Oh man, that is the best news I've had all day."

Dave came in then, his eyes obviously bloodshot. "Hey," he said to us.

"We can do it tomorrow," I said.

Dave sat back into his ancient chair. "Cool. Cool. Coolness. Coolness." He pumped a fist in the air and Jason met it with his, gently. "You guys are the greatest." He smiled. "Jas', were you guys still going to do that frat party tonight, too?"

"Yeah, man. They've got electricity, after all." He looked up, the soft fingers of his hair shifting away from his eyes as he did. "Hey, you guys interested in a good party?"

Bart and I looked at each other. "Yeah, sure."

"Aw-rye. We're playing for this party at CU. At like ten o'clock. Oh, it'd blow those guys' minds if you showed up."

Bart mimed some air guitar and then his head exploding. "You think we should play?"

Jason put a hand to his cheek. "It ain't formal, not really. It's more like a house party, just jamming and stuff. But yeah, we'd love to jam with you guys. Oh man."

"Sure, I'm up for it." Bart cracked his knuckles.

"It couldn't hurt to bring guitars," I said. Oh, why the fuck not.

"Just stick with me," Jason said. "This is cool. They'll have food and everything. And beer, of course. Hey, come back to my place and meet the other guys."

Break On Through

So me and Bart and Kevin and Chris ended up walking to Jason's house not far from the theater, while Ziggy and Colin went down the main street to the used record shops we'd seen on the way in.

Down in one half of a two-family house with low hanging tress in the yard, Jason's girlfriend had cooked up a humongous load of rice and beans. We shared dinner with a couple of other members of Stumble-fish, and then we got stoned and Kevin scored some of the fine weed for later, too.

Marijuana kind of messes with my sense of time, but after night fell and we weren't really stoned anymore, we took our van and theirs somewhere, and parked on the street a few houses down from what was once a very big house. Not a mansion, just a big old house, three stories high and surrounded all the way around by an open porch.

Jason had not called ahead to warn the hosts that he was bringing special guests and we were treated to a spontaneous display of four frat brothers dropping to their knees and bowing up and down in front of him. "Hey, I just brung 'em," Jason said. Whereupon they shifted the direction of their bowing to me and Bart and I waved. There were maybe twenty guys standing around, a clump of four girls in a doorway, chatting. A stereo played the J. Geils Band.

In the kitchen were two garbage cans filled with ice and bottled beer, and a third, smaller, with the expected keg. Bart fished us out two Sam Adams and we made our way to the obvious musician's corner at one end of the spacious common room. Chairs surrounded by bongos, tambourines, guitars in stands, stood against the wall. The J. Geils ended and no one started something else. Jason sat down in one of the chairs and picked a guitar out of a stand like it was his, which maybe it was. I got the Ovation out of its case and sat next to him. He oohed and aahed at it a bit and his fingers did a little hula dance as if they were drawn magnetically toward the fret board.

"Here," I said, holding it by the neck. "You try it."

"Let's tune first." He plucked a low E. "Cuz you know what that one is like and I know what this one is like. We can trade later."

The Ovation was good about holding its pitch if I didn't loosen the strings for transport, which I hadn't for the drive from Texas. We didn't bother with a tuner or pitch pipe and he adjusted his strings to mine. Chris was still in the kitchen, a beer in his hand, talking with someone. Stumblefish's drummer, another lanky surfer-ish guy named Doug, picked up a dumbek and settled it between his knees. "What are we playing?" he asked.

I looked at Jason and shrugged. He grimaced. "Oh man, I don't know."

People were angling themselves toward us in the room, though still talking and laughing. I cleared my throat. "I dunno. Why don't you just give me a chord progression and we'll get warmed up."

"Uh, sure."

He still looked tentative so I started a regular twelve bar blues. He fell into sync easily with the open chords and I switched to barring them up the neck. Doug patted out a beat and we began to chug along. Jason raised an eyebrow at me after we'd gone around several times and I went ahead and plucked out a solo. He played with a pick while I played with my fingers, but the Ovation was superb at ringing out over other instruments and we could hear me just fine. I played with a little melody for a while, coming back several times to this one E high up on the G string, the mellowest string on the guitar. And at some point that had used itself up and I told him to take it.

The twelve bar blues is a good one to start any jam with because it's damn near hardwired into anyone who grew up in the United States and wasn't locked in a closet until age ten or something. The one-four-five chord thing is like second nature—it's every Elvis song, every early Beatles song, every Bach chorale, too.

Yes, J.S. Bach.

You can get into mystical numerology or the science of acoustics or whatever you want but there's no denying the pull and the satisfying oomph of coming down off the five, onto the four, and then hitting the one again. The Batman theme. You're A Grand Old Flag.

So I felt pretty safe starting with this, on the off chance that Jason, nice guy as he was, turned out to be a complete 100% loser of a guitar player, it would still be monumentally hard to make this suck.

It did not suck and Jason was really halfway decent. Midway through Jason's solo turn, Bart came in and took the Miller out of its case, and it had held its tuning pretty well too, and he added a bass riff using the bottom strings. When the solo came back to me, I made something with a counterpoint to Bart's pattern and we played a little tug of war with that for a while. Jason rocked back and forth while he played, his head going one direction while his shoulders went the opposite. I was more of a front-to-back kind of man, nodding my head as I went.

The other two Stumblefishes came into the room—the other guitar player/singer and the bass player, and we wrapped up the blues thing because it would be just plain silly to try to add two more guitars to the three already playing.

"Cool," Jason said when we finished.

"Why don't you guys play some," I said, putting the Ovation into the vacant stand where Jason's guitar had been. "I want to drink my beer."

"Okay, man, okay." His band assembled around him. A standup bass was brought from some closet or other room. They tuned briefly. More people had come in while we were playing, and people were looking in the porch windows, too.

Stumblefish's regular sound was a kind of rootsy rock-reggae cross, and people started to dance and sing along to some of the tunes. They played maybe half an hour, forty five minutes, and I sat on a windowsill drinking my beer and thinking, *hey, good party*. Much better than the last party I was at, at Christmastime. Kevin and Chris sort of half-danced with beers in their hands.

When they were done, the singer/guitarist whose name I'd already forgotten announced that we were here and wondered aloud if we'd come up and play a couple of songs.

Me and Bart and Chris went up there and took their places, Bart at the standup bass, Chris with a set of bongos, and me with the Ovation.

"Our singer's out tasting the Boulder nightlife," I said. "So we're improvising this."

First we ripped out an instrumental version of Welcome, which drew cheers from some guys in the crowd. Oh yeah, we could kind of funk it up, the bombast of the power chord replaced by a little pseudo-flamenco scratch I used to draw the sound out longer. Bart wasn't even looking at me, he just followed me down the notes like a ladder. It did sound sort of forlorn without any lyrics though. "What do you guys want to do next?" I asked when it ended.

"We can do 'Here Comes the Sun,'" Bart suggested.

"Do you remember all the words?"

"Do you?"

"I bet between the two of us we remember them all."

I started it. It took him one time through the progression to find something he was happy with on the bass and then we were singing. Some people sang along, too, "It's alright..." and it was. I felt hopelessly folky and buzzed and happy about it. Someone brought us a new round of Sam Adamses at the end of the song and I took a drink while thinking about what to do next. "Hey," I said to Bart. "You can sing that Love & Rockets song. Mirror People."

"I can?"

"I've heard you sing it four times on this trip already in the van."

"Oh yeah. But do you know it?"

"It's Love and fucking Rockets, Bart." I mean, not to cut Daniel Ash short or anything, but the chord progressions are not hard to figure out. So Bart sang Mirror People and, I think, improvised some of his own words, but it wasn't as if anyone here didn't enjoy it.

I did a rendition then of "Me & Julio Down By The Schoolyard" and Doug played the dumbek with Chris on bongos and people danced.

"Yeah, okay, enough with the cover tunes. Let's do something of our own," I said then. "Let's try Walking. Like we did it in New Orleans."

"Yah!" Christian banged out a count and whooped.

Now I was singing something I could say I knew, where I knew how the guitar part and the lyrics fit together, where the five-four-one hit everyone in the gut the same, like I'd intended it to when I wrote it, and

I could actually sing and project this one a little.

Jason sat down with a tambourine, and with the three of them down there now swaying and chugging like the Plastic Ono band, the song was propelled along, and the words came out of my stomach as if of their own accord. Like I said, I was a rock forward and back kind of guy, and every time I rocked forward I spat out words, screamed them, my own version of Carynne's Janis Joplin voice tightening my throat.

We were, as they say, cooking.

Kevin waved his harmonica at me from where he stood in the thickening crowd. I twitched my face at him—yes! yes!—and kept going. He laid the wickedest blues riff on top of it, and I let him take the solo for a good while, and we passed it around, Chris pushing the tempo a little.

I brought the whole shebang to an end with a repeat of the first chorus, dragging everyone down a notch in tempo again and then grinding us to a halt. Before they could do anything else, though, I hit an eight-bar blues. The eight has a much more urgent feel to it than the twelve, and is more rock than blues. Kevin picked it up and ran with it. Which was good because I found I was completely out of breath from singing so hard.

Not until some time midway through that jam did it occur to me to think, hey, I'm happy. I'm having a good time, and I'm noticing I'm having a good time. And I'm playing, and I'm feeling like, well, like myself. People use that expression, oh, I haven't been myself lately. It's kind of nonsense, because when I'm not myself I don't really have the ability to tell. But when I come back to myself again? It seems obvious, like how you can't tell if you're asleep until you wake up.

I was waking up to the fact that I was awake now and it felt good.

I stayed up there when Stumblefish came back and picked my way through their tunes, my fingers on autopilot, my ears in control, fully in the moment and discovering each note as it came along. And when their second set was over, Jason and I traded guitars and just jammed, him falling in love with the Ovation before my very eyes and me getting to know the feel and sound of his Takamine (not a bad guitar either). We were sitting back for a while, quiet, pulling on fresh beers and talking shop when some campus rent-a-cops came and officially closed the party.

If there was one thing that would have made my night better, it might have been to get laid, too. But I settled for a grilled cheese sandwich at Denny's (one of the few places open late at night in Boulder, according to Jason) with Bart and Chris and Kevin. And a bowl of vegetable beef soup.

Get Off of My Cloud

So we got to see more of Boulder than we otherwise would have. That afternoon Bart and Chris and I had lunch and wandered around the pedestrian mall in the center of town, poking around stores selling nifty Western minerals and kites and mountaineering gear. In a bookstore our publicity photo was on the cover of *Rocker*, what do you know. I didn't buy it. We hung out for a little while in the mainstream record shop where Jason worked, shooting the shit. He was looking forward to tonight, and I guess I was, too. The mountains stood like a curtain on one side of us and I found myself kind of orienting to them as we walked around, like knowing where downtown was in New York by the World Trade Center.

We went back to the hotel to change clothes and pick up the guitars before heading over to the hall. I was sorting through T-shirts when Ziggy came to the door. "Hey," he said, and sat on the bed where I was laying shirts out.

"Hey," I said, not looking up from my sorting.

He sat quietly for a moment, but only a moment. "I want to apologize for the other night."

"For what?" Black shirts in one pile, white shirts in the other.

"For picking a fight with you. For getting all bent out of shape about Jonathan. I know it was stupid. I don't know what I was thinking." He leaned on one arm, making a dip in the bed as he bent toward me. "So, I'm sorry."

"Apology accepted," I said, pulling an oversize white shirt with black letters on it from the pile. I folded it apart from the others and started putting the others back into my duffel bag. I should have discovered this I'm-busy trick with the laundry before.

Out of the corner of my eye, I could see him suck his lower lip into his mouth. "You're still mad at me, aren't you."

"Mad at you for what? I said apology accepted." I shrugged and looked into his face so he'd believe me. He didn't move for a few more moments.

"I feel like you're slipping away from me," he said.

No shit, Sherlock, I thought, but didn't say it. You're only figuring that out now?

I looked back at the shirts in my hands. We were supposed to have a laundry day in San Francisco that we were going to miss from staying the extra day in Colorado. Hopefully the hotel there could do what we needed. Big city hotels did have their advantages.

He still hadn't moved. I didn't want to fight. I wanted to tell him to stop driving me away, but I knew that would turn into a fight. Is this what people mean when they say things in movies like Just give me some space? I need some space?

"Don't worry about it," I said, after a while.

It was the advice I was giving myself.

Over the Hills & Far Away

As promised, power had been restored at the theater and we did our soundcheck and hung around with Stumblefish, eating catered cold cuts and drinking a kind of canned soda called Blue Sky. Carynne called around six frantic and trying to figure out what we were doing in Boulder still. I told her, and she told me she had decided to fly out to San Francisco to meet back up with us after all. She had a friend at the University of Washington she wanted to visit in Seattle, too.

There's not much more to tell about waiting around. Ziggy was keeping his distance again after I'd brushed him off. Me and Bart watched the first half of Stumblefish's set from back of the second floor balcony, while college kids and sunny Boulderites danced in their seats and occasionally recognized us. They were some groovy dudes, Stumblefish, and I found myself thinking it was too bad they lived two thousand miles away from us, because it would have been fun to jam with them again.

We heard the rest from the backstage wings. And then roadies and band members were clearing their gear. And then the inevitable moment arrived when it was our turn.

Maybe it was a good thing that at that point I was more worried about our undone laundry than I was about how the show itself was going to go. We started right in, and I went to autopilot, one part of me watching the crowd sing along to Welcome, one part of me thinking about the laundry, one part of me using minimum effort to keep me in sync with Bart and Chris. Ziggy was opening conservative tonight, warming up slowly, standing dead center at a mic stand, his arms in, building up his volume and inflection bit by bit.

By the third song he had the mic out of the stand and was about to lose the loose over-shirt he wore. We followed him up the ramp of energy, until we hit Intensive Care and began to break loose. Now I found myself feeling the altitude, the air too thin in my lungs as I danced and moved and played. Compared to the chest-crushing heat of Texas, though, it was almost pleasant to hyperventilate. Ziggy was feeling the thin air, too. I could hear the way he cut off the ends of his words, to hide the panting. Pace yourself, I kept thinking, save some energy for the drive. I tried to tell him that but I couldn't bring myself to step into his spotlight to say it out loud.

The crowd went wild with Candlelight, but I wanted the show to be over by then. Chris thumped and boomed out the beat and would not be rushed. And then, we took our bows, and I saw Jason in the wings and got him on stage to bow, too, and an actual real red curtain drew down, and then there was a frenzy of packing and handshakes and last gulps of Blue Sky cola and then we were in the damn van heading out of town and over the plains.

Won't Get Fooled Again

The route Carynne had mapped took us east to the Interstate, then north into Wyoming to hook up with I-80. Colin drove the truck first and Kevin had been planning to drive the van, but I wanted to drive while I was up and awake. I put in a tape of a Yes live concert which was too full of tempo changes and dynamic shifts to lull anyone into sleep. Just before midnight we passed through Cheyenne, and about a half hour later came to a truck stop on the outskirts of Laramie where we switched drivers and did the usual pit stop type things. Kevin took over from me and Chris drove the truck. Ziggy went to sleep in the very back of the van, and I kind of spaced out looking into the dark of the side of the road.

If there was something bothering me, it wasn't specific enough to give me a lump in my stomach or a flutter in my chest. Wyoming went by in a dark blur and I wondered if there was something more constructive I could be doing with myself than sitting there and staring. Go on, Daron, solve the problems of the world in your spare time.

Some hours later, as we neared the Utah border, we pulled off for gas in a place called Evanston, which struck me as funny because for all I knew we could be in Evanston, Illinois. I was finally beginning to feel sleepy, and although there was no glow in the sky yet, I think we could all feel morning coming on. "What do you think, boss," Chris said, yawning. "I see motels down the road."

A Best Western was next to the filling station, and something called a Whirl Inn National Nine was a bit further down the road. I tried to figure out loud how much sleep we could get. "If we crash for about six hours, we can be on the road by say eleven, we should be able to make it to San Fran by... ugh. I can't do math when I'm tired."

Everyone clustered around as I opened the day book. "Bizzy shuffled the media around a bit but we've got a dinner meeting with an interviewer from *SF Weekly*. If we hit the road by eleven, we can probably still make it." That gave us only five or six hours of sleep, but we could sleep in the van. "Yeah. We can crash out if you want."

Nods all around. We pulled the vehicles into the Best Western's lot and Kevin went in to see about rooms. he came out shaking his head.

"Full up," he said at the passenger side window. "Let's try the place down the road."

We pulled up at the Whirl Inn National Nine and I held my breath, hoping. I had gotten my hopes up for a few hours in a real bed, and I was starting to worry if we kept driving we'd end up headlines somewhere about having died in a ravine or something.

But Kevin came out with three actual metal keys in his hand and we pulled ourselves and our guitars up to rooms pretty much identical to ones we'd stayed in earlier in the trip, though I couldn't remember which city that had been.

Bart was showering when the knock came at the door. I was in a clean T-shirt and not much else. It was Ziggy, of course. "Can I come in?"

I walked back to sit on the bed and he walked and sat with me. "Yeah?"

"I was hoping maybe we could go back to rooming together."

"Rooming," I repeated, giving it an obscene sound. "Do you miss it that much?"

"It's not the sex," he said, petulant and wounded. "I just want a chance to fix things up. It makes me sick the way we've been."

"Yeah, I don't like it either. But, dammit, if we'd never—" I found energy rising up my spine and had to stand up. I had no pockets to put my hands into this time and I pawed at the air like I was playing a high piano. "I think we should just leave it alone."

"I miss you," he said. "It hurts that you've become so cold." His eyes were still dark with smudged eyeliner, his hair show- and sleep-tousled, and despite his hunched, contrite posture, he still looked like danger and poison to me.

"Ziggy, please." I turned to face him. "Listen to me. I'm not saying this because I'm trying to hurt you or play some game, okay? I really think it's better if we let it go." This was one thing I could say, and say sincerely, whether he was lying to me or not.

He stared at me, his mouth slightly open and his eyes frozen. He sounded like he could barely breathe when he said, "Let what go."

That was the perennial question, wasn't it? "Whatever it was we had. Blame it on me, if you want," I said. There were so many things I could call him on, lies, tricks, games he'd played. But throw that all out the window, and what leg did he have left to stand on? What protest could he make? "I don't want help. I don't want to figure it out. I don't want anything." I wanted his hold on me ended.

His shoulders started to shake as he sucked in a rough breath. But no tears came out of his eyes. He looked like maybe he was holding them back, but I couldn't judge what was real and what was an act. "Does what I want count?"

"If what you want is something other than jerking me around by the short hairs, then maybe."

He exhaled hard and stood up. I heard the shower squeak shut and Bart's towel flapping. "Then I want another chance," he said quickly.

"Another chance."

"I don't mean now. Later. I know we have to get through this first. I mean…" He broke eye contact and shook his head then. "Never mind."

He walked out of the room then, not stomping, not hurrying or dragging, just walking like he'd come over to borrow a cassette tape or a pair of clean socks.

I got in bed. Bart came out a few seconds later and threw himself down on the bed. We were both asleep before we could say anything more.

Going to California

When the wakeup call came I was lying face down on top of my left hand and my thumb was numb. Bart picked the receiver up and then lay back groaning. Sunlight lined the blackout curtains like white fire. I sat up and shook my hand. "Shit."

"Wha'd you do?" Bart said, standing up and yawning. He had a severe case of bed head.

"I think I slept on my hand." I could barely make a fist and pins and needles were starting to tingle over the back. "I guess I was too sleepy to notice."

"Get in the shower. Hot water will fix it up." He started making his bed, then smacked his forehead and left it. "I'll meet you in the restaurant for breakfast?"

"It'll have to be quick," I said as I went into the bathroom. The little room was still humid from Bart's shower a few hours before, the exhaust fan rattling weakly as I flipped on the light.

My right hand felt weak, too, and the tap was difficult to turn. I pissed while the water heated up and then got in.

I didn't remember any dreams from the night before. The drive seemed like it had been a dream, maybe, one long series of barely changing images. And Ziggy, that had been sort of unreal. As real as I had tried to be, as honest and truthful and open as I could be, I had no bearing on whether his reaction was calculated or genuine.

Maybe there was no difference. He wanted another chance, he said. Well, that was probably true, no matter how I interpreted it. Maybe for him there was no real answer to anything, as if giving an honest reaction would somehow betray his actual nature and therefore be dishonest somehow…? Man, I was out of it. I decided to put off shaving until later.

We had our first pit stop in the mountains west of Salt Lake City and had lunch on the border of Nevada. I drove after lunch. Nevada is a lot more nothing and I was once again struck by how huge the states are out West. All of New England and part of Canada and New York would fit inside Nevada.

We had dinner at a Denny's in Sacramento and I remembered that we gained an hour from the time change, which meant we'd probably even be on time for the newspaper interview we were supposed to do. We got slightly mixed up getting off the San Francisco/Oakland bridge, where I-280 and 101 and a bunch of other stuff does the mangled highway thing. But at not quite nine p.m. Pacific time we arrived in the lobby of the hotel.

I decided I liked urban high rise hotels with their valet parking and multiple restaurants, as we left the van and truck idling in the loading circle. The place lacked the easy bustle of the New Orleans hotel, but people were at least awake and moving about, bell staff and guests in business suits and evening wear traipsing around.

The hotel wasn't perfect—they'd mixed up our reservation somehow, as Carynne told me when she came half-running half-shuffling up
to me with a horse-hoof clop from the clogs on her feet. I was trying to
convince a bellman to let me carry the guitars myself. She had already
checked us all in hours ago. Because of the mixup we ended up with our
rooms scattered over two different floors.

"Hey, whatever," was my reaction to that news.

She handed me a card key and then flitted to the others, exchanging
greetings and pecks on cheeks. I walked into a lobby lit by giant golden
globe-shaped lamps that were somewhere on the tacky side of expensive. The others trailed in after me and I waited for them to catch up.
Carynne had not told me the room number(s).

When we got up to the suite, I found Digger was not there yet, but
a message from him was. He'd called from the airport to say he had
some other business to take care of and would catch up to us later.
Carynne sat on the couch in the larger room of the suite while I un-
packed a few things.

"Did you hear from that reporter?" I asked, all nonchalant, like I
hadn't really thought about it for the past thousand miles. Actually, I
hadn't really thought about it, but it had been in the back of my mind, as
were the interviews we'd had to blow off from this afternoon.

"Which reporter?" she said. Then, "Oh, the newspaper woman. Let
me check the messages in the other room. I've been sitting in the lobby
for the past hour." She picked up the phone. Then, she put her hand over
the receiver and said to me, eyebrows drawn together seriously, "This
one's the major newspaper, you know."

I knew. Bart emerged from the bathroom with his hair wet-looking
and somewhat tamed. "Do I look presentable enough to talk to a
reporter?"

"You look fine." My left hand felt a little weak, as if carrying a case
had tired the fingers out. I touched each finger to my thumb, pinky, ring,
middle, fore, then fore, middle, ring, pinky, back and forth. The rhythm
was steady enough but the fatigue persisted.

Carynne hung up. "This is pretty cool. People can leave voice messages for you and you can retrieve them without having to talk to an

operator." She looked at me twiddling my fingers and frowned, her red-brown eyebrows crinkling. "The reporter's name is Susan Walsh. She just left a message fifteen minutes ago saying she's on her way here. I guess the desk told her you were here since I'd checked us in."

Susan Walsh was in fact sitting down in the hotel restaurant having a quick gourmet overpriced hamburger and fries because she hadn't had time to eat yet that day, as she explained one she got settled in our suite with me, Bart and Ziggy. She noticed she'd gotten ketchup on her own sleeve and felt the need to apologize. She was wearing what in the seventies would have been called a pantsuit and now I wasn't sure what to call it. Just a suit, I guess, but a woman's suit, kind of casual and yet she looked uncomfortable in it. The suit was white and her shoes were black and looked like they'd been through a lot. Carynne, back in manager mode, retrieved glasses of water for everyone and then disappeared.

Centerfold

Susan Walsh set a tape recorder on the coffee table and cleared her throat. "Oh, yeah, " she said brightly, as if she was picking up a piece of earlier conversation, even though we hadn't had any conversation yet, "Michael said to apologize for him."

Blank stares from our side. "Who?" I said.

"The guy who was supposed to be here instead of me. He normally covers the whole entertainment beat." Her lips pursed. "He said you knew him."

We looked at each other. Ziggy leaned forward, from where he sat between me and Bart. "I think someone's having delusions of grandeur."

"You're probably right," she said, blowing a stray piece of brown hair from her face. "He's a jerk anyway." She sat quiet for a moment while the rest of us waited for the interview to begin.

"Yeah, so..." Bart said, after a moment. "What did you want to know about us?"

"I brought some questions," she said, opening her soft-sided briefcase. I was starting to think she was younger than we were, a college freshman or something. She pulled out a spiral bound notebook, the "college-ruled" kind, which reinforced my impression. "I guess I'll just ask them and you guys answer whatever you want, okay?"

Bart smiled, stifling a giggle and shot me a glance. Ziggy, still leaned forward, clasped his hands between his legs. "That sounds like a terrific idea," he drawled.

She smiled and exhaled a short huff. "Okay. So how did you guys get started as a band?"

Bart: "We met in jail."

Ziggy: "Be nice, now. Actually, I met the two of them cruising in the park."

I didn't know if she hadn't read the press kit, or if she just wanted it in our own words. "Bart and I were in a band together when we were at school. When we moved to Boston we met Ziggy and started playing clubs there." I paused for a moment and she tossed out the next question before I could say more.

"How would you describe yourselves? I mean, as a band."

Again Bart was the first one out of the gate. "Well, you remember the New Wave. We're the New New Wave. We're everything that was good about the New Wave, but also everything that was good about the Old Wave."

"The Old Wave?" I said.

"We're the perfect intermingling of dark and light, musical color and form, rhythm and spice, musicianship and showmanship, love songs and social commentary, fun and tears." Bart's tongue was so firmly implanted in his cheek it was a wonder we could understand him at all.

She actually said "Ooo."

I was already deciding this was one clipping I would not read.

Loves Me Like a Rock

We were still sitting there on the couch some half hour later, Ziggy telling a long involved story about where he got the idea for Cross to Bear, most of which I was pretty sure was fiction, when there was a thumping knock on the door. Carynne must have left the room entirely since she didn't answer it. I got up and opened it.

"Hey, kiddo!" Digger stood there with the strap to a rolling Samsonite suitcase in one hand and a briefcase in the other. I pulled the door wide and he rolled in. He was overdressed in a three piece suit, dangerously shined shoes and an overcoat. His tie was askew. "How's it hangin'?"

"A little to the left," I said, which had been Remo's customary answer to that question, once upon a time in my childhood. (An answer which I hadn't really understood until I was a bit older.) "Uh, we're..." I jerked my head toward the journalistic assemblage.

He dropped the briefcase on the king-sized bed and held up both hands. "Don't let me interrupt."

Susan Walsh stood up then and looked at her wristwatch, an incongruously large and bulky-seeming thing on her thin wrist. "Oh, god. I've got to be somewhere else in fifteen minutes."

Ziggy turned off the tape recorder and handed it to her. "Then let's go down and get you a cab."

It was only after they were gone that it sank in — smooth move. Outside the windows, the sky was the nighttime glow of city-reflected light in low clouds. The long drive and anxiety about arriving were still circulating in my system as if I had trouble realizing that we were really here and that, hey, I didn't have to be anywhere or do anything for twelve or more hours. I sat down in the stuffed armchair by the window and stared.

Digger came up and sat on the arm. "So, how was the trip."

"I was going to ask you the same thing."

"Anything other than what I'd guess?"

"Nope. The usual. You?"

"Here neither."

He was chewing gum and the sound of it squishing around in his partly open mouth was languidly rhythmic. "You been in touch with Mills?"

"A little."

"We've got you added to a few early Fall festivals, and dates are lining up in bigger venues, pending partly on a big single hitting this summer."

"Windfall?"

He shrugged, and I couldn't tell if it was because he didn't know what song BNC would pick or because he didn't know which one I meant. "You eat?"

"Couple of hours ago," I said.

"Hungry?"

"Not really." At that moment all I really wanted was to be alone, to have some quiet. Even so, I was being more curt than usual. But so was he.

"Remo's coming in tomorrow at noon," he said.

"You talked to him?"

"What are you, surprised?"

I knew if I answered that things would escalate. "Who's picking him up?"

"He can take a cab. He ain't poor."

"Why don't you get yourself something to eat, get settled in." I looked out the window hoping my expression was sleepy and not sullen. I went to the bed and lay down on top of the bedspread, my shoes on, and rubbed my eyes with both hands. "I'm bushed."

"Sure thing. See you in the morning." He picked up his bags and left, the door shutting with a heavy, hotel-grade click.

I lay there a few moments, wondering why I felt so downright cross. Just a bundle of contradictions, that's me. I resented him for not being closer to me, but when he got buddy-buddy I couldn't stand it.

To get my mind off Digger I wondered where Bart had gone off to, and that led me into worrying about Carynne and Ziggy and whether she was doing alright. Anxiety crept up my throat and I sat up suddenly to dispel it.

Hey, this was San Francisco.

Hey.

I swapped my sneakers for boots, put on a plain black T-shirt and my leather jacket. Then I took the jacket off to shave in the sink, running hot water and steaming the mirror. I brushed my hair and teeth. I brushed my hair again and put it into a ponytail, then took the ponytail out and left it down. I put the jacket back on, then decided to rinse my face one more time and got the cuffs of my sleeves damp.

I didn't see anyone in the elevator on my way out.

The Wild Night Is Calling

If in other towns I'd had trouble because there was nowhere to go, in San Francisco I almost had the opposite problem. It was hard to decide where to go for all the choices. In the end I took a cab to Castro Street where, even with the night bay chill in the air, there were people on the street, spilling out of late night bookstores and cafes, and sauntering to the disco-techno beat leaking out of bars.

In another city or in another neighborhood the same break beats and remixes might have poured forth from a venue with limousined and fur-coated women waiting at the door, or club kids with torn jeans and Crayon-hair. But with evidence of neither in sight, and men in T-shirts one size too small all around, the incessant beat was a siren song for me.

I had no doubt in my mind what I would find through those doors.

I picked a smallish place, pool tables, a long bar, glass cases with some kind of local baseball trophies (jeezus, a gay baseball league!) in it, two pinball machines, no dance floor. A long narrow place, sandwiched between a restaurant on one side and a hardware store on the other. I somehow expected the floor inside to slope like the street outside. Various pairs of eyes watched me as I made my way from the door toward the back and to an open spot at the bar.

I do not have a "type." I had so rarely had a choice of options, that I had never thought much about what I liked. I got a Rolling Rock and slipped up onto a stool still warm from the man who had sat there before me. With both elbows behind me I scanned the crowd. I rotated the Rock slowly in my right hand, the texture of the raised painted lettering under my fingers like Braille as I divined my future. The complicated codes of eye contact seemed the same here as elsewhere.

A man with hair that was either black or well-gelled brown, in a white tank top, jeans, and combat boots came over and bought himself a drink and talked to me while waiting for it.

"Hey, I haven't seen you here before." His mustache reminded me of Matthew's.

"First time, here," I replied, supposing that was a variation of *do you come here often*. "I'm from Boston."

"Boston, great town. I have a lot of friends who moved here from there. You like it there?"

"Yeah, it's okay. I used to be kind of weirded out by it, but I'm used to it now. I'm originally from New York." I pulled on my beer and glanced at the crowd occasionally. "Where are you from?"

"Nowhere," he said, taking the drink from the bartender and leaving bills on the damp wood. He turned around so we both faced outward. "I'm from here, now. I live right around the corner."

So. The rest of the conversation was about as clichéd as the first part and the only part where I got a little balked was when he asked me my name, and I told him. His was Paul.

Things got a little funny when we reached his place and his room-mate, who was watching TV in their shared living room when we came in, did a double take at me like he thought maybe he recognized me... I just kind of waved as Paul hurried me through to his bedroom without introducing me. Which was probably a blessing because by then I was anxious to get on with it, and didn't want to deal with either stopping for a conversation with a third person nor getting into the kind of psycho stuff that I imagined could ensue if Paul got hung up on me being "somebody."

I filed that eventuality away for future pondering and insomnia and let him undress me instead.

I learned that I was Paul's type. He liked short, boyish men who—with his broad chest and longer arms and legs—he could kind of envelop from behind. He told me this in short, choppy sentences in between thrusts and *oh yeah*s and grunts. His bed shuddered and squeaked and the motion made me feel weightless, like I was sinking and floating at the same time.

And yeah, I forgot all about my previous anxieties for a while, which was, maybe what I had really been looking for.

After we were finished we lay in bed and he smoked a cigarette and I wished I had a little of that fine Colorado weed. The contact high and nicotine buzz of lying close with him felt good. He smoked some kind of all-natural cigarettes, in a green package with white letters on the side that read "The next best thing to rolling your own." The smell was rich and almost a little sweet, much better than the usual.

And then I disengaged myself from the sheets and started getting dressed.

"You got somewhere to be?" he said sleepily.

"Not exactly," I said, my jeans on and me fiddling with the pockets to get them straight on the inside.

"I don't want you to think I'm kicking you out now. There's plenty of room if you want to crash here." His arm stretched across the space I'd just left. A mustached Adam reaching across the ceiling of the Sistine.

"Nah, I should get back," I answered, sounding, I thought, convincingly casual and non-anxious about it. I tried to come up with something to add, like: *I've got some business to take care of tomorrow*, but something that vague bordered on a lie. I put on my shirt and picked up my jacket.

"Suit yourself, sweetcheeks. Thanks for a lovely evening."

"You, too." I leaned over him on the bed and kissed him on the lips, and he tasted salty and smoky and good.

The TV was dark in the living room, the roommate nowhere in sight. I got myself a glass of water from the tap in their kitchen and guzzled it down, then left the empty glass upside down at the edge of their already very-full dish drainer. Out on the street things had gotten quieter, a few couples walking up or down, the restaurants and bookstores dark, the all-night diner on the corner spilling yellow light onto the sidewalk.

I stood in front of it, waiting for an empty cab to troll by, writing a song in my mind about the fog glowing under a hidden moon, cracked with black fissures of sky.

Legend of A Mind

The lobby clock showed two a.m. when I walked to the elevators, now feeling a little itchy for a shower. When I got up to the suite I heard people laughing inside and I knocked instead of opening the door with the key.

Bart opened it. "Here you are!"

I stepped past him and saw sitting on the couch Carynne, Chris, and Remo. Remo stood up and came toward me. "Jeezus, where you been?"

We shook hands first and then kind of hugged with one arm each. He was wearing his old dun-colored denim jacket, so soft it felt like flannel. I felt grungy and wondered what I smelled like. "I went out to see the town a little."

Bart nodded. "Probably snuck off to see an ABBA cover band or something and didn't want us to know."

I figured the less I said about it the better. Three out of the four people in the room knew about me, but that didn't mean that I was ready to tell the fourth or that I wanted them to discuss my sex life regardless of what they knew. Besides I had more pressing things to talk about. "So, what the hell you doing here? Digger said you weren't getting in until tomorrow."

Remo sat back down in the arm chair where Susan Walsh had sat earlier. "That birdbrain. I told him twelve thirty my plane gets in and somehow he decided that was in the afternoon. We thought maybe the two of you had gone out for a drink together."

"Did you check the hotel bar?"

Carynne nodded, her eyes said we-thought-of-that-already.

Remo rubbed his hands together. "Well, we'll see him soon enough. So tell me how you been. These guys have been filling me in on the tour adventures."

"What's to tell?" I didn't want to go into the angst of the shows and ruin everyone's jocular mood. "You knew about the Boulder delay."

"Yup." Chris stood up. "We were just getting on to what fun we had in New Orleans."

"I'm gaining weight just thinking about the meals we had last time there," Remo said, patting his stomach.

Chris waved to everyone. "I'm too fried to stay up. Need my beauty sleep," he said. As he made his way to the door we exchanged shoulder slaps and then I went and sat in his spot on the couch. Now I was aware that the three people I had explicitly told were all around me and I was trying to remember if any of them knew that the others knew. Ah, fuck it.

"So did I tell you I'm going to have my own signature series guitar?" Remo patted his knees like bongos, t-tap-tap-tap.

"From Ovation?" I said, my mind snapping back to the conversation.

"No. Takamine. Remember they custom-built me that twelve-string? I ended up getting a six-string just like it. More than one, in fact, to have backup for the road. And one thing led to the other."

I had played a Takamine in Boulder, Jason's, and told him I'd liked it. "That is so cool. So where is this beast and when can I play it?"

He gave me a shame-on-you glare. "You don't think I dragged it all the way up here when I'm not even the one with a gig."

I gave him a hurt look back. "No fair."

Then he broke out grinning. "Instead I brought you one you can keep."

"No way!"

He laughed and Bart and Carynne laughed, too. "You can wait until tomorrow, can't you?"

"No, no, I'm an instant gratification kind of person." I pressed my hands together in supplication. "You can't leave me hanging like this."

"Alright, come on." He made for the door, out of his chair like a sprinter, and I chased after him. Bart's footsteps sounded behind me as we hurried out into the hall like kids on Christmas morning.

"I'll see you guys tomorrow," Carynne called after us.

Follow You, Follow Me

Remo's room was halfway down the hall and he fished a card key out of the breast pocket of his jacket. His was a standard room, two double beds and a window that had the same view as one of ours, no historic bridges in sight, just downtown buildings and other hotels. The hardshell case lay between the two beds.

Remo took his jacket off (so as not to scratch the guitar with the brass buttons while he played) and then popped open the case and propped the guitar in his lap. He dug a pick out of the jacket and rang the strings. Steel, they had a brash sound unlike the Miller's mellow nylon. He plucked out a riff and then spun through a few familiar chord progressions.

"Ah, jeez, I can see your hands itching," he said as he swung the guitar by the neck to me on the other bed. I took the pick, too.

I let the pick slide down the strings—*p-p-p-ling!*—and then damped the sound with my fingers, running the calloused tips of my left hand up and down the neck. Then I bore down, E major, A major, D major, G major, climbing the circle of fifths one stroke at a time. I watched my fingers fit to the strings as I tried the different chords on, until I had been through the whole major cycle. I lit off on a little bit of Welcome and looked up while I played. Remo was smiling.

Bart smacked himself in the head and jumped to his feet. "Be right back," he said as I twinkled the melody up high on the neck.

"What do you think?"

I held the strings quiet. "Sweet." The fret board was soft to the touch, the action so low, I was hardly aware of the string tension.

"She's for you."

The wood was beautiful, golden like lions on a sunny savannah, a rosette of tiny leaves and flowers creeping around the sound hole. "Thank you." I said, then, "that sounded weak." I tried with more enthusiasm. "Thank you! I mean, really. Jeezus."

"Hey, what are friends for," Remo said, leaning his elbows back on the bed. "Hey, sit up straight when you play that thing."

When I played sitting down I had a tendency to hunch, to curl myself around the instrument, pointing my ears down toward the sound. For a flash I thought of Paul, curled around me, and I might have blushed a little. My fingers played whatever they seemed to want, almost like the guitar was playing itself. "I bet Bart went to get another guitar."

"Smart boy." Remo stood up and fetched himself a can of soda from the sweating icebucket on the dresser. "Has Digger been talking to you much about business?"

"Yeah, I guess. He keeps me up to date on BNC, clippings, licensing. And there's some new thing he wants to talk to me about." I put the pick down and looked up at him. "Why?"

"Just seeing..." he said, looking at the can in his hand and not at me. Someone, probably Bart, knocked, and he went to open it.

Bart had both the Miller and the Ovation, one case in each hand. "Speedy delivery," he said as he laid them down on the bed. He flipped open the Miller's case and I swung the Ovation toward me. We tuned for a few moments—nothing was too far off—and Remo put down his empty can and picked up the Takamine.

"Play me something, boys," he said.

Bart raised his eyebrows at me.

And we began to play.

Your Mama Don't Dance

I think I told you about how Digger got drunk at one of my sisters' piano recitals. I haven't told you about my own, though. When I was ten years old, my youngest sister (Courtney, five years old) and I were forced into piano lessons.

I'm not sure exactly how I had escaped doing it that long since my older sisters had been taking lessons for a while already. Now, you'd think with me being interested in music I would have preferred piano lessons over falling in the mud at soccer and other un-fun after school activities I was typically forced to participate in.

You'd think. But I didn't want to do it, maybe because Claire insisted, and maybe because even my two picture-perfect older sisters—who went without complaint to ballet and gymnastics and even ballroom dancing lessons at the local Catholic school—even those goody-goodies complained about piano.

There's also the fact that on weekends Digger would often drag me off to Remo's house where they'd sit and drink beer and watch sports on television and I'd play with Remo's guitars—so I'd known how to play the guitar since I was like seven years old, and thought of it as "my" instrument. This was before we started sneaking out to see Nomad play.

Come to think of it, I already knew a fair bit of piano from Remo as well, and I was reluctant (or afraid) to show that maybe I hadn't learned to play the correct way, and that if it was wrong, that I would have to change.

Anyway, plenty of reasons to hate piano lessons.

The teacher's name was Beaumont or something, but she told us to call her Madame B. (Digger always called her Beaujolais after a kind of wine and now it's the only name I can remember.) She was not, in all likelihood, the world's greatest piano teacher. She did have the distinct plus in Claire's eyes that she lived only two blocks from our house which meant we could walk to lessons.

I don't know if I was really such a music snob at that young age or not, but I probably was. Madame B's claw-like hands shook all the time except when she played and she always smelled like the dust in her couches. Her couches had carved feet and lace doilies hanging all over them and looked like they were as old as the woman herself. We were probably more afraid of her hands than anything else—she could hook you on the shoulder with her claws if you made a mistake (or talked back).

Of course, remembering those lessons now it seems obvious to me that my mother had some kind of special rate going with Madame B, for two kids for the price of one or something, because it was just when my older sisters convinced her to let them quit (Lilibeth so she could spend more time practicing flute and Janine clarinet, which they both played in the school band) that Courtney and I were forced to go. We had our lessons together, too, side by side on Madame B's big old piano, neither of us wanting to be there, and me in particular wanting to spend as little time as possible with my little sister and her baby piano-plinking fingers.

Like I said, a snob. We went once a week to Madame B's and were forced to practice a half hour a day each at home on the badly-tuned standup piano next to the TV in the living room. That is, until our recital came up, when Madame B. had the brilliant idea to have the Marks siblings play a duet. Maybe Lilibeth and Janine had had a big hit with such a demonstration, I don't remember. Now there was suddenly a kind of open antagonism between little Courtney and me, as we each thought the other would "ruin" the performance, and we each practiced our part fervently, trying to go faster than the other to make it look like the other was falling behind, etc. And of course, the sick thing is, the piece got better and better. About two weeks before the recital we began to like playing it together, and we went from war to truce to allies faster than you can say "Fur Elise."

The day of the recital came, and Claire of course dressed us up, me in a little suit and Courtney in a dress of mostly white satin bows, and we trooped to Madame B's house, where she threw open the parlor doors and brought in chairs from the dining room and kitchen and had folding chairs, too, arranged in a long gallery in the living room. The piano stood at one end, a side board with wine and cheese at the other end. All the current season's students and their parents were there. After each student's piece or pieces, everyone would politely clap, the respective relatives a bit harder for their particular kid.

The youngest kids went first and the show progressed to the older ones, but with me ten and Courtney five, we didn't fit that plan, and Madame B. put us near the end. Now that I think about it, maybe it wasn't really youngest to oldest, but worst to best, which often came out by age. It wasn't really Madame B's way to ever tell you if you were doing well. If you obeyed her she smiled and told your parents you had talent, and if you didn't obey her she told your parents you needed to practice more.

The result of all this was we had to sit through quite a few not-so-great little girls and boys, struggling through their simplified renditions of Bach or what have you, some of the slightly older kids, my age and older, plunking on through wobbly versions of the theme to "The Entertainer" and "Jesu, Joy Of Man's Desiring." But eventually our turn came, and Courtney and I got up there, and bowed to everyone (we had even practiced that part in the living room at home, with Courtney's stuffed animals on the couch as the audience), and sat down and played. And at the end we stood up and bowed again and people clapped.

I probably would classify this as a happy memory if it weren't for my parents' reactions. Claire's two comments were one to Courtney, an obviously condescending "That was so lovely, honey," and one to me, about how much I embarrassed her by getting up there with jelly on my face. (From a jelly cookie, I assume.) I don't know if this is memory or only what I wished I had done at that point—I reached up and wiped my face with the back of my good suit's sleeve.

I then scampered away to find Digger and ask him what he thought, but the lack of enthusiasm or depth in his "Great job, kiddo" led me to believe that he'd been at the wine and cheese during our performance. Courtney shared my disappointment and we stopped being nice to each other after that. After a multi-day argument during which I went to bed without supper twice, I quit piano against Claire's wishes (what could she do, drag me there in chains?) and that was the end of it.

I don't remember what song we played.

Superstition

Three guitars going at once can be a bit much so we ended up kind of freeform rotating, first me and Bart, then me and Remo, then Remo and Bart, although most of the time I think I was playing and the two of them traded on and off, while I traded lead with whomever I played at the time, back and forth.

We played all our usuals, the stuff we knew in common, Simon & Garfunkel, Beatles, whatever, Remo sometimes taking us toward the Allman Brothers and Bob Seger. We did some of our stuff and some of Nomad's stuff that was easy to improvise on. The music was fluid, as soon as something would wind down somebody would pick up something new, and it became sort of entrancing after a while. Though I had a wide-awake moment when Remo was carrying the lead on a piece I wrote and it was almost startling how fucking good he was.

Maybe an hour later Bart shook out his hands and said good night.

I got up to leave, too, but Remo said a little awkwardly "Wait one more second," so I told Bart I'd be along. We were all three wearing jocular smiles but Remo's eyes went somewhat serious. Bart, who never missed those sorts of things, waved goodbye with a little twitch of his eyebrow in my direction.

I sat back down on the bed, the Takamine in my lap. "Something on your mind?"

Remo put ice into two glasses and poured cold water from the bucket into them. "I wanted to ask you about something before Digger came around." He put one glass down on the bedside table for me and held the other one in his hand. It gave him something to look into when he wasn't looking at me.

"I haven't told him yet, if that's what you're wondering."

He laughed. He looked into the glass of ice water and laughed. "Wow. No, that wasn't what I was going to ask. But put that thought on hold for a moment, okay?" He sat back and sipped. "No, what I was going to ask was how much you knew about Digger's business."

"Why do I smell trouble."

"Well?"

"Not all that much, I must admit. Some kind of accounting, isn't it?" I thought for a moment. "At a multimedia agency called WTA. I haven't really asked him about it. It'd just give him another shot at telling me I'm stupid."

He pointed his chin at me in that therein-lies-a-tale way. "Yeah, he's in the accounting department. You know who WTA is?"

"I don't know what it stands for. But I couldn't tell you what RCA stands for either."

"But you know the gist. They represent movie stars, supermodels, retired athletes turned TV personalities, et cetera."

"Yeah, okay. I figured it was something like that. Like William Morris, right?" I hadn't realized quite how showbiz connected it was, though I should have guessed from Mills' enthusiasm about it back when. "Is there something wrong with this Agency?"

"Not per se. The thing to remember is that Digger's not an agent there. He's an accountant. He's not like a big deal-maker or what have you. He's the guy who makes sure they get paid when they're supposed to, and then pays out to people what they owe."

"Yeah, okay, accounting."

"But think about your old man for a moment." He pointed at me with the finger of the hand holding the glass, ice cubes tinkling.

"Always looking to move up. Always wanting to be where the action is."

"You got it. But there's no way he's going to move from accountant to agent within an agency like that. So he's got to go out on his own."

"Like he did with us. Managing us on the side." I put the guitar aside and sat forward. "Where's this all going, Remo."

He waved with his free hand and drank down a goodly gulp of water. "I think its going to create a certain amount of bad blood with certain people. I think he's using you as an example of the kind of fame he can create as an agent/manager. And, I think he's using your money to finance the plan."

"He did ask me about buying in."

"And how much did you give him?"

"Nothing yet."

Remo looked worried. "I wouldn't be saying all this if I didn't think there was a reason to worry."

"And that is?"

"I don't think the gamble is going to pay off."

"How can you be sure?"

"I can't. But he's been known to mishandle money, you know. The word *gamble* is a little too apt sometimes. Digger wants to live the high life."

I decided to start sipping water myself and picked up the sweating glass. The water was cold in my throat and I coughed. Smooth. "He does seem to be doing alright by us."

"That's true. Maybe I'm short-changing him a little. But he should still have told you if he's using your money."

"Do you know that for sure?"

"Well, what's he said?"

I thought about it. "He told me today that some model, Galanga Gorman or something, is going to sign on. And he said he wanted to set up an LA office."

"He already did."

"What do you mean?" I emptied the glass and put it down.

"He rented out an office suite in the same building where Nomad's back offices are."

"No shit."

"Yeah, he called maybe a month ago to ask me if I knew any place, and as it turned out the whole fourth floor of our building was vacant, so there you go."

"A month ago?"

"He's got a secretary in there and everything."

"I don't suppose there's any way I can find out if he actually started spending the band's money without asking him directly, is there." I pushed my hair out of my eyes.

"'Fraid not."

We both sat back with an almost audible *hmm*. Remo put his glass down on the table with a clunk. His voice got even more serious. "I don't want to bring up a lot of old shit, but you know, I've still never told you the whole story of why we left Jersey."

"You said you had to move the band to LA for business."

"Call me a coward, but we moved partly to separate ourselves from your dad. You know he had been calling Artie without telling me, as if he were our manager? He got one of our advance checks cut to him."

"What!" My mouth was hanging open in shock.

"Yeah. He paid it back, but I was never sure exactly what was going on. I really don't know, to this day, how much of it was a miscommunication between me and him, like, if I'd let him think he had more to do with us than he actually did. I mean, yeah, I let him help out sometimes, but he offered, you know? I thought he was doing it as a friend, making calls, or agreeing to take calls during the day for me when I couldn't be available because I was working. Whatever. I don't know if he needed that money for something like a gambling debt and he got lucky enough to clear it and pay us back. Or if he really thought he was within his rights to start managing our money or what."

"Wow."

Remo was nodding. "I should have told you all this before, but, once you got the deal going with him, I didn't want to make waves."

I swallowed hard. "He did actually do everything we asked. Thus far. And our relationship with BNC's been much better. I mean, he really pulled us out of a hole there, when it looked like Mills was going to bury us…"

Remo shook his head. "That's the whole thing with managers—you want someone you can trust, but that nobody else can." He yawned then. "He's a good dealmaker, I have to give him that. Just don't let him get too crazy with the money, that's all."

"Thanks." I stood and stretched, remembering suddenly that I still had not showered. "I better get out of here."

"Sure thing."

But as I was walking toward the door I thought of one more thing. "Hey, Reem, how did you know about him wanting to break off from WTA in the first place?"

Remo shrugged and yawned. "He asked me if I'd sign up as one of his clients."

"And wha'd you tell him?"

Remo shrugged. "I put him off. See what he says. I'll have to tell him 'no' one of these days."

I nodded. I was only recently developing the ability to do that myself.

Life's What You Make It

At 10:45 in the morning I was awakened by the sound of the door opening partway and then the chain clunking hard against the door while a sort of Spanish-sounding woman's voice muttered an apology. The door shut again and I found myself staring at the ceiling, as if my eyes were awake before my brain was. I glanced at the clock on the table next to me, the red numbers' glow made faint by the morning light. I guess I had remembered to put the chain on the door last night but not to shut the curtains.

Bart rolled over and yawned. "One of these nights you're going to put that chain on before I get home," he said, which gave me a Twilight Zone

186

moment, like he'd read my mind. We both lay there staring at the ceiling, at opposite edges of a king-sized bed so big it wasn't even like we were in the same bed. I felt awake, much more awake than I would have expected after the crappy sleep I'd been getting. Then I sat up and decided I was not as chipper as I'd first thought. I felt tired, like I was wearing wet clothes, every move heavy and full of effort. I let myself collapse back and the bed bounced.

"Getting up?" Bart pulled the soft hotel sheet up and drummed on his chest.

"I don't know."

"What time did you get to bed? I must have slept right through it."

"It was after six a.m. I took a shower and everything."

"Jeez. And to think when we do this again next time it's going to be three times as long, with fewer days off in between."

He meant touring. "But less driving," I pointed out. I was starting to have an inexplicably bad feeling about the tour that was, even as we lay there like lumps, being booked. I was thinking about Tread and that weird little gun he carried stashed in his gear in their bus, only on bus tours of course, no way to get a firearm through airports, he'd explained. He'd never explained what it was for, nor why he was showing it to me. And at the time I'd been too busy acting nonplussed to ask. I remembered the blunt look of the thing, the weird averse-to-touching-it feeling that tingled in my hands as he'd showed it and then stowed it. "Hey Bart?"

"Yeah."

"Do you really never worry about money?" (Don't ask me to explain how the question was related to the gun memory other than maybe an oblique Warren Zevon reference.)

"Not generally, no. Though I used to fake it sometimes just so I wouldn't seem like the trust fund kid that I am. Although it's a fine line, because if everyone knows you've got plenty of dough, you look stingy if you gripe about the price of things or what have you."

A tiny red light blinked from the ceiling—a smoke alarm, I guessed. "Forget the price of things, or paying stuff. What about getting paid? Like, would you accept lower than scale for a piece of work just because you know you don't need the money?"

"Heck no," he said and his voice cracked a little with morning dryness. "It's not a question of money, it's fairness and dignity."

"But is it fair for musicians who don't need the money to take what might be given to another guy who needs it more?"

"Don't give me that philosophy theory type stuff. If I take under scale for a job, then that ends up dragging the scale down. Talk about unfair. It'd be different if, say, it was a friend who I knew was strapped in his budget. Or say we knew he was doling out a major chunk to get like Tony Levin to come into the session or something. I mean, I'd pay *them* to work a session with Tony Levin." We both lay silent for a while, watching the alarm blink, and then he said "Did that answer your question?"

"I guess."

"Or did you not ask the question you really meant to?"

"I think I was getting to something."

"Band stuff?"

"Do you think Digger's a good manager?"

"I don't really have a point of comparison, but, he seems okay. I could imagine it being a lot worse, anyway."

"Yeah." Going on what Remo said last night, I had only vague suspicions, no actual accusations to level against him.

"Why do you ask?"

"Just wondering what we're going to do when the trial period is up. It'll be, oh, just about when we're supposed to hit the road again."

"Hmmm."

"Ditto. Something to think about."

Neither of us moved for several long beats and then Bart lurched wearily to his feet. Once he was in the shower I started the process of digging through my clothes. We'd missed a laundry day with the extra time in Boulder, which meant getting dressed took more brainpower. It also meant I should've probably been getting my laundry done then. But I had other things to think about.

Papa Was A Rolling Stone

At noon I went around to Digger's door and knocked, figuring I'd maybe get in the drivers seat for once. The too-loud voices of daytime TV came faintly through the door and then it opened. He stood there in a white undershirt and boxers, bloodshot and unshaven. If the can in his hand had been beer instead of Sprite he could have passed for a trailer park movie extra. "Hey, kiddo."

"Just wondering if you wanted to have some lunch."

"Feeling sorry you blew me off last night, huh?" He gave me what could only be called a loving sneer. As a matter of fact, I did feel kind of weird about yesterday, but I wasn't about to apologize and his remark made me want to tell him to go to hell. He backed up, his way of inviting me in, and I went in. I probably should have said something like *meet you downstairs* or whatever, but hey.

The room was on a corner of the hotel, a half-suite with windows on two sides and the bathroom around the bed from the door. He went directly into the bathroom and began running the water. Digger always shaved with the water running very hot, which used to drive Claire crazy because he could use up almost as much water in one long, painstaking shave as a normal person did in the shower. Once my sisters got to be teenagers there was never enough hot water in the house. I sat down in a chair by the window. He could talk while he shaved.

"Did you know Remo came in last night?" I said. I could see him when he leaned forward to be close to the mirror.

"Sure did," he said. "At least, I found out this morning. Good thing, or I'd be at the friggin' airport now."

I thought you said he could take a cab. That was what I was thinking. But if I said it I knew it would be pointless antagonism. I could have said something about the mixed up hotel reservation, too, but it seemed better to let the subject, which I'd brought up, drop.

"Oh hey," he said, feeling under his chin. "You know that new James Bond movie?"

"No, what new James Bond movie."

"It's coming out at the end of the year."

"Uh huh." Like I'd know about that.

"They're trying to update the old Bond franchise, make it appeal to the younger crowd. Do a soundtrack album of hip songs. A radio-ready thing."

"Great idea," I said, not sure where this was going, but guessing.

"I brought the idea to Mills, you know the studio owns BNC anyway, and it looks like it'll be a go. Mills a'course wants you to do a song."

Aha, relevance dawns. "Something new, or use something old?"

"Something new. Increase your radio presence, give fans one more thing to go out and buy."

"Who else would be on this thing?"

He moved the razor with small jerky movements, not smooth like you'd expect. Maybe this explained why he cut himself so often. I was once again glad I'd trained myself onto the electric shaver. "Pretty much all from the BNC roster. Mills can tell you more."

Uh huh. I thought about what Remo and I had said last night, about Digger wanting to be a deal maker. I was going to wait until we were sitting down eating somewhere to bring this up, but this opening was too good to pass up. Some time in the past few minutes I had finally decided on my strategy to get the most out of him. "Pretty sweet," I said, nodding. "Hey, old man, did you ever think maybe you should get into something a little more exciting than accounting?"

"Ho ho!" he said, and put the razor down to rub his hands together. "Just a sec." He bent over the basin and began rinsing his face, filling up his hands with water and thrusting his face into them. I tried hard not to wonder if that was what I looked like when I rinsed my face.

He sat on the bed, drying his face and neck with a towel. "Things are moving faster than I thought."

"Yeah?" Here it comes, I thought.

He went to the closet, where his polo shirts and slacks were hung and picked one of each. "What will really make things work is the interaction between the different types of entertainment: movies, music, TV commercials."

TV commercials? Or should that be: *TV commercials!* I stifled any outrage, though. I had a point to make.

"I figure if I can manage a few talents in diverse areas I could, you know, maintain that same kind of, of…"

"Synergy." A word I'd always liked, after discovering a band named that, Larry Fast and Peter Gabriel doing electronic movie soundtracks.

"Yeah. Synergy."

"So what's the next step?"

He was putting on his shoes. "Plans are all in place," he said, thudding his feet on the floor.

"Like the LA office you opened?"

"Yeah." He didn't give even a hint that he knew that I knew he'd fudged the truth with me on the phone yesterday. He picked things up off the dresser and put them in his pockets, loose change, keys, etc. "Hotel restaurant okay? Or do you want to go somewhere else?"

"Up to you. I'll eat anything."

"Not from what I remember," he said, but amiably. "Let's just go downstairs."

"Fine."

We walked to the elevators and their fake-gold doors, neither of us saying anything as we moved through the hall, making me feel conspiratorial somehow. I couldn't just call him on the little white lie, could I?

A hostess seated us by wide windows overlooking a busy street. While I tried to figure out how to ask him what I wanted, we chit chatted about stuff like soundcheck and other things Digger didn't really know jack about. Tour small talk. Instead of "How's the weather," "How's the set up?" or what have you. It wasn't until we each had an overpriced burger in front of us that we began talking again for real.

"So tell me what the dirt is with Carynne flying home." He hunched over his plate, grease and red meat juice dribbling from his pinkies as he held the burger in both hands.

"What'd she tell you?"

"Something about a family member being sick, but come on, everyone says that when they mean something else."

I took a bite to give me time to think before I answered. "It's her personal business."

"Do you know?"

"I don't think we should discuss it any more."

He looked hurt. I wanted him chummy right now, so he'd tell me more about his schemes, but I couldn't be so chummy that I'd spread dirt about C. "Let it drop, alright? Jeez, she's just a kid." Yeah, and older than me, but hey.

He took another bite as if he were saying *oh, alright*—and we were back on an even keel. We ate for a while. He asked a passing water-re-filling boy for a bottle of ketchup. I didn't wait for the ketchup to start eating my fries.

Finally I just gave up. "So how much of DMA do I own?"

"What?"

"Where's the money coming from, Digger?"

"Aw, c'mon, it's not like that…"

"Did you get some 'adventure capital' after all?" There it was—my face was reddening as I talked, I couldn't help it. "How deep into the till are you, Dad?"

He sat back, his hands in his lap. I kept eating my fries, wondering if I'd ever learn to play nonchalance as well as he usually did—or if I really wanted to.

"Look, things started to move really fast. I had to take the chance. It's not that much, only maybe twenty thou—"

"Maybe?"

I was amazed to see him blush. "Well, you know I established a line of credit for the band, too, so it's not really like I'm taking your money…"

"Not really?"

"I mean, it'll all be paid back."

I put both my palms down hard on the table. "No. This doesn't happen."

"Really, kid, it's okay. I haven't taken any of your actual money. I'd never do that without your okay…"

"So instead you're running us into debt?"

"Uh…"

I took that as a yes. "It stops now, Digger."

"What, what stops? The ball is rolling, it's all right. I don't need any more."

"When were you going to tell me? Or did you figure as long and the bills got paid back, I'd never have to know?"

He grimaced. Yeah, that's exactly what I thought.

I was out of things to say at the moment—my plan had only gone so far as to confront him about it, and now I wasn't sure what to do. I took another cue from Ziggy's book and walked out without saying anything more. There was a new guitar waiting for me upstairs.

The Politics of Dancing

I was neither worried nor upset by the fact that Ziggy was nowhere to be found when we left the hotel. Digger and Carynne were both around, and managing him was their job now.

As it turned out he was sitting on the loading dock of the music hall when we pulled up, holding hands with Susan Walsh, who looked much more comfortable in a UC-Berkeley sweatshirt and jeans than she had yesterday. The crew and gear had arrived some hours ago and I walked onto the stage to find my rig already set up and Colin half asleep backstage with his Walkman on. He opened his eyes when I tapped him on the shoulder and quickly hit the Stop button.

"Hey," he said opening his eyes wide like they were yawning.

"Hey." I didn't ask him what he was listening to, because I was pretty sure it was *Prone to Relapse* and I was pretty sure he was embarrassed about it for some reason. "We're here."

"Cool. Let me show you around." He led the way from the dim cinderblock back into the wood-paneled, curtain-hung front. The place had the shabby look of a very old theater, carpet worn thin by the current generation of combat boots and high tops. Renovation money had been spent only on the sound system, it seemed, from the look of the black grilles peering like giant insect eyes from rough cut holes high up in the old paneling. The huge and many-dialed control board nested halfway up the orchestra section of seats.

Colin introduced the man standing behind the board, an almost freakishly tall and skinny guy with no hair and tattoos of black knotwork on his scalp. "Graham," he said and shook my hand. "Really looking forward to it, man."

"Thanks." I couldn't stand too close to him or I had to crane my neck when we talked.

"You'll never believe who was here last week," Colin said. "Robert Fripp and the League of Crafty Guitarists."

"Cool." I had seen the show they did at University of Rhode Island and was now reasonably sure we would have good sound. I've seen plenty of nice-looking set-ups that still produced crappy sound. But if it was good enough for Fripp... "Not too much bass no matter what Bart says, okay Graham?"

"Okay, boss," he said, just like Chris or somebody.

I went to the stage. Chris was taking his place behind the kit. He yelled in Colin and Graham's direction. "Should we get miked up?"

"Already did it," Colin yelled back as Graham's hands went to the controls.

Chris spat out a little roll on the snare and then extended it into a long trip with the sticks over the rest of the kit, cymbals, toms, blocks, and ended with a steady bass drum thump. Out in the hall the sound reverberated, the PA pumping it up so it came back twice as loud to us as it went out. In the wings there was another board, a short-haired blonde woman in a tank top on a stool behind it. She spoke into a microphone and her voice came out of the monitors at my feet, softly spoken but loud in volume: "I'll need all four of you to do monitor levels."

"Yes, ma'am," Chris said with a salute of the sticks in her direction.

Bart and Ziggy came up, Ziggy half in stage clothes already—a pair of black pants criss-crossed all over with silver zippers and a black fishnet tank top. "Hey boss," he said, his mouth all shining teeth, and took a hold of the cordless mic waiting for him at center stage.

We played something soft, Rain's opening, and something loud, the chorus and bridge of Welcome, we played a little individually, just us three without vocals, then all together again, backing vocals, lead vocals... the permutations shifting as Graham and Colin and the monitor girl nodded and their fingers moved over the sound boards like some kind of big pianos.

"Hey, Col', we getting a dub from this?" I said into my mic. I was already wishing I had a tape of the show and we hadn't even played it yet.

He gave me a thumbs up from where he sat in the fold-down auditorium rows, a few seats over from the main board. And it clicked for me, duh, he'd been listening to a private dub from some previous show earlier, listening for pleasure. From Colin's record collection I wouldn't have thought we were really his cup of tea, but hey, no one ever expects me to like half the stuff I like either.

"You guys happy with that?" came the woman's voice.

I was about to say yeah when Ziggy cut in. "I'd like to give a spin through Intensive Care, hey guys?"

Three shrugs: sure. We played the song all the way through and when we were done Zig said, into the mic held close to his chest in both hands, "So we're doing that one tonight, right?" His voice echoed slightly from the PA in the empty hall.

"Instead of Windfall?" I just talked to him, no microphone.

"Why not both?"

Bart took a couple of steps toward us. "Where do you want to put it in the set?" We'd substituted the song in a few times, but not added it to the regular set.

Ziggy stuck the mic in the stand finally. "Why not open with it? It has that nice build."

I was shaking my head already. "I like opening with Welcome better. We know that works." With sound like this the quiet intro would be delicious, and an auditorium crowd would fall hushed for it. And, actually, I had already formed an idea in my head of Remo standing in the wings listening, and what I hoped he'd think of it. "Let's not mess with it."

"Why not?" Ziggy rolled his neck back and forth like he was stiff. "Come on, Daron, we've been doing almost the same set every night for weeks. It's getting stale."

A glance at Bart told me he was staying out of this one for now. I rested my hands on top of the guitar. "I think it's fine."

"This is a hip crowd here, you know. They're here for the new stuff. We've got to get playing it some time."

"We can add Intensive Care in the encore, after Candlelight. Kick it in then."

He shook his head. "I think we should take out Walking and put it in then. That song's never fit that set anyway."

"You're out of your mind. That's the perfect place to change the pace." I looked at Bart again and he took a step backward.

"It would be a change of pace if you took out Rain, and put Way of Life in instead." He had his bottom lip inside his mouth as he looked at me, the challenge there, but soft, like he hoped I'd give in without a fight.

"Sounds like you've thought this one out pretty thoroughly," I said.

"Yeah." He waited to see what I was going to say.

Did he think I wasn't going to notice he was trying to take out songs that I'd written and put in ones that he had? Or was I being paranoid? Get a grip, Daron.

I looked away, out at Colin who was standing up now, eyes on us. You're so hyped up wanting Remo to hear you, not the band but you, that you can't even consider changing it? "We open with Welcome. We'll put Intensive Care in after Candlelight to kick it out at the end. There's plenty of room for Way of Life between Cross and Right Hand."

Bart did speak up. "But then we lose that nice transition, that sustained D."

He was right. It was one of my favorite moments to throw them zingers, too, plucking out quotes of songs we knew, if the mood was right, or just to stand quiet and gather energy for the next three song push. "You're right."

Ziggy folded his arms over his fishnetted chest. "I'm telling you it's getting tired."

"It's getting tired or you're getting tired?" My voice sounded sharp suddenly, snippy.

But Ziggy could out-snippy me any day. "Me, I'm getting tired. Tired of your bullshit. We've been bending backwards for you this whole trip, dammit, with your prima donna bullshit and I'm sick of it. Sick and tired of it." He made a little motion with his arm like he was throwing something at the ground. "Throwing" a tantrum, maybe.

I clenched my jaw, willing myself not to admit he might be right. He had done it again—flipped our roles, this time making me out to be the over-sensitive one.

He was still yelling. "What's the use? I know these two will agree with anything you say, but I've gotta speak up when I know you're driving us into the ground."

"Aren't you being a little extreme," I said, but I said it quietly and he ranted right over me.

"I wish I'd never signed that stupid paper. There's nothing fair about giving you the final say. I don't even know why I bother. Where would Way of Life be without that chorus? Some stupid ass shit, probably."

"Ziggy..." I let out a long breath, trying to swallow my annoyance and dampen him down. "Zig, calm down."

"Or what, you'll fire me? No, goddammit, I've got things to say."

"Okay, fine. Look, you made your suggestions. I've taken your suggestions for set order before. I just don't think it's going to work this time."

And then, things to say or not, he did a textbook dramatic exit, and stomped off, stage right. I held up my hands and Bart mirrored me. I heard the rattle of Chris letting his sticks fall as he got up.

"Curtain eight o'clock," Graham announced through the PA. "You're on at nine sharp."

Fame

The girl behind the monitor's name was Bailey. She unlocked a little office upstairs in the back so Carynne could make a few phone calls, but C. instead sat and motioned for me to close the door behind me and join her. "Mister Zee's off the edge," she said as she sat down behind an empty desk.

I sat on the desk. "God, maybe he was always like this but I didn't notice because I was too worried about other things. Speaking of which," I looked at the billboard with old concert flyers tacked to it instead of at her, "how are things with you cend him?"

"Thankfully null. He's latched onto that reporter-groupie."

"Oh god, she was a riot. I couldn't believe it."

"Bart told me." She was looking at the small, neat unpainted nails on her left hand. "What do you think he's going to do?"

"Sulk a bunch, take it out on Ms. Walsh, and then sing like a banshee tonight."

"So you're not worried."

"No. This time last year I would have been beside myself. I would have been on my knees begging him to forgive me, or I would have been floating around out there in a state of panic, waiting for the other shoe to drop." I sighed and swung my feet, drumming the heels of my high tops on the metal desk quietly. "Now, he can try what he wants. I'll deal with it when it comes."

"You're not worried about stage fright."

"No. Not anymore." I was only mildly surprised to find that true. "He can try what he likes up there—I'm ready for him. I don't even know what got into me..." I trailed off and sat there, wondering if that was what she'd wanted to talk to me about.

She leaned forward on the desk, her hands in her lap, her chest against the edge of the blotter. "Is it true you turned down an offer to do a beer commercial?"

"Yeah, you knew about that."

"No."

"Don't you remember, like a year ago. They wanted to feature us in the commercial, us talking about the band in little snippets, it was going to look almost like a mini MTV style documentary, make us look way hip, and the beer too, by extension."

"Why didn't you do it?"

"They wanted Welcome as the background music, and wanted to use it as a jingle, you know, people walking into a bar, and here's this anthemic 'welcome'—as in 'welcome to beer country' or something. I just couldn't."

"How much money was it?"

"That's the thing. It wasn't even that much money. They were like practically acting like we should be grateful for the exposure and all that, like they were making us this career-making offer and ought to suck up to them. I was having none of it."

"What did you tell them?"

"In the end I told them look, I can't do this. I'm not even fucking old enough to drink."

She laughed then like I'd told a good joke, which I guess I had. Then, smoothing her lips together, she added. "You know Zig wanted to do that commercial real bad."

"I know." We sat like that for a few more seconds. "Hey, don't you have calls to make?"

"Daron," she said, her face serious. "Has he talked to you about outside projects like acting or stuff like that?"

"Ziggy you mean?"

She nodded. "There's nothing about that kind of stuff in your contract."

"Why would I care if he wants to act or something? Unless it interfered with a tour or our schedule or what have you. He can dance in the fucking Nutcracker for all I care. Why do you ask?"

Carynne slicked her dark orange hair back from her face and it cascaded forward in a wave. "I think you better ask him about that. Maybe not today, but you ought to bring it up."

"What do you mean?"

"Ask him, Daron, not me. Maybe it's nothing. But ask him."

Good Times Bad Times

Carynne picked up the phone like she really was going to make some calls, and I took it as a hint I should leave. Although if she was going to make calls there was no reason why I shouldn't stay. But I had a feeling she wasn't doing business—no day book out—so picking up the phone was a signal instead. Right? Take your cue, Daron.

I sat in the back row while the opening band did their soundcheck, and listened to them run through a nice piece of work with one twelve string guitar and one electric guitar. I could not remember their name. Halfway down the room from me, Graham stood next to his stool without moving, facing the stage.

Backstage I found Remo slinging a laminate over his head and talking with Digger. "There's what, two hours to showtime?" he was asking.

"Something like that," Digger said. "Hey kiddo, how's it hanging?"

"A little to the left. First band goes on at eight. We're on at nine." I stood there with my hands in my pockets.

"They did a nice job with catering," Digger said, with a little jerk of his head toward the green room. "Might as well enjoy it."

So we three trooped into the green room. I was still full from our large late lunch but opened a can of 7-Up and sat in a folding chair with it fizzing between my knees while I listened to Digger and Remo banter. They could both do the same thing: say essentially nothing but in a kind of jocular, engaging way, so if you didn't speak English you'd think, hey, what good buddies those guys are. They talked about the cold cuts, the condiments, each one's sneaking suspicion that Levi's had subtly changed the cut of 501 jeans, ripping each other about getting gray hairs. Maybe I was being cynical. After all, when Bart and I got together, what did we talk about? When we weren't talking about work, that is. Every conversation wasn't some soul-baring, topic-of-import type discussion. Still, I had the feeling Digger and Remo were more being friendly to each other than being friends. For some reason that made me sad.

C. came in and had to conference with Digger on something and Remo sat down next to me, his folding chair turned backward so he leaned his arms on the upright back of it. "What do you guys do to kill time?"

Chris and Kevin were playing cards. Bart and Ziggy were not in the room. Colin was eating a sandwich and staring into space. I shrugged. "Whatever we feel like. We'll eat dinner after."

"You feel like playing a little more?"

"Sure." Truth, my thumb was feeling a little sore from playing so much last night, and I'd already played an hour today, plus the sound-check. But I would not have said no to him.

I fetched the Ovation from the stage where it sat in a stand behind an amp. The hollow body knocked against my knee as I pulled it toward me by the neck, the sound so small in the largeness of the empty hall. Back in the green room, Remo was tuning the Takamine he'd given me (of course I'd brought it along) by ear.

"Hey I started writing something today," I said as I sat down next to him and hitched the Ovation up under my arm. I dug a thumb pick out of my pocket and tucked it onto my finger.

"Let's hear it," he said. He took a sip from a can of Coke and then put it under his chair.

I played out the riff I'd been working on, a Travis-picked pattern, kind of a folky pattern but I played it with open chords, a suspended fourth here, then open fifths, chords that would have had some dissonance in them if played with a strum. I didn't explain, I just played it through twice slow, watching Remo watch my fingers, first my left and then my right. He strummed the chords lightly, hitting the top E and then sliding a finger up the neck to play it an octave up. He watched my left hand go through the chords once more and then began to pick the strings in tandem with me, the fuller, mellower sound of the Takamine making the Ovation seem harder and brighter than usual.

He pushed the tempo a little and then said "The implied E. Nice."

I nodded; he'd known what I was aiming for, understood it without explanation. "It rings."

We played it through again. "Here's the B section." This was three more of those chords, a slight variation in the color, and then, the E we'd been waiting for, though I didn't play it with all six strings. He grinned at me.

People were walking back and forth, making sandwiches, pausing to watch, talking. I was aware of them but unaffected by them at the same time. My fingers seemed to move of their own accord now, the pattern preprogrammed.

"What the hell kind of melody do you put on top of something like this, kid?"

He started on the A section again and I showed him, the brittle twang of the Ovation carrying the notes easily through the run of his picking, even though I played low on the neck. And then, in the chorus of the B section, I showed him how the tune changed and echoed itself. We were both into the groove now, looking at each other's faces and not at our hands. I carried the tune up the neck and played it again, with variations for a while, until Remo passed the rhythm part back to me.

We played in unison again for a few measures and then, using his first two fingers to walk up the scale, he played me a melody that fit sinuously into the pattern. It wasn't anything like the one I'd played, but it fit. I don't know how to describe it other than to say it was as different as he was from me. The tune had a cohesive beauty that was revealed gradually on the first round through, and shone on the second.

I believe I said "Oh yeah."

When the lead came back to me, I found it had changed in my mind, and what I played now was somewhat in the form of mine but the color of his. We played with that for a while until the moment arrived, as it always does, when we reached the end and stopped. Sometimes when you're jamming, the end approaches from far away, and everyone sees and feels it coming, and then you end. But sometimes it happens suddenly, whoom, and everyone stops, barely aware that we've stopped playing until we hear the quiet. Okay, it doesn't happen like that every time. Not every bunch of musicians is as tuned in to each other as every other, and sometimes different egos can be battling for control or the last word. But this time, we felt the end coming and we let it go with one last icicle bright arpeggiated strum from the Ovation.

Remo took a sip of his Coke. "What do you call that one?"

"How about 'I wish I had a tape recorder.'" We both laughed and I shook my left hand out.

"Thumb bothering you?"

"No," I said, but that was so obviously a lie, what with me rubbing the joint with my right, that it didn't come out like a lie. It came out like something meaningless I had to say, like please or thank you, and neither of us gave it much weight.

Remo laid the Takamine back into its case and slouched into the chair. "I'm gonna move my old bones to the couch."

"Sure." We both went to the couch and sat there drinking soda from cans and not needing or wanting to say much and kind of nodding our heads from time to time, whether in agreement or in time to inaudible music who could say.

Remo and I were still sitting on the couch backstage in comfortable silence when Digger came in.

He had a piece of curled-up paper in his hands. "Feast your eyes on this." He handed it to me—that soft, strange paper that came out of fax machines, smudged black on the edges where he'd held it. At the top was the BNC logo and then a long list of dates and cities.

"Are these all shed and festival dates?" I asked. There had to be thirty five cities, at least.

"Not all. You'll note the date at MSG." He pointed down the list.

There was one in New Jersey, too. "What's… oh, this must be Garden State Arts Center." Practically in our old backyard.

And Mansfield, Massachusetts, that was Great Woods. I hated seeing shows at Great Woods, crappy sound, bad seats, and the traffic getting out of that parking lot was hell. But maybe playing there would be different. Chris and Kevin abandoned their game and came to look over my shoulder.

"Shit," I said appreciatively.

Digger was beaming even though the dates were probably BNC's doing as much as his. "Have you been watching the European charts?"

"Heck, no. I've been living out of a suitcase for weeks."

"Candlelight's hit number four in France, number seven in the UK. Mills wants a six-week European tour in September/October." Digger's expensive shoes tapped the concrete floor.

"Great. Good. Vun-der-bar." I handed him back the fax.

"Nothing like steady work, eh?" said Christian.

"You said it," said Remo, who clapped me on the shoulder and smiled.

Everyone was still kind of clustered around me, having their own conversations now. I held the Ovation by the neck and parted the crowd with it.

As I put the guitar back into its stand I heard again that same sad sound of the body's hollow echo. I sat on the stage's edge, then, swinging my feet into the front row's airspace, looking into the empty seats wondering, who's going to sit here tonight? Did they buy the tickets? Win them from a radio station? Get them in graft from a rep or promoter's cousin or program director? Or did they shell out top dollar? Will they come with their girlfriend/boyfriend/spouse? Will they be younger than me, or older? Do people take their kids to see concerts?

Digger never took me to a big arena show or music hall like this. We went out to honky tonks and bars where the bartenders would let me have a root beer while Nomad or some blues band or whoever played. And of course I'd never asked him if he'd want to go with me and whoever I was scamming a ride with to the Meadowlands or the Capitol Theater in Trenton—it was unimaginable, me in the back seat with a couple of burnouts or whoever, rolling joints for them on our way to see Rush or Styx or Journey, trying to imagine bringing Digger into a situation like that. I didn't go to a lot of shows. I wasn't really friends with these guys and their souped up Camaros or father-borrowed Cadillacs. But I knew where the parties were, I played the guitar, and I never made a move on their girlfriends, so they took me along.

What were those guys doing now? They'd be mid-twenties. I could picture, for some reason, myself backstage at the Garden State Arts Center, then walking out from a soundcheck, the sun still up in the sky, out to the parking lot all divided by little banks of evenly spaced trees, and finding them sitting around the tailgate of a car, in baseball shirts with three-quarter sleeves, the stereo still playing Pink Floyd "The Wall," passing a joint and arguing over where were their seats, anyway.

You Ain't Seen Nothing Yet

So, the show already.

If Ziggy could be a moody bitch, so could I. The two of us were all business now with the bitchiness and bastardy, and people stayed out of our way. Bart didn't try to lighten the mood—maybe he wanted to see what would happen. Zig and I worked ourselves into a fine stew not speaking but giving one another glances that were by turns angry, pitying, regretful, and immature, and once in a while making comments to bystanders that betrayed our state of mind like "We're going to kick some ass tonight" and "God I hope they don't throw stuffed animals."

We'd both learned by then that whatever state of mind you're in when you're offstage changes when you get there, and it does not always change the way you'd expect. Any images you have of what the show is going to be like are never the way it goes once you're in the moment.

Once you get out there on the knife edge, everything's real-time improvisation and whatever script you think you're going to play from vanishes. It's like sex that way, the give and take can still surprise you even if you're following a well-known set list.

We opened with Welcome. Johnny Rotten was right, anger is an energy, and we launched into things hard. The song begins soft, but it can be done with intensity. I let loose with a little crying riff before the verse like a horse neighing in the starting gate, Chris picked up on the tension and gave the cymbal roll an extra push, and when the spotlights hit, Ziggy came in literally growling the words.

I had that feeling as I played, as I picked out a lead line and carried it up, that the notes were coming out of my throat even though I wasn't singing, like the notes were pouring out of me as I breathed. That happens at the best of times, and usually takes me several songs before I can reach that kind of peak, before I can give myself over to the total that way. But here I was, ripping, my head thrown back, feet planted, two hands moving, and then the chorus came and time to really sing. One part of me did its job singing, while another part of me kept playing, and whatever part of me it is that does things like tries to come up with a script or thinks about what I look like up there got pushed to the back of the bus.

The crowd feels that kind of energy. They were out of their seats and we gave them no chance to sit down between songs. I like a smooth set, with only a few breaks for patter in between. We kicked right in to Do It Up—it's a pretty simple tune, both musically and lyrically, a party song, or as close to one as we come to doing, and we'd put it second in the set to carry the tempo forward from Welcome's ending and to give people a little good-time feeling before we start hitting them with the heavy stuff, the theatrical stuff.

Ziggy was with me on this, we were at the edge of the stage side by side facing the audience, being as loud and steady as you can imagine. We exchanged looks, we kept going. I left him up there to step back and face Bart—we traded riffs like a game of catch and I could see Chris's eyes when he looked up at us, bright, a little maniacal. He knew we were riding the wave, too.

I had a brief moment of pause as the song was coming to a close—it seemed impossible somehow that so much communication could be going on without us speaking to each other. But look what happens when we do speak to each other...

I pushed through the pause by deciding to test the envelope. As I threw out the notes of the closing riff, I changed it, I started the chug of Intensive Care's hook; it's an almost Hendrix-like bit of work with three string chords all over the lead.

They were with me. Ziggy's mouth was all teeth as he turned to me before he began to sing.

We dropped the volume down so the grinding menace in his voice had a chance to build.

And here it was, the real-time knife edge thing, happening all around me. Ziggy must have been thinking I was out of my mind, or maybe that he'd won the argument after all. Of course I wasn't thinking about that at the time, because that would have pulled me out of the moment. But it was happening all the same. And it felt good.

Intensive Care can be an ugly song, or it can be sort of erotically painful. After we'd been through the chorus the first time I found myself away from my mic, sinking to my knees facing him, as he crawled over me like a predator, like he'd bite my neck if he weren't busy singing, his knees touching mine, and then he pulled away in time for me to get back on my feet and sing the chorus again.

It was, I guess, sort of like old times.

Here's where it started to go wrong. As we were finishing up Intensive Care, I knew it was up to me to either steer us back onto the set list or take us somewhere new. Just as I was about to start into Wishes, thinking that after that we'd get back into the regular set order, my thumb locked up. Not exactly locked—a tendon or something caught suddenly and threw me off by a half a beat. I needed to crack it but couldn't stop then. I got the song going, and Bart picked the riff up and then I did take a step back and shake my hand.

It ached but was okay, or so I kept telling myself. How long had it been aching and I hadn't been paying attention? And that brought the thought into my head about all the people backstage and wherever who saw that flick of my hand and were now worrying about it. I could feel their anxiety and there was no way I could send a message—I'm okay, forget it—not even by playing, hiding it. And that opened the door for the general thought of what they were thinking, looking at me up here, Digger and Remo, Colin and his bootleg tapes, excellent sound man Graham.

I was out of the now and into self-conscious land again.

I suddenly wondered if Graham could tell about me.

And then Ziggy took a step toward me, sneering, accusatory with the line of the chorus "Oh, I wish."

I took a step back, short of breath and wondering where my cup of water was, and how I was going to need a sip of it when this song was over. Ziggy sang on, coming closer to me with each repetition:

Oh I wish, I could tell you more
I wish, I could even the score
I wish, I could walk out the door...
Those are the wishes I whisper...

I stood my ground, breathing hard and thoughts spinning through my head. I planted my feet apart and kept my hands doing their job, until we were nose to nose, our foreheads pressed together, wet and more wet, me canted forward like I was leaning into a strong wind to keep the guitar free of his body, him holding the cordless mic to the side a bit so he didn't hit me in the chin with it.

I wrote this song. I wrote it one day when I was pissed at him, I don't remember exactly when or which time, and even though I knew some of the lyrics were clunky, cliched, or didn't completely scan, he hadn't dicked with them or smoothed them out. I didn't know if it was that he didn't bother, or if he knew damn well who the song was meant for and decided to leave it alone for some reason related to that.

But now he was singing it to me, annunciating the words carefully with little snarls and held out syllables, and he was making it make sense this direction, too.

I thought you were the one for me
But a river runs its course
How well I know that you know me
I don't have to say, because...

We hit the chorus together and stayed together, physically I mean, still head to head, the crowd screaming at the edges of my awareness, and all of those what-do-they-think thoughts were driven forcibly out of my mind.

On the last verse he broke away, spinning on his heel and going back to prancing in front of the audience. But when he started the last verse, I sang it with him. That whole body singing feeling had returned and I played the melody and sang a counterpoint harmony at the same time, dragging the tempo down a notch as we ground toward the end...

Forget the life that has to be
Live instead the truth
I'm on the highway west of me
You're on the way to the moon...

And I stuck with that line "You're on the way to the moon," and Bart and Chris picked it up with a thump-kick line, and I let my hands free and clapped on *You're* and *Moon,* and the audience clapped with me, me and Ziggy repeating the line again and again until it had no meaning anymore, and then we reached that moment where we did all finally stop.

I dumped my cup of water over my face and down my shirt. There were cheers and whistles in the silence while I picked up the Ovation and slid the thumb pick on, checked the tuning, and stepped back to Chris to tell him we were back on the set list now, and to hit it whenever he was ready.

The Loadout/Stay

I haven't yet succumbed to the temptation to write a song about being on the road. I mean, jeezus, it's all been done before, said before, it's almost a cliché in and of itself to just be out there living the lifestyle.

But if I was going to write a road song, I think I'd try to write about the transition from stage back to the real world. Because this is where it gets tricky. This is where you're energized and tired at the same time. This is when you look forward to relaxing or partying or sex or whatever, but it's also a depressing let down to have to deal with all these people.

They say when Tom Petty tours, he's in the bus and already on the road to the next place before the lights come up in the arena. He travels in a bus separate from the Heartbreakers. I don't know why, but I can imagine that being a dangerous time to be around him. Maybe he's learned over the years that it's better to cool down in the dark isolation of the bus, than to mix and mingle. Maybe someday I'll get to ask him about it.

Up to that point, with me, it was not always the same. Sometimes I'd come down and be left with a serious jones for something, sex, drugs, something to fill the proverbial hole. Other times I just felt fine. And sometimes, the rarest thing, I'd get weirdly angry, like something was not right and I couldn't find it to fix it. The same way I can't predict what kind of a show I'm going to have from my pre-show mood, I can't predict what I'm going to feel like afterward. I can have a shitty show sometimes and then feel fine, relieved even. We can have a good show and I'll get angry. I just don't know. It's this anger thing that makes me wonder about Petty's decision.

Remo, on the other hand, always seems the same. Before the show, a mixture of restless and smug, if you can imagine that. And afterward, a kind of keyed-up satisfaction not that different from the way he was before. I wish I knew what he was like when he was my age (or what he would have been like if he were playing these kind of shows then). Remo doesn't even do drugs anymore, shrugs them off like why bother, though he usually lets himself have one good scotch afterward. That scotch is his reminder that yes, he's living the good life.

We came off the stage to a flurry of congratulations. Remo was impressed, I could tell by the look in his eye, and it was funny to me that although I'd worried about it so much beforehand, now that I had his approval I was unconcerned about it. Digger was whistling appreciatively. Colin gave me two thumbs up as he skipped onto the stage to start breaking down. Bailey, from her stool, gave me a closed-eyed nod like—well, alright—and the promoter's guy wanted an autograph.

I sat down on a chair backstage and peeled my soaked shirt off. I held it balled up in my hands while I sat there, elbows on knees, like I was waiting for my ears to stop ringing. (I took my earplugs out, too.) I stared at a piece of concrete floor about two feet in front of me while I waited to find out what kind of a come-down I would have tonight.

My managers were here, my crew was taking care of things. There was nothing I had to do then but sit there and feel.

I looked up and there was Ziggy, leaning on the back of the couch, ankles and arms crossed, looking at me. I gave him the chin up—*hey*. He gave it back and sat down in a chair next to me.

"Well," he said, cucumber cool, "that worked out well."

"Yeah, I guess it did." I let my wet shirt drop to the floor with a dishmop sound and cracked my knuckles. "My thumb is killing me."

"Here." He took my hand in his and rubbed it gently, first the ball of muscle in the web between the thumb and forefinger, then the tendons in the knuckles. I let him. It felt good. It hurt some, but felt good. Shit, man, I wanted to say, if this is what antagonism gets us, then let's have a screaming fight every soundcheck. But that's not what I actually said.

"Hey, Zig," I said, my voice quiet in the bustle of the room, "do you think about what you're going to do next?"

"What do you mean, like, how far in advance are we talking?" He looked from our hands to my face and back down again.

"Long term. I mean, do you imagine us playing like this forever?"

"What, like the Rolling Stones or something?" He laughed. "No, I don't figure we will. But maybe when we get old we'll be saying 'oh, but we know better now.'"

"Well, for theory's sake let's say that we stick with our principles and we don't succumb to nostalgia reunion bullshit. Do you think about what you're going to do next, after the theoretical band's days are over?"

He stopped rubbing my hand and held it still. I would have thought his hands would be sweaty but they were dry. "Yeah, I think about it. You know your old man thinks I should make a movie."

"No shit."

"Yeah. That guy who directed Why The Sky, he's developing something, Digger's kept in touch, and maybe he wants me to do it." Now he was looking across the room at Digger, who was in earnest conference with the promoter's guy, the two of them hunched toward each other in one corner. "So but that's possibly the short term, I mean, they're talking about trying to do principle lensing before we hit the road again. The whole shooting schedule is like eight weeks."

"Man," I said, somehow not at all surprised.

"But if you want long term, I figure, I don't know, acting, singing, there'll be something, I hope." He put his hands to his face then, rubbing his eyes with his fingertips. "What about you?"

"There'll be something," I echoed. "Start another band, write soundtracks, I don't know."

"Now wouldn't that be the shit, if you wrote the music for movies I was in." He smiled, a regular this-thought-makes-me-happy smile.

Wow, this is almost like a real conversation, I thought. We're sitting here talking to each other meaning what we say. Hallellujah.

It wasn't until he got up and walked away I wondered if he'd heard more than I'd meant. "Well, okay then," he said as he stood up. "Okay then." And he walked away.

And here I was still wondering what kind of a come-down this would be. I motivated myself to find a dry shirt. Now I was even feeling a little chilly, the loading dock was open and foggy air was coming in. I put on my denim jacket. Didn't Journey do a song about San Francisco? I hadn't written a song about a city, yet. I didn't plan to.

Dirty Deeds

It was when I made one more trip to the men's room that I overheard something I probably wasn't meant to. Okay, I know I wasn't meant to by the people talking, that is. There were some ceiling tiles missing from the men's room ceiling, you see. Some kind of duct work going on. Since this was a back of house area it wasn't like a public hazard or something. The ladder was even still standing there. Anyway, something about the acoustics of the place meant that I could hear Carynne's voice perfectly when I stood at the urinal.

She must have been in the women's room on the other side of the wall. And she must have been talking to Susan Walsh, the fill-in entertainment reporter, given what she was saying. But there was a moment there where I thought she was talking to Ziggy.

"Listen, I'm not judging you. I'm not some kind of prude, far from it. But you have to accept the facts," she said. "You're wrong if you think sex can't wreck you in this business just as badly as drugs can. Maybe worse, since you can go to rehab for drugs but once your reputation is shot, there's no going back."

I could hear a female voice replied softly but not make out the words. I could smell a clove cigarette, too, and wondered if they were inside the handicapped stall or something.

"Trust me, been there, done that, but you're too old to be getting away with it if you want to actually keep a job at the newspaper or pursue a career there. There's nothing wrong with groupies and there's nothing wrong with a consensual fling. But you have to know Ziggy's not serious about you, right?"

She didn't sound the slightest bit jealous when she said that, either.

"Oh good. Look, I wouldn't even bother saying any of this if I didn't think you had a good head on your shoulders. If you were just some dumb chick, you know? You gave into temptation this time. I know. And he can be really persuasive. I know. Most of what I'm saying, I guess, is just don't do it again. Don't think you can get away with this over and over, even though temptation is going to only get worse if you stay on the celebrity beat. Guys are always looking for an easy lay. They aren't thinking about whether you could lose your job, or get banned from venues, or any of that stuff. But you could. This business puts women into two categories. Worthless sluts, and everyone else. Thing is, once you get into the slut category, it's pretty much impossible to climb out. Once you're considered worthless, you will never get someone to return a phone call again. Not a manager, not a publicist, not an artist. it's not fair, but it's the way it is. I mean, tell me seriously, what would your editor say if he knew?"

A higher pitched answer this time but I still couldn't make out the words.

Then Carynne again. "Of course not! I won't tell. I have no plans to. If I did, I wouldn't have bothered to tell you all this. Women have to stick together and help each other when we can. But stay out of the boys' pants from now on, all right? Or don't, but don't expect to have any professional contact with them if you do. That's the bottom line."

Through all this I had been afraid to move, because I was afraid they'd hear me and then be freaked that someone had overheard. At that point, though, someone else came into the men's room—a venue employee type I didn't recognize, and went into a stall. A short while later he flushed, a long, noisy flush from the industrial-grade toilet, and when it got quiet again, the voices were gone.

Once your reputation is shot, there's no going back. That was her message.

I wondered if it applied to me, too.

I Got You

The promoter's guy, it turned out, had friends who ran a Moroccan restaurant and they often took bands there after a show for a little decadence and graft. Unlike some towns, Frisco had several competing promoters and they wanted to curry some favor. Pun intended. We went along with free food on principle.

I was about to get in a van with a few of the others when Carynne pulled me toward a cab. I figured it didn't look like a big deal that we went together, what with there being some amount of chaos as people were getting into vehicles, and also no one else could tell what an iron grip she had on my arm.

She told the driver where we were going and then waited until he'd pulled out into traffic to say anything.

What she said was "Jeez, Louise."

"Something bugging you or did you just want to get away from everybody for a while?" I asked.

She looked me over. "I'm not so much with the getting away from people usually," she said. "That's you."

I shrugged. "Make a note in the day book for the next tour that I get cranky if I'm forced to talk to too many people in a day. But seriously, is something up?"

She sighed and looked out the window. Then she looked back at me. "I can't do what he does."

My mind was still on the conversation she had with the reporter in the ladies room. "Ziggy?"

"No, stupid. Digger. Did you see that list of dates?"

Oh. "Car', come on, trust me, it's not Digger's name that is opening those doors. It's BNC."

"Tch. You can't really be that naive."

"Naive? Enlighten me. If it's not BNC, he's been name-dropping the agency, and working his connections. What's the big deal?"

She gave me a murderous look, like I wasn't taking her seriously enough, which I wasn't. "Daron! Honestly. That's what I'm saying. He's got way more connections in much higher places than me. I can't do what he does!"

I put my hand on her arm, to show her I was serious. "You can. Okay, maybe you might not have done it as fast, and maybe you would have leaned on Mills and your uncle a lot more…"

She sucked in a breath like she was panicking a little and trying to tamp it down.

"I'm not about to fire you, you know," I said. "And I'm not about to let you quit, either."

"Shit, Daron," she said, her shoulders slumping. "It just seems… a lot bigger than I can get my head around."

"Are you seriously saying I should keep him as manager?"

"Set aside for a minute that you have issues with him or whatever, the bottom line is, does he get you the work that you want and do you make the money that you want? This is like fuck-you money we're talking about, you know."

"What about the fact he's borderline embezzling from me?"

Her mouth hung open a bit. "Define 'borderline,'" she finally said.

"Opened a credit line using the band's money or contracts as collateral, used it to rent an office in LA and hire support staff. All without telling me."

She chewed her lip. "That doesn't sound that far outside the realm of—"

"It's not a Moondog Three office. It's the Digger Marks Agency office and he's been on the West Coast trying to drum up other clients. Movie stars, directors, that sort of thing."

"Ohhh. Yeah, that's definitely the slippery side of the slippery slope." She winced. "But is it because he's your dad?"

"What do you mean?"

"I mean, parents make unilateral decisions for their kids all the time without asking. And it sounds like otherwise he's busting tail for you…." She thought a moment. "But no, that's still pretty weasely. You have to set some really firm boundaries when you work with relatives. I should know."

"Yeah, well, I told him it stops now. I don't figure I can take back what he's spent, really, but I can demand some ownership."

She chuckled. "That's brilliant. Did you think of that yourself?"

"Yeah, I did. Seemed better than just telling him to go to hell and being stuck when he runs off with the money." I shrugged. "Basically if he doesn't cough up paperwork and a deal to my satisfaction, I'm sending him packing. I think he'll do it legit, though. He… Something Remo said makes me think he wants that more than money. To be a legit player. He fakes it until he makes it."

"He's pretty damn close to making it," she said.

"Just don't leave me defenseless," I said. "I need you actually road managing this tour. I want you double-checking everything he does, anything he sets up, and I want you building the biggest damn Rolodex you can, so that if we do have to fire his ass, you've insinuated yourself with all his contacts."

"Piece of cake," she said. "I can totally play it like I'm his secretary when I need to, like anything they'd tell him they can just tell me." She batted her eyelashes innocently.

I laughed. "I know you can bust balls when you need to."

The cab lurched to a stop and the cabbie pointed at place across the street, explaining in broken English that it was best we just get the hell out now and walk over there. Carynne paid him and I could see what was creating the traffic jam.

Ziggy was signing autographs on the sidewalk outside the restaurant.

"Speaking of busting balls," she said, and got out of the car.

One Way or Another

The Moroccan place was total decadence, everyone half-sitting, half-lying on these pillows on the floor, the walls all padded with complicated patterns like the set of a movie in a harem. I half expected the low round tables to come complete with a hookah.

Chris and I and Bart sat with our backs to the wall and our legs splayed, drinking beer and eating with our fingers. (There's apparently no silverware in Morocco.) Colin and Remo sat across from us. Remo didn't say much during the meal, told a few anecdotes about weird food on their last tour outside the US, and what have you. Chris and I talked about all kinds of shit, what to do with the Allston house, movies we were missing seeing while on the road, the food. We were shoulder to shoulder in a slouch when I thought again, what if he knew? Would he sit here with me like this?

Telling him was on my to-do list. I hadn't forgotten that.

I made a rolling motion with my fingers under the table and looked at him. He nodded with his eyebrows and went to the men's room. I followed a few moments later, and jeers were made about all the beer we were drinking.

I took a piss at the urinal, first. When my hands were dry, he pulled the joint out of his jacket pocket and held it out to me. "I lost my lighter," I said.

"Asshole," he said with affection, "it was my lighter to begin with."

"Ah, sorry."

He chuckled and grumbled at the same time and pulled a lighter out of his back pocket. We each took a hit and sat in silence.

I was suddenly sure I was going to do it.

He took another hit and handed the roll back to me. "Hey Chris," I said, my fingers pinched together. "You know I'm gay, right?"

He looked at me, like he was stuck for the answer, not sure if I was shitting him or what. I felt awkward for having phrased it that way, and tried to keep things moving before he could convince me to play along with the joke.

"Cuz I want your advice about something." I felt a little dizzy, but there was none of the gut-wrenching nausea I'd felt some previous times. Maybe the pot was helping that.

"My advice?" he didn't quite stammer. "I, Daron, look, I—"

"Chill out. Chill out. So—you didn't know."

He shrugged and I handed him back the joint without taking another hit myself. "It didn't... It's just a surprise is all. I mean, you seem really nor—" He shook his head. "It's none of my business, is what I'm trying to say."

I nodded. "It's cool. I thought you should know for sure, though. Anyway I want to ask you something."

"Go ahead, shoot." He leaned against the sink, casual-like.

"When you quit your job to play with Highway Death, and your father went apeshit, did you like, tell him you were doing it, or did you just do it and then wait for him to find out?"

He laughed. "Oh I told him alright. Once I decided to do it, I couldn't wait to tell him. I couldn't wait to shove it up his... I mean, I wanted a confrontation, I wanted to tell him how I felt about all his bullshit over the years and how I wasn't going to take it anymore. I was going to stand up for myself and told him to blow it out his ear."

"And then he went apeshit."

"Yeah, but it wasn't like I wasn't ready for that. If I'd gone to him and like begged or something, or said *hey Dad I'm thinking about maybe quitting*.... he would have gone apeshit anyway, and I wouldn't have been ready. But I was like immune to it when I went in fighting. I was like *piss off, you old fart!* and then he couldn't touch me."

"You mean, it just rolled off you like water off a duck."

"Yeah, and also he couldn't like physically push me around. I'm not the scrawny kid I used to be and I was, you know, *in his face*. He knew better than to try pushing me around because he'd lose."

"So what happened?"

He took a long drag and held it before he answered.

"Well, you know, we didn't speak for a long time, and then like one night Miracle were playing in Brockton and he shows up with some drinking buddies of his and kind of begrudgingly made this gesture of okayness. I didn't tell him of course that we were only getting like $75 for that gig. I mean, we still don't get along, but hey, it's not high on my list of priorities."

"Aha." We stood there for a while. The roach was dead.

"So, why did you want to..." he started to ask, and then he said, "Digger approves of you, obviously."

"But he doesn't know." I couldn't quite bring myself to use the word *gay* twice in one conversation.

"Ohhh," Chris said, the original subject of the conversation dawning on him. "Well, shit. It does come as kind of a shock. Did you want me to break it to him?"

"Fuck no! But thanks for the offer, buddy."

"Gotta say it's going to take some getting used to. For me. Shit, I feel like a heel for all the times I tried to drag you out to pick up girls…!"

At that I had to laugh. "It's really okay. Don't feel bad. I've tried not to be obvious about it."

"Well, you succeeded." He whistled appreciatively. "So, are you going to tell him? Your dad, I mean."

"No clue. Maybe, maybe not." I was having the urge to lie down on the pillows out there again. "It's none of his business."

"Damn straight," Chris said, and we went back to the others.

While You See a Chance

There was a bellydancer waving silks and hands in front of the table when we returned, dollar bills forming a green counterpoint to the blue sequins of her costume. She coaxed Digger up and danced with him to the too-loud piped in music, circling around him with her scarves while he did a kind of drunken boogie, chugging his fists forward and back like a Rock-em Sock-em Robot.

I sat on his pillow next to Remo and joined the general jeering and laughing. Bart darted forward suddenly with a dollar in his hand and stuck it into Digger's pants, producing howls of laughter from the rest of us. The dancer led him back to the table and snake-charmed him down onto a tuffet and then made her way sinuously away to dance in front of some other patrons.

"Ho ho, very funny," he said as he threw the dollar onto the table, but he was enjoying himself. "I can't stand these fucking teases! God help me!" He turned to me and Remo. "Hey, kids, what say we head south of market after this. It'd be like… old times."

Remo opened his mouth but nothing came out as he looked at me, maybe wondering if he should be trying to rescue me from the old man or what. I said "Yeah sure, if you're payin'!" I was thinking about what Chris said, about being in your face and then they can't touch you. There was nothing that could hurt me in a strip club but my own ugly feelings. When I was fourteen I didn't know that. Now I did.

So here's Remo and me and Digger, Digger walking slightly ahead of us and gesticulating in the grand way of drunks, down a pretty steep sidewalk. He wasn't drunk enough that we had to worry about him falling down or anything; if anything I was the drunkest of us all, but I'm a pretty quiet drunk. We followed him to a place he seemed to know and took up residence with a round of cocktails at a table along the runway. This place was smaller, more cramped, than the old Foxy Lady had been. The Lady had been a free-standing building of course, on a little highway in New Jersey, between two strip malls and down the way from a diner. This was some kind of urban industrial space that had been subdivided many times and whose ceiling was barely high enough for a stage show.

These girls were smart. They pegged Digger for a horny old bastard who thinks his money makes him important and who likes to throw it around. I don't know exactly what kind of thing is legal to do in these places—I thought I remembered there being laws about there being no touching allowed but maybe that was New Jersey—but some of these girls who really wanted to milk him would climb right down off the stage and crawl into his lap. I was fascinated by the way they'd stalk down and then put a hand on one of his shoulders and then the other, and then one leg over one of his legs, and then the other. As soon as they leaned close enough, Digger's face would go slack, eyes rolled up into his head, like he'd gone to another planet, or Heaven maybe. And then when she'd back away he'd come alive again, and whistle, and wave more money in the air.

And I wondered a couple of things like, is that what he looked like having sex? or was this better than actual sex somehow for him? And, is that what I look like when Ziggy crawls onto me on stage? I could imagine him doing this, somehow, peeling off his clothes and teasing, the audience crowded around the runway, until that moment when his hard on would spring free, and he'd lower himself to a willing mouth (mine), people pushing each other to be the one to reach out with a tongue and take him in.

Fuck. Maybe I did have a little too much to drink. Funny, somehow deciding it was over between me and Ziggy had given me license to fantasize about him again.

Yeah, so maybe it wasn't as over as I thought.

Remo caught my eye and smiled wryly as Digger hooted and hollered. I gave a shrug. Let him have his fun.

Then Digger turned to us. "You see anything you like? For a little extra at this place, you know, you can have what you want."

Remo shrugged. "Ah, jeez, Dig, I can't keep up with you anymore. I'm too bushed."

"Ha, bushed," said Digger. "I'm going to get myself bushed, ha, bushed. How about you, kiddo, do a two-fer with the old man?"

"What?" My eyes snapped open like faulty window shades and I stared at him.

"Jeezus, kid, these girls love it. One in the front and one in the back. My god, you can bone them all night that way."

I think I said "what" again, stunned and off-balance, waiting for him to say he was kidding.

He wasn't kidding. "It's a bargain, too. Almost two for the price of one." His face was open, red, eager. "C'mon."

No you go ahead, is what I was trying to say, but the words wouldn't come, I couldn't encourage him to fuck one of these girls for money. "You're joking," I finally said.

His lips went sour. "You were always a pussy when it came to women, weren't you."

"Excuse me?" I would have stood up, but Remo had a hand around my wrist under the table. "Are those the two choices, be a pussy, or be a fucking suck-my-dick whoremonger?" Oh yeah, I was drunk and flying high and kept thinking of the words In Your Face.

"Jeezus kid, I didn't mean it that way. But show a little respect here for what I'm offering you. I mean, Christ, I never would have thought you'd turn out to be the same prude your mother was."

"I get my dick sucked plenty, thank you." Remo's fingers were digging into my arm like he was trying to warn me off, but there was too much booze in me and the chance was too good for me to let it pass. "But I guess it's nice to see I'm not the only pervert in the fucking family."

"Pervert, who said 'pervert?'" He was looking around like some culprit would show up, his hands held out like he was balancing something. Girls were clattering by in their high heels, waiting to get his attention again and then moving on. "This is all perfectly legal, you know. Like gambling or drinking. If you don't want to, hey, okay, but don't go judging me for my choice of recreation. You're old enough to know every man's got to get off somehow. You don't judge it."

"You mean that."

"You fucking bet I do."

"Alright, then don't you go judging me either."

"Shit, kiddo, you think I care if you smoke weed or screw your Girl Friday there six ways from Sunday? I don't care if you're digging up corpses and fucking 'em in the eye sockets. Well, I mean, as long as you're not getting arrested or having to go to rehab or otherwise killin' yourself." His voice was not mollifying or joking now. We were staring into each other's eyes across the table and I wondered if Remo's other hand was clamped onto Digger's wrist, too. "Fuck no, Mister Big Time rock and roll star. You do what the fuck you want. And don't you dare judge me."

"I won't judge you if you won't judge me, is that the deal?"

"Yeah, sure."

I was wishing Ziggy was there right then because I would have given him a deep tongue kiss. Instead I decided I'd said enough. Just enough. "Well okay," I said softly, maybe too soft to be heard over the music. "Okay," I said louder, sitting back. The tension went out of both of us and Remo let go. I suppressed the urge to smirk and instead I put some cash down on the table. "I gotta get some rest." I still couldn't bring myself to say he should get himself a girl but the money probably said the same. Remo and I stood up at the same time.

Digger smirked, wiggling his head back and forth as he eyed us through slits. "Oh all right. I'll see you in the morning probably, before you head out."

Remo clapped him on the shoulder and we all nodded to each other and then Remo and I made our way to the street.

Take the Long Way Home

Remo and I walked for about a block in silence, climbing the hill toward the hotel, me propelled upward by energy and the feeling like I couldn't quite get enough air into my lungs. Streetwalkers called to us, homeless-looking men shifted toward us and then away. It felt almost like New York.

"Wow," I said when I started to speak again. "Wow."

Remo chuckled. "I seriously thought you two were going to get into a punch-up."

"There was only that one moment there, when he called me a pussy."

"And then you called him a pervert."

"Yeah well." Our boots tapped out a few bars.

Then Remo said "So you didn't tell him."

"But I came close."

"Are you going to?"

"No." I knew it with the same certainty I knew I was going to tell Chris earlier. "No, I've said enough."

"What are you going to do when he finds out? Cuz you know he will, Daron."

I sucked my teeth. "You know what? I think he already knows. I think he would have pressed the issue in there if he didn't. He doesn't want to hear it, though." It was like Claire, tolerating anything the neighbors didn't know about. Plausible deniability meant he could pretend. "Maybe, there'll be a day when he'll finally decide to confront me about it, and then, we'll have a huge fight. But I've got my ammunition for that fight, if it ever comes." The wind was cold and wet on my cheeks but I didn't much mind, the heat draining away from my reddened face. "But I think he knows that, which is why he'll leave me alone." I slowed down a little and we walked side by side. "It's nobody's business but mine."

Remo nodded to himself. "So… you gonna keep him as manager?"

"I don't think so, but at the same time, you don't get off a horse that's taking you somewhere. I'll wait until he slows down."

"Was I right about the money?"

"You were right about the money."

The clammy breeze shifted and starting pushing us uphill. We went for a little bit before Remo said, "Have you thought about maybe talking to someone else at WTA? I mean, look at the dates you have coming up. You shouldn't be knocking on doors anymore. People should be knocking on yours."

"So, I tell him I'm firing him for someone else."

"He won't be mad."

"Like hell he won't."

"Okay, he'll be ripshit, but then it'll pass." Remo sighed. "How long do you think you'll be together?"

"The band, you mean?"

"Yeah."

I shook my head. "I don't know. After the album comes out in the summer, and after the worldwide tour… who knows. Me and Ziggy seem to have a fine creative battle brewing." At that moment I couldn't picture us starting from scratch again with new material. "And you know he's going to make a movie?"

"No shit."

"Sure sounds like it."

Then Remo said, "You gonna stay in Boston?"

"For now, I guess. Chris and I bought the house we live in. I'd probably, I don't know, sell him my half if I was going to move." I turned to look at him and the wind blew my hair into my eyes. "Why?"

"You ever think about LA?"

I shrugged. "Why, there a good gig there for me?"

"Great gig, in fact. Real established band, tour every summer, new album or no. It's really picked up the last couple of years, too, lot more jams. Not quite the Grateful Dead but you know what I mean. Seriously need another guitar player."

"I don't know, Reem."

"I'll confess you a secret. I keep hoping something goes wrong with M3 so Nomad can have another crack at you."

I thought I was all done with blushing tonight, but no. "I… that means a lot to me."

"The door's basically open, man. Unless I get so old I have to pack it in completely."

We could see the gold lights of the hotel as we rounded the corner. "Hey, Reem?"

"Yeah?"

"If I hadn't been there, would you have, I mean, would you and Digger have…?"

He let out a burst of laughter. "I don't think so. Fifteen years ago, maybe, but not any more. I… lost my taste for it, I guess, about the time you…" He frowned slightly. "About the time he started dragging you out to the bar. I started to get less enthusiastic. Since I moved to LA, nope." He must have seen the look on my face (which was probably a mask of sudden and intense curiosity) because he closed the subject down then with, "I get my share of groupies, son."

"You fancy a nightcap from room service?"

"I could do with a ginger ale."

"We can get that from the vending machine."

"I've got a six of it in my room."

"Well, alright then."

Point of Know Return

Some time later, after everyone else was asleep but before dawn, I found myself sitting on the windowsill, tired, very tired, but not ready to lie down yet, rubbing my left thumb in my right hand and thinking. Bart was asleep on his edge of the bed and I wasn't quite ready to get under the covers yet myself.

In less than a week we'd be home. Remo had told me over ginger ale about another movie he'd been hired to score; he wanted me to come out and play on it. And then the summer tour, and then probably Europe after that, and Asia. It would be a year before we went into the studio again. If we went into the studio again.

It could be over in a year. That thought was weirdly comforting.

Equally comforting was the thought that we could keep changing, that in a year's time we might be ready, all four of us, to go in some new direction. There was no predicting it. I was looking forward to arriving at that moment, at being in the moment, and doing it, whatever it was.

My next fight with Ziggy, could be tomorrow, could be next week, I was sure something would come up and I was eager to meet it head on.

I'd told him it was over. I had a vague sense of loss now thinking about it, remembering that time of getting to know what he liked, and having someone who knew me as well. But I suppose everyone wishes for the perfect match.

He'd asked for a second chance. I had to decide whether to give it to him.

I wondered if Digger was lonely, or if Remo was.

I did not feel lonely at that moment, staring out over a dark city where sex workers and club dancers and cab drivers were on their way home. I had the slight urge to take out the Takamine and play, but that would wake Bart and aggravate the thumb.

I felt alone and that felt strangely good, a feeling I could not come up with words for, a feeling like the moment when the soloist takes off from the orchestra, into the bars the composer left blank, a feeling that could not be expressed with the written score and could only be stated with a fingerprint personal sequence of notes, flying from fingers moment by moment, each one truer than the last.

End of Volume 3! Continued in Volume 4...

Excerpt from *DGC*: Volume Four

Living Colour

Inside the new rehearsal space, Carynne was already talking with Louis, which was to say Louis was talking and she was nodding a lot. He was gesturing toward the rafters but I couldn't make out what he was actually saying. He hadn't struck me as the talkative type so it must have been important.

I laid the guitar case on the stage and then went to join them. Chris started adjusting drums. Ziggy prowled the edges of the space and the stage like a cat, checking everything out.

"Basically what I'm telling the boss here," Louis said, as I stood next to him, "is that what I'm going to set up in here is like a toy piano, but when we get on the road it'll be more like a Rick Wakeman set-up."

"Okay."

"What I'm going to do, basically, is learn your set, so I can, for lack of a better term, play along. Except I'll be playing with lights instead of sound."

Ziggy wandered into the conversation.

"There'll be some specific cues you want, colors, or effects, and I'll work those in, but you know, a lot of it will be mixed live."

"Waitasec, you mean you do it by hand?" Ziggy said. "You play the light board like an instrument?"

"Yup."

I was glad Zig was the one who asked that, since I hadn't quite realized it was going to be that intensive.

"Some of the stuff, we really need to work out together, though," Louis said. "Like you mentioned you had that one effect, Daron, some show with a single white spotlight? That you liked a lot."

Ziggy and I both nodded.

"If it's a spot from above, it can be a great effect, but only if you can hit your mark." He said this last to Ziggy. "We'll have a follow spot on you too, of course, most of the time. But this sort of thing, you have to get back to center stage, and of course every stage is going to be different." He shook his head a little. "Come on up and I'll show you the way I mark the stage."

Bart was up there, chatting with Chris.

"Are we going to use fog at all?"

"I don't think so," I said. I glanced around at the others. "Definitely not."

"Good. You'll be less likely to lose these then, too. Some guys just use an 'X' for each mark, or three parallel lines that show the angle of the front of the stage. I use your initials so if you wander around you don't get lost."

We chuckled at that—he'd said it like a joke—but I got the feeling it was no joke.

Next to my mic stand was a 'D' made with two different colors of tape stuck to the boards.

"You guys make it fairly easy since you've each got a stand, but just in case." Louis pointed upward. "I hung some cans; I'll play with them tonight. But ignore me. Do whatever you have to do; don't be stopping or starting a song just because I'm screwing around. I'll have plenty of time to figure out the whole set."

I slung the new Stratocaster over my shoulder.

"One more thing, the song we need to talk about the most, though, is Candlelight."

"You think?" I asked.

"Yeah, I think. It's going to be the song the crowd knows best. It needs something special, and especially since it's got so many mentions of light and dark in the lyrics. We don't have to talk about it now, but we'll need to soon."

"Okay."

"That's my spiel. G'wan, get to it, I'll get out of your way now." He hopped off the stage and back to where he'd set up his "toy piano"—a control board about the width of a DX-7 but twice as deep.

I turned to Ziggy. "What do you want to warm up with?"

He stood with his feet crossed, hands in his pockets, thinking. "How about Walking in Time? An oldie but a goodie."

We hadn't played the song in approximately forever, but it was easy on the voice compared to a lot of our songs so it made sense. I doubted we'd play it on the tour, either. But, well, I had asked him what he wanted to do.

I turned to Chris. "Hit it."

It's a simple song, just a basic one-four-five blues progression, and a song any of us could've faked our way through if we didn't remember. But that made it easy to remember.

And Ziggy took it as a warm up, just breezing through the lyrics without too much effort, at least for the first two verses. I started to noodle a little, playing a countermelody without really thinking about it, echoing off the last few notes of each line. When we reached the bridge, I had thought we might break off since I didn't intend to play a solo, but he answered me right back, picking out pieces of the lyrics and sort of scatting them back at me, more melodic than a rap but less wordy. Chris and Bart just kept chugging along and letting us fly. And at some point we changed from me answering his vocal riffs note for note to unison, and I couldn't have told you which one of us was leading that improvised melody.

When the song came to a close, the silence of the small theater seemed loud. So did my heart and breath. We were standing face to face, maybe a foot apart.

Yeah, I missed you, too.

Oh fuck.

Want more of Daron's Guitar Chronicles?

Join Cecilia Tan's Patreon to get access to exclusive (sexy) bonus
scenes (you know the ones!) and more stories featuring the DGC cast
of characters, including the Daron "Christmas Special" stories!
Visit: https://patreon.com/ceciliatan

Or keep up with all of Cecilia Tan's new books and writing
on her reader mailing list:
Sign up: https://ceciliatan.com/connect

And check out the DGC website at https://daron.ceciliatan.com for the
"liner notes" explaining cool stuff about the music biz and the 1980s,
links to cool music and videos, where Daron answers comments that are
left for him.

NOW IN KINDLE UNLIMITED:

Vol 1: March 2024
Vol 2: April 2024
Vol 3: May 2024
Vol. 4: June 2024
Vol. 5: July 2024
Vol. 6: August 2024
Vol. 7: September 2024

Thanks for reading Daron and Ziggy's story!

The first draft of most this volume was written in 1995, shortly after I had gotten my masters degree in writing. At the time Johnny Cash, David Bowie, and Prince were very much alive, weed was very much NOT legal, and the term "Generation X" was just starting to be accepted as the name for Daron's and my generation.

If you didn't live through the 1980s, and even if you did, you might not know just how much of this story is real. Daron and Ziggy are fictional, but most of the places they visit and the music they listen to is real, as are the homophobia, paranoia around AIDS (and the atomic bomb), and wacky ways of the music industry they encounter. There are extensive notes that go into detail on some of the history on the DGC website, which is found at http://daron.ceciliatan.com

Also on the website: bonus material! There are stories from Ziggy and other characters' points of view, and there are some "adult only" scenes, as well. All the bonus material is accessible by members of my Patreon, as well as a la carte for one-time donation on the website.

You might have noticed that each chapter is titled with either the title of a song or album. In the first few books I mixed in some classic rock with songs from the 1980s, but as the series goes on, I start to stick with songs that are contemporary to the year in which a book takes place. Some fans of the series have made playlists on Youtube of the songs in each book, so you can listen to the music while reading, if you like. If you make a playlist of your own, please share it with me!

About the Author

Cecilia Tan has been writing professionally since she was Daron's age in the 1980s. She sold her first fiction in the early 90s, and her short stories have appeared in *Nerve, Ms. Magazine, Strange Horizons,* and *Best American Erotica.* She is the award-winning author of over 35 books in many genres, including romance, fantasy, erotica, science fiction, and baseball nonfiction. In 2010 she was inducted into the Saints & Sinners LGBT Writers Hall of Fame.

Also by Cecilia Tan

The Magic University series:
The Siren and the Sword
The Tower and the Tears
The Incubus and the Angel
The Poet and the Prophecy

The Struck by Lightning series:
Slow Surrender
Slow Seduction
Slow Satisfaction

The Secrets of a Rock Star series:
Taking the Lead
Wild Licks
Hard Rhythm

The Prince's Boy
The Hot Streak
Mind Games
The Velderet
Royal Treatment
White Flames
Black Feathers
Edge Plays
Telepaths Don't Need Safewords
Watch Point
Bonds of Love (Silk Threads)

Nonfiction:
The 50 Greatest Yankees Games
The Binge Watchers Guide to the Harry Potter Films